Ro Thunder

V Plague Book Three

DIRK PATTON

Dirk Patton

Text Copyright © 2014 by Dirk Patton

Copyright © 2014 by Dirk Patton

All Rights Reserved

This book, or any portion thereof, may not be reproduced or used in any manner whatsoever without the express written permission of the copyright holder or publisher, except for the use of brief quotations in a critical book review.

Published by Reaper Ranch Press LLC

PO Box 856

Gilmer, TX 75644-0856

Printed in the United States of America

First Printing, 2014

ISBN-13: 978-1511492409

ISBN-10: 1511492406

This is a work of fiction. Names, characters, businesses, brands, places, events and incidents are either the products of the author's imagination or used in a fictitious manner. Any resemblance to actual persons, living or dead, or actual events is purely coincidental.

Rolling Thunder
Table of Contents

Also by Dirk Patton 6
Author's Note 8
1 12
2 23
3 29
4 36
5 48
6 52
7 59
8 68
9 77
10 88
11 98
12 109
13 120
14 129
15 143
16 153
17 165
18 173

19	183
20	195
21	206
22	213
23	223
24	231
25	243
26	253
27	261
28	268
29	283
30	298
31	310
32	317
33	325
34	335
35	346
36	357
37	366
38	376
39	382
40	391
41	395
42	401

Rolling Thunder
43 408

Dirk Patton

Also by Dirk Patton

The V Plague Series

Unleashed: V Plague Book 1

Crucifixion: V Plague Book 2

Rolling Thunder: V Plague Book 3

Red Hammer: V Plague Book 4

Transmission: V Plague Book 5

Rules Of Engagement: A John Chase Short Story

Days Of Perdition: V Plague Book 6

Indestructible: V Plague Book 7

Recovery: V Plague Book 8

Precipice: V Plague Book 9

Anvil: V Plague Book 10

Merciless: V Plague Book 11

Fulcrum: V Plague Book 12

Hunter's Rain: A John Chase Novella

Rolling Thunder

Exodus: V Plague Book 13

Scourge: V Plague Book 14

Fractured: V Plague Book 15

Brimstone: V Plague Book 16

Abaddon: V Plague Book 17

Cataclysm: V Plague Book 18

Legion: V Plague Book 19

The 36 Series

36: A Novel

The Void: A 36 Novel

Other Titles by Dirk Patton

Fool's Gold

The Awakening

Author's Note

Thank you for purchasing Rolling Thunder, Book 3 in the V Plague series. As you've probably already guessed from the title, this is the third book in the series. If you haven't read the first two books, I would encourage you to do so first. Otherwise, you will be lost as this book is intended to continue the story in a serialized format. I intentionally did nothing to explain comments and events that reference Books 1 and 2. Regardless, you have my heartfelt thanks for reading my work, and I hope you're enjoying the adventure as much as I am. As always, a good review on Amazon is greatly appreciated.

First and foremost, I would like to thank my beautiful wife, Katie, for all the support she gives me every day. I couldn't write these books without her love and inspiration.

There's also a young man currently serving our country that deserves special recognition. Being the dumb Army grunt that I am, there have been a few Air Force related errors creep into my writing (no I'm not going to tell you what they were) and he has become my go to guy to help ensure I'm accurately depicting Air Force personnel and how they operate. Any errors are either my mistakes or changes to make the story flow better. Many thanks to Air Force SSgt Z. May the gods of war make you fleet of foot, strong of arm, stout of heart and low of profile.

I also want to give a special mention to all the readers who have sent emails and contacted me on Facebook. Thank you all for your wonderful words of encouragement. I'm so glad you're enjoying my work.

Last but not least, I can't fail to mention the real Dog. Somehow he'd know that I forgot him, again, and would most certainly make me pay. Now leave me alone and go get the damn squirrel.

Have a question or comment? You can email me at dirk@dirkpatton.com, visit my website at www.dirkpatton.com or like my Facebook page at www.facebook.com/DirkPattonAuthor or follow me on Twitter @DirkPatton

Finally, if you enjoy my books, PLEASE post a good review on Amazon for each of the books in the series that you have read. Good sales are driven by good reviews from real readers like you and the more I sell, the more I write. Funny how that works, huh?

Dirk Patton

Rolling Thunder

Rolling Thunder

Crying parents tell their children

If you survive, don't do as we did

A son exclaims there'll be nothing to do to

Her daughter says she'll be dead with you

The Fixx – Stand or Fall

1

I pressed harder on the accelerator as I heard two more blasts from the shotgun. Sergeant Jackson of the Murfreesboro Police and a few dozen others were making a last stand. A horde of infected had breached the defensive wall we had set up to buy time for evacuees to board trains that would take them to safety. Not all of us made it onto those trains. Some were paying the ultimate price and falling to the unstoppable rampage of the infected.

I didn't hear any more shots and would have liked to think it was because I had driven out of hearing range of the battle, but knew better. The handful of defenders who had been caught before boarding the train wouldn't stand up to the thousands of raging females for even a minute.

Glancing in the small mirror mounted to the dash of the purloined ambulance, I noted that Rachel was still unconscious. She had been flattened by a massive explosion when a truck stop's underground fuel tanks had touched off. I didn't know how badly, if at all, she was injured, but I had taken a cautious approach by putting on a cervical collar before strapping her to a backboard. Just in case.

I'm not a religious man and couldn't summon up a prayer for her, but I fervently hoped she was just knocked out with no other trauma. In the new world we found ourselves in, a world where survival of the fittest was truly the law of the land, any incapacitating injury was a death sentence. In the seat next to me, Dog let out a series of low whines as he looked into the back at Rachel's still form.

As I drove, I looked over the cab of the ambulance. The vehicle had a compass integrated into the dash, which told me I was driving north. Between the seats, a sturdy laptop mount held a rugged looking computer. Driving with one hand, I raised the lid and the screen flared to life, displaying a login prompt. Shit. I can use a computer with the best of them but don't ask me to hack into something. Blow it up? OK. Shoot it? No problem. Hack into it? I'm not even sure what that really means.

Closing the lid to get rid of the light from the screen I caught a brief glimpse of something shiny on the outside. Clicking on the overhead light, I saw a single strip of tape with some writing on it. Leaning forward, I could make out

EMTsROCK99, hand written in black sharpie. Raising the lid again, I typed this in one handed and was rewarded with the display changing and showing a detailed road map with a pulsing blue dot that had to be the ambulance's location.

By now, I had driven at least ten miles and felt safe enough to stop so I could figure out where we were and where we were going. Pulling to the side of the road, I made sure the doors were locked and decided to turn on the red and blue emergency lights on the roof while I was stopped. There were still people north of the approaching herd, and they would be fleeing to safety in a panic. All I needed was for a van load of refugees to plow into the ambulance. I hoped the emergency lights would help us avoid that little problem.

I played with the map for a few moments, zooming in, then out and scrolling around. We were currently sitting on Tennessee state highway 10 and were about thirty-five miles south of Interstate 40. Highway 10 ran north from Murfreesboro and stayed to the east of Nashville. I wanted to avoid the large city if at all possible.

The original attacks had not included Nashville, but the second wave of infection just a couple of days ago probably made that a moot point. The day the second wave hit, I had briefly spoken on the radio with a Royal Air Force humanitarian aid flight and was told that they had lost all communication with Nashville. I had a pretty good idea why that had happened and didn't feel like confirming my belief the hard way.

Still staring at the screen, I ducked involuntarily when a helicopter flared into a hover just in front of me, a hundred feet in the air. A blinding spotlight lit up the inside of the ambulance. I recognized the sound of a Black Hawk helicopter and dragged my pack out of the back, digging through it for my secure comm unit. It took me a minute to find it and get the earpiece inserted in my good ear, then another couple of minutes as I tried different channels to communicate with the helicopter.

"US ground forces on secure comm calling unidentified Black Hawk," I said into the throat mic.

"Devil three seven on station over you." A voice with a heavy Boston accent replied when I hit the right frequency. "Identify yourself and state your status."

"Major John Chase, Fifth Group. I have two souls with me, one injured, and need evac. Can you comply?"

There was a long pause before the voice responded. "Negative. Aircraft is already over capacity."

I wasn't surprised.

"Do you have a medic on board?" I asked, glancing at Rachel in the mirror. "The casualty needs assessed and possibly treated."

"Wait one," was the reply.

A long moment later the spotlight winked out and in the ambulance's headlights, I could see four ropes drop to the ground beneath the helicopter. Four figures slid down them to the pavement. One wore a large pack. The other three had rifles strapped to their bodies and immediately set up a defensive perimeter the second their boots hit the ground.

Killing the ambulance's emergency beacons and headlights, I stepped out to greet them, Dog jumping to the ground next to me. Another figure slid down a rope to the asphalt and the helicopter pulled up and away before going into a tight orbit around the area.

Rolling Thunder

I walked forward and first met the medic, who I directed to the back of the ambulance. He clicked on a low power light and looked at the bloody shirt wrapped around my head, but I waved him on. Rachel was the priority. The last man who had fast roped out of the helo walked up, stopping a few feet away and looking me up and down.

He wore First Sergeant's chevrons on his uniform and a green beret on his head. His name tape read Glendon. He glanced at my oak leaf and nodded a greeting. He wasn't being disrespectful. You never salute a superior officer on the battlefield. If you did it would be like holding up a big neon sign for the enemy that reads *"kill this guy; he's important!"*

"Could have used you guys back in Murfreesboro," I said, checking on the location of the three men who were watching our perimeter.

"Was that you? That big explosion?" He asked, and I recognized the Boston accent I'd heard on the radio. Guess I hadn't been talking to the pilot.

"Yep, that was pretty much the end of us. The herd is only a few miles behind, but we held it long enough to get two trainloads of evacuees out of town."

"Sorry we weren't there, Major. We were northwest of Nashville, picking up one of the civilian leadership when we saw the explosion. Decided to come investigate."

Civilian leadership meant a member of congress, or one of the President's cabinet. Being as we were in Tennessee, I had a reasonably good idea which it was.

"He's on board with his family right now and isn't too happy that we've delayed to help you."

A small grin spread across his face. I knew how he felt about politicians. They talk tough, but tend to rant like children when they're scared. To a man, the military enjoys inconveniencing them as much as can be gotten away with without stepping over the line. I grinned back and motioned for him to walk with me so I could go see how the medic was doing with Rachel.

"Well, you have my thanks for dropping in. Tell me what's going on. Is Nashville safe? What about Fort Campbell?"

"Fort Campbell has fallen," he said, all traces of the grin gone from his face and voice. "The defensive line at the southern Tennessee border has also fallen. Nashville is chaos. Whatever the hell happened a couple of days ago... well, half the people in Nashville turned, or went crazy, or whatever the hell you want to call it. The other half is doing the best it can to survive, but there's no coordinated effort. After the packs overrun one group of survivors, they move on to the next. You don't want to go anywhere near Nashville."

I nodded, dismayed but not surprised by anything he was telling me. We reached the back of the ambulance and looked in. The medic had removed the cervical collar and was running his hands over the back of Rachel's head and neck. She was still unconscious. Dog stood watching, one of the rare times his ears weren't straight up. Sergeant Glendon raised a hand to his earpiece, listened for a moment then excused himself and stepped away to hold a conversation.

"How is she?" I asked the medic.

"What happened to her?" He asked without pausing his examination.

"That huge explosion you guys saw. She was maybe a couple of hundred yards from it and got knocked flat. She was on her back, unconscious when I got to her."

"She's got a big lump on the back of her head, probably from hitting the ground when she got knocked down. I can't find any other signs of injury but with her unconscious, I can't do any of the tests I'd normally perform for spinal injuries. Why did you put her on the backboard?"

He stopped what he was doing and turned to look at me.

"Just seemed like the right thing to do," I said with a shrug.

"OK, well, like I said, all I can find is the lump on her head. She probably has a pretty bad concussion. There's no sign of it being worse than that. Her pupils are fine. Equal and reactive to light. Her vitals are all good. There's really nothing I can do for her at this point."

He started packing away the equipment he had used.

"So, should I leave her on the backboard?" I asked.

"For now, I would. It won't hurt anything. If she wakes up and can feel and move all her limbs, unstrap her. And try to keep her from taking any more blows to the head for a few days. If she wakes up and has problems..." He stopped talking and looked at me with a helpless expression.

"Yeah, I got it," I said, letting him off the hook. He packed up the last of his equipment and turned to me.

"Want me to take a look at your head?"

I had forgotten I was injured too. Nodding, I climbed into the back of the ambulance and sat down on the bench next to the medic. He carefully untied the bloody shirt, unwrapping it from around my head. As soon as the pressure came off, the pain hit and I could feel blood running down the side of my face.

"Damn, Major! Your ear is almost completely torn off."

Well, that explained why I could hardly hear out of it. The medic worked fast. First, he numbed me up, then cleaned the raw edges of skin where the infected had ripped my ear loose. Opening a couple of drawers in the ambulance, he found a suture kit and set to work.

"This won't be pretty," he said as he worked. "Sorry, but I don't do this a lot. You'll probably have a hell of a scar, but at least I think it will save the ear."

Dirk Patton

I grunted, not really giving a damn about another scar. It's not like I could have ever been a male model to begin with. Not that I'm ugly, but... hell, you get the idea. Anyway, it took him about ten minutes to sew me up, bandage the ear and treat the gashes on my face where the female had slashed me with her nails. As he was finishing, Sergeant Glendon appeared at the back of the ambulance and looked in.

"Sorry, Major. We've got to get our asses in gear, and you'd better do the same. The Air Force has a big present on the way for that herd of infected."

"What's happening?" A nuke was the first thought that went through my head. God help us if we started popping those off on our own soil.

"They're calling it Rolling Thunder."

Rolling Thunder

2

Rolling Thunder was a bombing campaign during the Vietnam War... uh, conflict, from 1965 to 1968. It was basically carpet bombing of North Vietnam with the declared objective of demonstrating America's commitment to our South Vietnamese allies by disrupting NVA and VC supply lines and demoralizing their troops.

Despite millions of pounds of bombs being dropped, it didn't do either. But that wasn't because the idea of waves of B-52s dropping thousands of bombs at once is a bad idea. It was the politics involved, and... well, I digress.

"Carpet bombing to stop the herd?" I asked.

"Yes, sir. Everything south of I-40 is about to get rearranged, big time. First wave of bombers will be overhead in twenty mikes."

He must have already called for a pick up as the Black Hawk came out of its orbit and dropped to a hover just a couple of feet above the pavement. The medic shouldered his pack and I thanked him as he jumped out of the ambulance and ran for the waiting helicopter.

Neither of us wasted any more time. Glendon stuck his hand out and I gave it a quick shake, then he was running for the Black Hawk and calling in the guys on the perimeter over the radio. I slammed the back doors to the ambulance and ran for the cab, Dog beating me there and leaping in and across my seat.

I had just been looking at a map before the helicopter's arrival, and I knew I-40 was thirty-five miles away. And I only had twenty minutes to get there. Waiting for the last of the soldiers to board the Black Hawk that was blocking the highway, I shifted the ambulance into drive and held my foot on the brake.

As I waited for the helo to clear the way, I did the math in my head. Thirty-five miles in twenty minutes. Shit. I was coming up with over a hundred miles per hour. Not that big a deal in a sports car, but an ambulance isn't built to haul ass on dark, twisty highways.

The last man climbed aboard the hovering helicopter and it roared off into the sky. I floored the accelerator and grimaced in frustration as the ambulance slowly picked up speed. It seemed to take forever to reach sixty, and I kept the pedal nailed to the floor. Slowly the speedometer climbed and was passing eighty as I came to the first curve.

A yellow sign with a sharply hooked arrow warned me to slow to fifty, but I kept the throttle pegged and steered for the inside edge of the pavement. The curve was long and sweeping, a sheer rock face right next to the highway on my left and a guardrail on the right protecting a drop-off that, in the dark, seemed bottomless. The speed held at just over eighty as I fought the steering wheel to control the drift towards the guardrail. The wheel fought back, the dual rear tires chattering in protest as I entered the sharpest part of the curve.

There were several crashes from the back as equipment and supply drawers flew open and spilled their contents. The big, top-heavy vehicle threatened to roll up on the outside tires, but I had held it tight enough that there was room to slip to the right and compensate.

Finally, we roared out of the end of the curve, the speedometer quivering on eighty-six, and directly ahead was a long, steep hill. Our speed climbed to just over ninety for a few moments, then we started up the grade. For every quarter mile traveled, the heavy ambulance lost almost ten miles per hour. Shit. We weren't going to make it out of the area in time.

As the grade leveled out, our speed started climbing again, then we crested and started down the backside of the hill. Quickly, the speedometer which only registered up to one hundred, was maxed out. The downgrade wasn't as long as the climb had been, but the ambulance hadn't been designed to run at the speed I was driving.

The wheel bounced in my hands and even though there was power steering, I was having a hard time keeping us in a straight line. The downgrade bottomed out, and so did the ambulance. We screamed into a right-hand curve marked at sixty and I almost turned us over as I battled with the brakes and steering.

Coming out of the curve, there was a fairly level stretch of road ahead and I pushed on the throttle as hard as I could. The engine roared and the wheel shook, but I was able to get the speedometer maxed out once again. I had noted the time on the dash clock when I'd gotten back behind the wheel and risked taking my eyes off the road long enough to check it. We had been driving for seven minutes. Maybe we had covered eight miles. I kicked myself for not having noted the odometer reading as well.

We got another minute on the straight, then another yellow warning sign flashed past. This one was marked forty-five. Standing on the brakes, I cut our speed to seventy as we blasted through the curve. Coming out of the other end, we climbed a small hill and crested it doing nearly ninety. The ambulance's headlights, on bright, glinted off chrome and glass in the road ahead. Much too close.

It took me half a second to see that the road was completely blocked by a jack-knifed semi, no more than three hundred feet in front of us. I jammed both feet onto the brake, pushing so hard my ass rose out of the seat as all my weight shifted to the pedal. The tires screamed and the front end wanted to turn, but I fought it for all I was worth. If we went sideways at this speed, the big vehicle would roll.

Dog slammed forward off the seat, bouncing off the dash and wound up on the floor when I stood on the brakes. This probably saved his life as we were still going too fast when the front bumper hit the wrecked truck and the air bags deployed with a loud pop and a huge burst of the white powder that's used to keep the material from sticking.

Rolling Thunder

3

I can honestly say I've never had an airbag deploy in my face before, and I don't ever want one to do so again. It's not a pleasant experience. I sat there for a minute we didn't have, slightly dazed but intact. Dog started scrambling on the passenger floor and succeeded in pushing his way past the deflated airbag and back onto the seat.

He looked none the worse for wear, but had a coating of fine, white powder frosting his fur. Sneezing violently, he shook, re-filling the slowly clearing air with another cloud of the damn stuff. Coming back to full alertness, I glanced at the clock. Nine minutes gone. Checking the mirror, I was thankful to see the backboard holding Rachel was still strapped securely in place. She looked like she'd come through the crash better than either Dog or me.

The engine was still running, and I batted the airbag out of the way and shifted into reverse. I was flooded with relief when the ambulance started moving backwards. Stopping, I threw the selector into park and spent a few seconds slicing the airbag off the wheel with my Ka-Bar.

Dirk Patton

I stepped out of the vehicle and tossed the heavy fabric away as I went forward to check the damage. The front of the ambulance was dented and banged up, but the heavy-duty bumper had done its job and protected the vehicle. I didn't readily see anything that would prevent me from continuing to drive it.

The semi I had rammed into was a different problem. It was a specialized trailer for carrying the forty-foot shipping containers from the rail yard back in Murfreesboro, and it was loaded. Currently, the full length of the trailer and container were effectively blocking the road. On either side of the pavement were rails that protected drivers from steep drop-offs. There was no going around with the ambulance. Leaving Dog inside to guard both Rachel and the vehicle, I climbed over the rail and made my way past the blockage.

The trailer was still connected to the truck, and both had remained upright on their tires. There were no other vehicles visible, but I was starting to get worried that I was stumbling around a roadblock that had been set up to ambush unwary travelers. Rifle up and ready, I moved forward, slowly circling the cab. Moving in front of the truck's grill, I scanned a full circle but didn't spot anything concerning.

Rolling Thunder

My internal clock was bonging like Big Ben, warning me that the bombs were about to start dropping. Turning to face the truck, I looked up at the windshield and saw the problem. An infected male sat in the cab, pressed forward against the inside of the glass as he tried to reach me. The poor bastard must have turned while he was driving. Fortunately, for me, the truck had stayed upright and I should be able to move it out of the way.

Stepping to the passenger door, I lowered my rifle, drew the Kukri and tried the handle. It was locked. Hoping for better results on the driver's side, I walked around the cab, took a deep breath and pulled the door open. I stepped back quickly as the male tumbled out onto the ground. He was no longer smart or coordinated enough to use the steps built into the outside of the truck's body to climb down. Before he could clamber to his feet, I buried the Kukri in his head, stepped over the body and climbed into the cab.

The keys dangled from the ignition, which was still in the *on* position. Depressing the clutch with my left foot, I wiggled the long gear shift until I was satisfied it was in neutral, then hit the starter button. There was a loud whine, then the diesel engine roared to life and settled into a smooth idle.

Dirk Patton

Clutch pedal still pressed to the floor, I stared at the markings on the shifter, trying to figure out how to get into gear. Any gear. The damn thing appeared to have eighteen speeds. I wasn't sure which one would get me moving, so I pushed it into what I thought was fourth.

Giving the idling diesel engine some throttle, I let the clutch out slowly. The truck jerked hard and died. Needing a higher gear, I restarted the engine and tried sixth, this time getting the rig moving. The left front corner of the trailer was jammed against the guard rail. I kept feeding in throttle and the truck dragged it free with a horrible screech of tearing metal.

I drove far enough to clear room for the ambulance to pass, shut off the engine and climbed down. Trotting back, I paused long enough to grab the dead infected's belt and drag the body to the side of the road so I didn't have to drive over it. Running back to the ambulance, I piled in, shifted into drive and floored the throttle.

We slowly accelerated around the truck. I checked the dash clock with a brief glance. Fifteen minutes gone and we'd covered maybe ten miles. We were going to be well short of I-40 when the Air Force started dropping their bombs.

Rolling Thunder

One thing about the Air Force. They are always on time. Usually to within a couple of seconds, and I didn't have any reason to believe anything would be different this time.

I pushed the ungainly ambulance as hard as I could, and to its credit, the crash into the semi didn't seem to have affected it one bit. It still drove like a chuck wagon being pulled by three lame horses.

Sixteen minutes. I started trying to think of any alternative, but when thousands of bombs began falling from the sky, it would be luck that kept us from getting our asses blown into a few million pieces.

Glancing at the clock again, I saw we were at eighteen minutes. Raising my eyes back to the road, the switches for the red and blue emergency beacons caught my attention. Would the pilots try to avoid dropping on our location if they saw an emergency vehicle's lights? Worth a shot, I thought as I flipped on the overheads.

Nineteen minutes. The high intensity red and blue lights from the roof alternately lit the hood of the ambulance and the trees along the side of the highway as I kept racing north. For the moment, we had left the sharp curves and steep grades behind and were running on a fairly straight and level stretch of highway. The speedometer needle was buried beyond one hundred and the wheel vibrated in my hands like a living thing trying to escape my grasp.

I was splitting attention between the road and clock when we hit twenty minutes. A few seconds later the deep, bass rumble of multiple seven hundred and fifty and one-thousand-pound bombs, sounding just like distant thunder, reached my ears. I tried to press harder on the throttle, but it was already pressed as far down as it would go and was probably embedded into the floor by now. The rumbling steadily rose in volume. Thankfully, for the moment at least, it was well behind us. In the rearview mirror, I could see a constant ripple of flashes across the horizon as bombs detonated.

Carpet bombing is exactly what it sounds like. Bombs are dropped in sufficient quantity to literally *carpet* the terrain. These aren't the smart bombs that you see on the news with a camera in the nose and the target getting bigger and bigger until the image blinks out on detonation. These are just big, dumb, iron bombs that aren't really any more sophisticated than what was used in World War II. They are devastating as all hell, but I wondered just how many the Air Force still had in inventory.

Rolling Thunder

They really hadn't been used in large quantities since Vietnam. If there was a sufficient stockpile, then maybe the Air Force could destroy enough of the herds to make clean up by ground forces manageable. But then, just how many would be needed? The herds were reported as numbering in the millions. How many square miles did millions of people fill up? How many bombs did it take to carpet all that geography? That was for bigger minds than mine. Right now, I needed the ambulance to go faster as the bombs were getting closer.

4

I pressed on, wrenching the ambulance through curves that were thankfully not as sharp as some of the earlier ones, but still forced me to back off the speed to keep from rolling over at a hundred miles an hour. The bombing was getting closer.

Negotiating another curve, I held my breath when a small herd of frightened deer dashed into the road and we went up on the outside set of wheels as I steered to avoid them. It seemed to take forever for the tires in the air to come back into contact with the pavement. I nearly lost control when they did, fighting the instability with small corrections to the wheel and throttle.

Tactical and evasive driving skills were another part of my training from years ago, but that training had not been used since I'd left the Army. I was surprising myself how well I was doing. Remembering my uncanny ability to jinx myself, I shut down that line of thinking and focused on my driving as more bombs came down close enough to rattle the ambulance with their shockwaves.

Rolling Thunder

They kept getting closer, one so near that it lifted the back of the big vehicle completely off the ground for a moment. The tall, narrow windows in the back doors, as well as both side mirrors, were shattered by the shockwave. One of the four rear tires shredded from shrapnel and there was a hell of a racket as chunks of rubber tore off the damaged tire and were thrown against the undercarriage of the ambulance.

Fighting the wheel, I bled off some speed to regain control, absently noting the sign that said I was two miles from I-40 as we roared past it in the dark. As if seeing it was a talisman, the bombing stopped. Well, at least the bombing that was nearly right on top of my head. I couldn't tell if the Air Force was still pounding away farther south without the side mirrors and didn't feel like stopping to get out and look.

Less than two minutes later we reached the intersection with I-40, and I had to slow to navigate through some abandoned wrecks then, clearing the Interstate, accelerated again. Yes, I had been told the bombing was only supposed to be south of I-40. However, I knew that unguided, iron bombs were being dropped and to expect precision placement of them during carpet bombing would be foolish. I wanted at least a few miles of buffer in case some pilot was just a little too far north during his bombing run.

Pushing on for several more miles, I slowed to a more manageable speed as I passed a sign welcoming me to Lebanon, Tennessee. Soon I had to slow to less than thirty to work my way through the crashed vehicles that littered the highway. Houses and small businesses started appearing, but they all looked to be deserted.

Glancing down at the dash, I found the controls for the overheads and shut them off. No need to be any more noticeable than we already were. Besides, a bright red ambulance will draw plenty of attention, even at night. The dash clock told me it was almost 0530, and the computer map showed us slowly approaching what looked to be a medium-sized town. There was still no sign of habitation, and I started to suspect that Lebanon had already been evacuated.

I shouldn't have looked at the clock. I had been operating on adrenaline for quite some time and I could feel both my mind and body starting to shut down. In the old days, I would have popped a couple of *go* pills to keep myself awake and moving, but I didn't have any. There was probably something in the back of the ambulance that would do the trick, but it wouldn't be labeled with a name that meant anything to me and I didn't feel like experimenting right now.

Exhaustion setting in, I started eyeing the abandoned homes we were passing, looking for a good candidate to hole up in for a few hours of rest. I wasn't particularly concerned about the infected we had left behind in Murfreesboro. They were over forty miles away and had just had the snot bombed out of them by the Air Force.

Not that I thought for a second the carpet bombing had been very successful in stopping the herd, but it should slow them down. Assuming the herd was probably moving at around four miles an hour, as long as they weren't actively pursuing prey, that gave me more than ten hours before the leading edge made it to Lebanon. If they were even coming this way and not angling to the northwest to go to Nashville.

My sluggish brain didn't register the house on the left until I had already driven past. Hitting the brakes, I made a slow U-turn then turned into a long driveway that cut through a recently mown lawn. A couple of hundred yards from the highway, a neatly maintained brick house sat dark and silent. I was more interested in the large barn another fifty yards behind it. It was large enough to hide the ambulance, and was the best choice I'd seen so far. The other advantage was not having to go farther into town where we might encounter more infected or other survivors.

The driveway was smooth, packed dirt and I let the ambulance idle along at about five miles per hour. Headlights on bright, I scanned the house and saw no sign of anyone in residence, either infected or not. Blinds were open, and as we drew closer I could see that the front door was ajar, the entrance protected only by a screen door. This made me feel confident that there weren't any survivors inside, but there could still be infected waiting to invite me in for breakfast.

Stopping in front of the house, I tried to peer through the windows but it was pitch black inside. I couldn't see a thing. Relaxing a little, I felt it was a safe assumption that if there were any infected in the house, they would be charging out through the screen door in response to the clattering diesel engine. Releasing the brake, I idled past the corner of the house, following the road to the barn and coming to a stop a dozen yards from its closed double doors.

It was painted the classic red that one expects to see and looked to be as neatly maintained as the house and rest of the property.

Rolling Thunder

Shutting off the lights, I sat there for a few minutes to give my eyes time to adjust to the darkness. Without the headlights, I noticed the sky to the east was beginning to lighten with the approaching dawn.

I also noticed the horizon to the south glowed reddish orange in a few places from fires burning as a result of the bombing. Shutting off the engine, I told Dog to stay and stepped out of the cab, rifle coming up to the ready position as soon as my boots hit the ground.

Stepping away from the ambulance, I carefully scanned a full three hundred and sixty degrees, not seeing anything that concerned me. Keeping a nice wide buffer, I circled the barn, finding nothing to worry about. There was only a huge fifth wheel horse trailer parked on a cement slab behind the barn. It was empty and clean.

Back in front of the ambulance, I moved to the barn doors and banged on one of them with the steel toe of my left boot. I took a quick step back when there were a couple of answering snorts, then relaxed when a horse softly neighed from inside the building.

Pulling the door open wide, I exercised a great deal of caution, stepping back with rifle ready in case any infected were lying in wait. I hadn't forgotten the female in the forest that had shown the intelligence to set up an ambush and had no clue if the horses I could hear would be calm around an infected. After a few minutes of waiting and watching, and detecting no threats, I clicked on the flashlight mounted to my rifle and moved quickly into the barn, stepping sideways and putting my back against a wall.

Still no movement other than what I now saw were four horses in their stalls. I scanned across all the walls and looked up, but there was no loft and no place for an infected to hide. A few feet away was a large panel with half a dozen electrical switches. Figuring it was worth a try, I slid along the wall and flipped all of them up. The inside of the barn lit up as banks of overhead lighting popped on.

This wasn't an old barn. It was new, modern and cleaner than many houses I'd been in. It was obvious the owners loved the horses that were all looking back at me. This set-off alarm bells in my head. I grew up around horse people and knew that even as the world was falling apart, they would not leave their animals locked in stalls and untended.

Stepping away from the wall, I thoroughly cleared the barn, checking each stall to make sure someone wasn't hiding with a horse. Nothing. Shit. I hadn't wanted to have to check the house, but something was definitely off here.

The horses were getting agitated, most likely hungry and thirsty. I didn't want them to get too worked up and start making a lot of noise, so I spent a few minutes feeding and watering them from gleaming buckets that were neatly hung on pegs by each stall. That chore finished, I stepped out of the barn and closed the door behind me. I took a moment to wedge a short length of straw into the hinge side of the door so I would know if anyone opened it while I was gone. After I checked on Dog and Rachel, I headed for the house.

The back of the house boasted a large screened in porch that had a pair of matching chairs positioned so that they were facing the barn. A small table sat between them with a tall stack of magazines resting on its surface. Horse & Rider, Equestrian, Horse Illustrated, Cosmo and People; if it matters. Moving across the porch, I came to another open door that was only protected by a screen, slowly pulling it open and slipping inside.

The smell hit me when I was opening the screen door, and it was stronger as I moved into the house. Not the overpowering stench of a long dead body, but still the smell of death I knew all too well. I had the rifle up and ready, flashlight on as I moved deeper into the house, clearing rooms as I went. The house was as clean and organized as the barn. Until I entered the living room.

The space was a shamble. Every piece of furniture had been knocked over and broken glass from several photo frames and crystal vases twinkled in the light. In the middle of the floor, a large man who looked to be in his early forties lay on his back, the rug beneath him stained black with blood. He had been stabbed in the chest and stomach more times than I cared to count. I played the flashlight across the body and noted the condition of his hands and face. He'd put up one hell of a fight before dying.

Remembering the magazine selection from the back porch, I took a deep breath and steeled myself for what I expected to find next. Down a short hall that led to three bedrooms, I found her. She was young and pretty. Or had been. Now, she lay on a bed in the second bedroom, dead, vacant eyes staring at the ceiling.

She was nude, only a scrap of fabric still circling her waist and ripped underwear hanging from one ankle. Her wrists were tied to the headboard. She had been beaten, among other abuses. Since I couldn't see any knife or bullet wounds, I suspected she had been hit too hard, one too many times.

I stood there staring at the girl for a few minutes, getting my breathing under control. Finally, I came forward and yanked a sheet off the top of a dresser, sending knick-knacks flying, and covered her with it. As I was doing this, I touched her arm and was surprised the body wasn't cold. Not nearly as warm as the living, but she hadn't been dead for more than an hour or two. As I gently pulled the sheet over her face, I heard a vehicle turning off the highway onto the property.

Moving quickly to the third bedroom, located on the front of the house, I looked out the window and saw a mud splattered Toyota pickup coming towards me. I could make out two figures in the cab, but no details about them. Leaving the bedroom and returning to the front room, I stood well back in the darkness and watched the truck approach through the screen door.

It was several years old, dented and rusted under all the mud. Brakes squealed sharply as it came to a stop in front of the house. The doors popped open, but my attention was drawn to the shiny, dual rear wheel Dodge truck that was turning onto the dirt road.

I was willing to bet the Dodge belonged to the dead man since it looked like it would go with the horse trailer I'd found behind the barn. I stood still, gripping my rifle tightly, and watched the two men that got out of the Toyota. They were about what I expected. Young, dirty and stupid looking. Not unlike the ones that had taken Rachel when we were still in Georgia. They moved to the back of their ride and stood waiting for the other truck.

It pulled up a moment later, an older version of the first two stepping down from the cab. Father and sons? The older man was alone in the Dodge, and he waved the other two over to where he was standing. Opening the rear door, he lifted out bags of groceries and handed them to the two younger ones. When each of them had their arms full, he reached back in for two cases of beer, used his hip to close the door and they all started towards the front porch.

"It's my turn with the bitch," one of the younger ones was saying with a grin when I stepped out onto the porch with my rifle raised. All three froze when they saw me.

Rolling Thunder

"Good morning," I said pleasantly, then shot the older one in the knee.

5

He fell to the ground screaming and cursing me as the two younger ones dropped the bags in their arms and scrambled to get behind the Toyota. I fired again and one of them spun to the ground with a shattered hip. Turning quickly, I shot the third one in the lower back as he dove behind the pickup. He flopped to the ground and started dragging himself away with his arms. His legs weren't working any longer.

Stepping down off the porch with rifle at the ready, I roughly searched them. I removed a pistol and a knife from each, the keys for the Dodge from the older one and the Toyota keys from one of the younger. I walked over and piled the weapons into the cab of the Dodge and locked it with the remote on the key chain.

They cursed me. Spat at me. Screamed at me. I ignored them and said nothing. Didn't react to them at all as I worked, piling the three of them into the back of the Toyota, none too gently. By now the younger ones were frightened and pleading, asking what I was doing and why I was doing it.

Rolling Thunder

With them loaded, I silently got into the cab of the truck and started the engine. Driving around to the barn, I stopped next to the ambulance. Getting out, I ignored their renewed curses. Checking on Dog and Rachel, I disappeared into the barn for a moment after making sure the straw I'd stuck into the door jamb was undisturbed.

When I'd cleared the barn earlier, I'd noticed a cabinet that held several lengths of chain with open padlocks swinging from each. These are used to secure equipment at horse shows and events so it doesn't grow legs and wander off on its own. Tossing the chains into the Toyota, I climbed back in and headed across the pasture behind the barn.

The pasture was large, maybe half a mile across. At the edge, the forest that had been cut back was dense with large oak, elm and walnut trees. Parking near an oak with a particularly thick trunk, I stepped out of the cab. I walked around to the tailgate and dragged out the closest man, letting him fall to the ground. It was the one I'd paralyzed with the shot to his back and his head cracked against the tailgate as I pulled him out of the truck by an ankle. He was crying now, tears rolling down his face and snot bubbling from his nose.

Dirk Patton

"C'mon mister. What the hell? I didn't do nothing to you! Please! I need a doctor!"

I ignored his pleas, dragging him to the closest tree where I sat him up and hit him very hard with my forearm to make him stop trying to grab me. I secured him to the tree around his waist. Pulling the chain tight, I snapped the lock into place and walked back to the truck.

Five minutes later all three were bound to the same tree, the chains tight around their waists. Even if they had the use of their legs, they still wouldn't be able to get free. They had stopped cursing me. No more screaming. Only tears from the two younger ones and a look of stubborn resignation on the older one's face. I stood there for a few moments, looking down at them, then turned to go.

"What did they mean to you?" The older one called.

I stopped and turned back, wanting to raise my rifle and empty a magazine into each of them. Wanting to draw my Kukri and see how many body parts I could remove before they died. But I didn't. I wanted them to know terror and pain like they had inflicted before they died. When the infected arrived, they would know both.

Rolling Thunder

"They didn't mean anything to me," I answered before climbing into the Toyota and heading back to the barn.

6

I woke up eight hours later by the dash clock in the ambulance. For a moment, I was disoriented. Didn't know where I was or what had wakened me, then heard it again. Everything clicked into place and I scrambled off the gurney in the back of the ambulance and looked down at Rachel. She was awake and calling my name.

"Hi," I said, smiling down at her.

"What happened to me? Am I alright?"

She was still strapped to the backboard and couldn't move. The look on her face was one of true fear.

"It's a really long story, so first things first. Can you feel your legs? Your feet? Wiggle your toes?"

She looked at me and a whole new wave of fear washed across her features.

"I think I'm wiggling them," she said, trying to raise her head to look at her feet, but the strap across her forehead kept her secure.

"Hold on."

Rolling Thunder

I crab-walked my way to the foot of the backboard and gently unlaced, then removed her boots, wincing with every movement of my hands. The anesthetic had worn off, and they hurt like a son of a bitch.

"OK. Wiggle again."

I let out a big sigh of relief when all her toes started waving in the air, and the smile on my face was all she needed to let her know everything was working as it was supposed to. Quickly, I pulled the straps loose and a moment later Rachel was free and sitting up. She started to say something then clamped her mouth shut and scrambled out the back door, running to the far end of the barn and disappearing into an empty horse stall.

Grinning, I stepped out and looked around for Dog. He was stretched out on a pile of straw in a stall with one of the horses. They had both been asleep, waking when Rachel made her bathroom dash. Dog lay there looking at me with half-closed eyes, his tail lazily wagging just enough to rustle the straw.

Out of old habit, I reached to my breast pocket for a pack of cigarettes that wasn't there. Muttering a curse, I sat down on the back bumper of the ambulance. A couple of minutes later,

Rachel came back joined me. She surveyed the damaged back end of the vehicle then turned to me with an expectant look on her face.

I filled her in on all that had happened since she had been knocked unconscious by the exploding fuel tanks. It took a while and I made sure I didn't leave anything out until I got to our arrival at the barn. I told her about the bodies in the house, but didn't go into details about the three men I'd shot and chained up in the forest. Some things I do, and they damn well need doing, but that doesn't mean I'm proud of them.

We talked for a few more minutes then decided to walk down to the house to see if the water was still on. Rachel dug clean clothes out of our packs while I checked the clock in the ambulance and noted we were still ok on time. But it wasn't going to be long before we needed to start moving again in case the herd was heading our direction.

I had pulled the Dodge truck into the barn after hiding the Toyota behind the horse trailer, so no vehicles were visible to passerby. Walking around it, I raised my rifle when we reached the doors. Dog stood, shook the straw out of his fur and joined us. Unlocking the doors, I pushed one of them open a few inches and looked out at a sunny afternoon.

Seeing nothing out of the ordinary, I slowly kept pushing, sweeping through my expanding view with the rifle. No infected waited to pounce and no survivors waited to ambush. Stepping fully out of the barn, I told Dog to stay with Rachel while I made a full circle of the building to make sure we were alone.

It was a beautiful afternoon. The temperature was probably somewhere close to eighty, the sun was shining brightly, birds were singing in the trees and a gentle breeze mitigated what could have been oppressive humidity. It was out of the north and I glanced in that direction, seeing heavy storm clouds on the horizon.

Somewhere it was raining like hell. I knew there were a lot of streams and rivers in the area that flooded spectacularly from time to time, but had no idea if rain that far away would drain into this part of the state. Something to keep my eye on.

Reconnaissance complete, I rejoined them and we walked to the house. Again, leaving Dog with Rachel, I went to each end of the house to check our perimeter, staying behind bushes to move to the edge of the wall to scope out the front. Still all clear. At the back, we moved through the screened porch and into the kitchen.

Rachel checked the sink and smiled when water flowed from the tap. Keeping the rifle up and ready, I led the way to the bedrooms, bypassing the one with the dead girl. The master was obviously the man's room. It was neat and orderly, the bathroom just as clean. I did a quick clear of the room and left Rachel to get cleaned up.

Back in the front room, I sat down in a leather wing chair that had a good view out the front windows and screen door. I had only been sitting for a minute when I got back up and went to the unoccupied bedroom to retrieve a sheet that I used to cover the man's body.

I wasn't spooked or bothered by the corpse. It was just one of those funny little quirks of mine. Leaving a body lying out in the open is disrespectful. Covering it up was acknowledging that this was a person that didn't deserve what had happened to him. Strange? Maybe, but that's how I think.

Rachel took a long time in the bathroom. Getting bored, I left Dog to keep an eye out and wandered into the kitchen to find some food.

Rolling Thunder

The pantry was well stocked, as was the refrigerator. The power was still on so nothing had spoiled.

Taking my time, I put together a large meal for us, finishing off one of the half gallon cartons of milk while I prepared the food. I was still working when Rachel walked in, wet hair hanging down her back and soaking her T-shirt. Her dirty clothes were balled up in her arms. She poked around, opening doors until she found a laundry area.

"Give me your dirty clothes and go shower. I'll finish making the food," she said, stuffing her clothes into a washer.

"We really don't have time for that," I said, pausing to look at her over my shoulder.

"We have time if you'll get your ass in gear," she said. "By the time you shower and we eat, our clothes will be clean, and if we have to go, we can take them with us still wet. After a couple of days of tromping through the woods and fighting, we need to get clean. You smell like a slaughterhouse and look worse. You happy with all that blood on you?"

I looked down at myself and saw what she meant. My shirt was as stiff as a board with dried blood, both my own and infected, and for the first time I noticed the smell. Giving in to the inevitable, I took my weapons off and piled them on the table, stripped naked and headed to the shower with pistol in hand.

7

Getting clean always feels good. Getting clean with wounds in both hands and your ear nearly ripped off your head adds a new dimension to it, but I still felt better. Twenty minutes later I was freshly showered, dressed and sitting at the kitchen table with Rachel.

The clothes had washed quickly and were tumbling in the dryer as we ate. I hadn't realized how hungry I was until I started eating and couldn't remember the last food I'd had. As I thought about it, I realized it was the breakfast at Arnold Air Force Base, several days ago. Don't know why it mattered. It was just one of those things my mind had to work out before I could move on to anything else.

"So where from here?" Rachel asked as she pushed an empty plate towards the middle of the table.

"North for a little, then turn west," I answered around a mouthful of food. "I still think avoiding Nashville is a very good idea."

Rachel nodded as she leaned across and stole some of the food off my plate.

Dirk Patton

"How are your hands?"

"They're hurting pretty bad. I need you to inject them again."

Rachel reached across the table and I put my right hand in hers. She examined the palm first, then turned it over to check the back. Releasing it, she examined my left the same way.

"All things considered, they don't look too bad. No external sign of infection, but you're not out of the woods yet."

She stood up and circled the table, coming up behind me and bending to check my ear.

"That medic actually did a good job of sewing your ear. He wasn't kidding about it being almost ripped off. There's only about half an inch of skin that's intact. I can see some redness, so we need to get some antibiotic ointment on it. And you need another shot."

Great. Another shot in the ass! I started to make some sarcastic comment about Rachel just wanting me to drop my pants, but remembered the last injection she'd given me and decided I'd be better off just nodding my head and keeping my mouth shut. I finished eating while she folded our freshly laundered clothes, made sure Dog got his share, then we headed for the barn.

In the back of the ambulance, Rachel attended to my injuries. New bandages and another sore spot on my ass later, I told her to gather all the medical supplies we might need and went to check out the Dodge. The ambulance had gotten us out of Murfreesboro and clear of the carpet bombing, but it had taken enough damage that I was ready to trade vehicles.

The Dodge was one of the huge, dual rear wheel trucks you see retirees using in the summer to drag their giant fifth wheel RV trailers all over the country. It had four doors and a back seat big enough for three grown men to sit across without being crowded. In the bed was the hitch for the fifth wheel horse trailer parked behind the barn. The best part was the hundred-gallon auxiliary fuel tank that was full of diesel.

I was pleased, but not surprised. If you're pulling a heavy trailer long distances, you go through a lot of fuel and it's a pain in the ass to stop along the interstate where the prices are higher. A lot of guys add these tanks so they can fill them before a trip with cheaper fuel. Another benefit is they don't have to worry about pulling off for anything other than a restroom or food.

We spent almost half an hour getting the truck loaded and organized. When we were done, I stood there looking at the horses. I toyed with the idea of hooking up the trailer and loading them. There were saddles as well as pack gear in the barn, and the animals could come in handy if we found ourselves on foot again. Then the image of being tackled off the back of a horse by an infected female went through my head and I decided that maybe that wasn't such a good idea.

Opening the double doors, I walked around to each stall and led the horses out of the barn. There was plenty of food for them in the pasture and streams abounded in the area, so they'd be able to find water. They might not be as comfortable as they were accustomed to, but then I wasn't as comfortable as I had grown accustomed to, either. We endured what we had to if we wanted to survive.

Standing in the doorway with Rachel and Dog, we watched the horses wander out into the pasture and start grazing in the late afternoon sun. I raised my eyes and tensed when I spotted the shambling figures of two infected males making their way across the back side of the pasture. Knowing where they were heading, I told Rachel it was time to go, and we piled into the truck.

Dog seemed happy to resume his former position, sitting on the back floor and resting his chin on the console between the two front seats. Scratching his ears, I started the truck and backed out of the barn. Driving around the house, I turned north when we reached the highway.

The Dodge was almost new with only fifteen thousand miles on the odometer. Like most new vehicles, it had navigation built into a display in the dash. This is good for finding out where you are, or guiding you to a specific location, but not so hot for planning a route that will keep you out of populated areas.

Fortunately, the owner of the truck was also a little old school and went in for paper maps. Using the one folded into the glove box, I had planned our route to skirt the majority of Lebanon. Rachel sat with it open on her lap, guiding me through the turns needed to follow the course I'd charted.

We drove on small streets through everything from industrial areas, to neat little neighborhoods and what looked like Lebanon's version of a ghetto. Nothing moved. No survivors or infected, and the houses looked abandoned. Creepy was a good word and our communication was limited to quiet instructions on which way to turn.

Lebanon wasn't a large town and we were soon north of it, moving along US highway 231. My plan was to keep going until we came to state highway 10, where we would turn west to Gallatin. From there, a series of small highways would keep us well north of Nashville and eventually to Dyersburg, Tennessee.

Once in Dyersburg, I hoped we could cross the Mississippi River. I had spent some time scouring the map and had been surprised to find there was only one bridge that crossed the river between Cairo, Illinois and Memphis. I wasn't about to go anywhere near Memphis, and I'd heard reports that the upper mid-west had been hit hard by the nerve gas as well.

I didn't have a solid plan B in the event the bridge at Dyersburg wasn't passable. It could be jammed with abandoned refugee vehicles. It could be swarming with infected. It could be being used by survivors to set up an ambush. It could have been blown up and dropped into the river by the military so infected couldn't cross.

Rolling Thunder

The odds were not in our favor, but it was our best option at the moment. I had a couple of ideas for plan B if it was needed, but wasn't too fond of either of them.

We pushed on, driving through sunshine, but the storm clouds on the northern horizon were foreboding. The highway was completely empty. No wrecked or abandoned vehicles. No other traffic. It was like the world had just packed up and left us behind.

We hadn't driven long before coming to the Cumberland River. I slowed to under forty as we approached the bridge, scanning for any signs of an ambush. If someone like me was lying in wait, I'd never spot the ambush until it was too late. Fortunately, there aren't too many out there like me. If my wife Katie were here, she'd say that was very fortunate.

The bridge over the Cumberland was big, rising up from the shore to the midpoint of the river. Reaching the crest, I came to a stop and looked out the side window at the water below. I didn't know what a normal level was for the river where it went under the bridge, but I could tell it was higher than usual. A lot higher.

Neither bank was visible as the river had flooded into the trees on each bank. Looking around and feeling fairly secure, I put the truck into park. Leaving the engine running, I stepped out of the cab. Dog hopped out with me to take advantage of virgin territory for his mark and a moment later Rachel followed.

Standing at the railing, I leaned out and looked at the muddy water rushing beneath us. The surface of the river was maybe twenty feet below the bottom of the bridge deck. I watched for a few minutes, noting the level on the concrete pilings. It rose noticeably as I was standing there. Looking up at the northern horizon, I saw the storm clouds still piled up and the breeze blowing in my face was heavy with the smell of rain.

We all got back in the truck and I picked the map out of Rachel's lap and started checking our route for river crossings. After turning west, we had a crossing over what was labeled as Old Hickory Lake. On the map, it appeared to be part of a river that ran down from the north. After that, we had another half a dozen crossings, including the Cumberland again, before reaching Dyersburg then the Mississippi.

I re-checked, looking for routes that would avoid the rivers, but Tennessee is full of them and there weren't any better ways. I looked north of the route I'd planned, but there were just as many, if not more, bridges. Oh, well. Onward, and we'd deal with what we found.

8

We kept heading north and soon passed a sign that told us the turn for Gallatin was nineteen miles ahead. The storm clouds continued their push in our direction as we drove directly towards them. The entire horizon was obscured for as far as I could see to the east or west.

I didn't know this area of the country well, didn't know if it was normal for storms this large to roll into Tennessee. I briefly wondered if the multiple nuclear bombs that had gone off in New York were able to influence the weather this far away. That led to concerns that the storm might contain radioactive fallout. I have such cheery thoughts.

I kept my attention on the road ahead, alert for any problems we might encounter. While I drove, Rachel started fiddling with the big touch screen in the middle of the dash. She navigated through several menus and after turning the AC on high, twice, let out a sigh of frustration and stabbed at the screen.

Rolling Thunder

"What are you trying to find?" I asked, not pausing in my scan of the upcoming pavement and shoulders.

"I'm hoping Max made it out of Georgia," she answered. "There really wasn't anywhere else for him to go other than Tennessee and if he made it, maybe he's broadcasting, but I can't find the damn radio. Everything else – I can tell you how many hours this engine has been turned on, how many gallons of fuel this truck has used since it was built, but I can't find the... ahhhh, there it is."

Rachel stabbed another button and music started playing loudly. That got my attention. Since the morning after the attacks, there hadn't been any commercial broadcasts and I was very surprised to hear a radio station.

"What is that?" I asked, trying to watch the road ahead and the screen at the same time.

"Satellite radio. It's still broadcasting."

Rachel kept selecting options and soon brought up a menu of the satellite stations. Selecting the news category, she started picking stations, but every one she tried yielded silence as perfect as only digital radio can be. Getting the hang of things, she switched the system to the

FM band and had it scan. It swept through all the frequencies without finding a signal. She came up with the same results after trying the AM band.

Back to satellite, she started scrolling through everything that wasn't news and found many of the music stations still broadcasting. She stopped on one she apparently liked and turned the sound way up. Out of the corner of my eye, I could see her moving around as the music blasted and I turned my head to see her dancing in the seat with a smile on her face.

Dog's ears were straight up, and he was staring at her too. The song sounded familiar, but I didn't know what it was until I checked the display screen. Michael Jackson, Don't Stop 'Till You Get Enough. Are you kidding me? The world has ended, and I'm listening to Michael Jackson?

Rachel was really getting into the music, moving her shoulders and head to the beat and when it hit me, I roared with laughter. I tried not to look at her, but couldn't help myself. The more I looked, the harder I laughed. Tears rolled down my face and I had to slow the big pickup for fear of driving off the side of the road.

"What?" Rachel shouted over the pounding music without missing a move, a half smile on her face.

Rolling Thunder

"Did you ever see Rush Hour? Jackie Chan and Chris Tucker? You dance like them! How the hell did you make a living with moves like that?"

I barely sputtered the last line out, nearly choking myself as I laughed. Part of me knew her dance really wasn't that funny, but after what we'd been through we were both ready for any little bit of levity.

Rachel smiled sweetly at me and worked a raised middle finger into her dance. I could only keep laughing, finally getting it under control as the song ended. Both of us were smiling, and it felt good to have one minute to think about something other than the apocalypse.

"Oh, hell no!" I said when the next song started.

I recognized something by the Bee Gees and began stabbing buttons. I got the radio moved off of the offending station and for the hell of it, hit the menu that scanned the AM band. Rachel and I both jumped in our seats when a voice we recognized as Max blasted out of the speakers, the volume still high from Rachel's dance party.

"...tell you the truth."

Max paused and lit the usual cigarette he liked to smoke while broadcasting. I fiddled with the touch screen and turned the volume down to just below ear-splitting. Slowing quickly, I braked to a stop in the middle of the highway so I could concentrate on what Max had to say.

"We've made it out of Georgia and into Nashville, but I'm not sure we're any better off. This town is falling apart around us as I speak. I've got a lot to tell you, so make sure you're in a safe location and hunker down. I'll start with the more important stuff. What's going on for you folks within range of my signal.

"There has been a new outbreak, or a second outbreak, or whatever you want to call it. It's been a little over two weeks since we had the attacks and most of the people that weren't outright killed were exposed and infected. That seemed like it was going to be the end of it, but a couple of days ago, people who seemed completely normal suddenly became infected and started attacking those around them. The latest word is this was designed by the Chinese. I can't tell you if people are still turning, or if there will be more outbreaks, but watch your backs.

"Now on to the herds approaching Nashville. The Air Force took a playbook from the

Rolling Thunder

Vietnam War and tried carpet bombing the big one coming up from the south. It slowed them down, but we just don't have enough bombs to stop them. There was also a stand made in a town called Murfreesboro, but it only slowed the leading edge of the herd for a couple of hours. They're back on the move and are approaching the southern suburbs of Nashville. If you're still here, you need to do what I'm going to do and get out! They'll be walking through downtown in about five or six hours.

"Safety lies to the west, but there's a problem. The military has destroyed all the vehicle bridges that cross the Mississippi river."

Rachel and I looked at each other and she reached out to take my hand in hers.

"The only crossings still open are railroad bridges, and there's not many of those. The only way to cross the river is on a train, or take your chances and try to walk on the bridge. But there's steady rail traffic and if you get caught mid-span, you can either jump or get run over.

"Herds are also coming west from the eastern seaboard as well as moving south through Kentucky. The military was especially hard hit in the most recent outbreak, and there aren't enough soldiers left to defend us. Nashville is going to fall."

Max paused, coughed a couple of times and lit another cigarette. I wanted one so bad at the moment I could taste it.

"On to the rest of the world. The Navy has stopped the Chinese battle groups in the Pacific. It's not looking like there's going to be a land invasion. That's about the only good news there is. The US, with assistance from NATO, has launched more attacks against China, dispersing the same nerve agent that they used on us, and China is in complete chaos. Unfortunately, China also launched attacks on Europe, and the entire continent is in shambles.

"In the Middle East, Israel has launched pre-emptive nuclear strikes against Iran, Syria and several other radical Muslim countries. Russia remains neutral and is on full military alert. So far they haven't been attacked by anyone. Africa has disintegrated into civil and tribal warfare. Closer to home, Canada is in no better shape than the US as all its major cities were also victim to the nerve gas. Northern Mexico is in chaos and the Mexican army, with assistance from several South American countries, has set up a defensive barrier two hundred miles south of the US border.

Rolling Thunder

Everything south of that line has so far not been affected. Australia is also free of attacks and infection.

"I'm boarding the last train at midnight, heading west. You must get out. There's not anyone left to come help you. God bless you, and God bless America. What's left of it."

After a brief moment, the signal shut off and a blast of static sounded over the speakers. Reaching forward, I shut the radio off and leaned back in my seat with a long sigh. Rachel was quiet too, processing what we'd just heard.

"What are we going to do?" She finally asked in a low voice.

I picked up the map and stared at it. It took me a moment to spot our location. We were northeast of Nashville, maybe a forty-five-minute drive to downtown in the old days. Now, it could take hours or even days to cover the same distance.

Thoughts were swirling through my head. Some dismissed as soon as I had them, others quickly categorized as good or bad. After a few minutes of poring over the map, I looked up at the navigation screen in the dash and pressed a button to access the menu.

Several miscues later, I got the damn thing to display a listing for Nashville's Union Station. Selecting it as my destination, a small circle spun on the screen for a few moments before a map appeared with a route from our location to the train station. The path was highlighted by a thick, blue line. What I assumed was an alternate route was shown by a thick, yellow line. A female voice spoke over the truck's speakers telling me two route choices were available to reach my destination. Route one was forty-one point six miles and route two was forty-nine point one miles.

I stared at the screen. The blue route took us back through Lebanon to I-40, then west into downtown Nashville. The yellow route continued on to Gallatin as we had planned, then turned south on I-65 and into downtown Nashville. I wasn't happy with either choice, but the longer we could stay north of the city, the better off I thought we'd be.

Reaching out, I selected route two, which took us through Gallatin. The voice told me to proceed in my current direction of travel for sixteen point four miles. I stepped on the throttle and roared north towards the approaching storm.

9

"What's the plan?" Rachel asked again, eyeing the navigation screen as I drove.

"We've got two ways across that damn river," I said. "Fly, which unless you have a skill you've kept to yourself, isn't an option. Or, catch a train. We're going to catch a train. I'm not happy about it, but I don't see any other way at this point."

Rachel thought about what I had to say then nodded her head. Dog was just happy to be along for the ride, as usual.

"Can we make it into Nashville? This map looks like we have to go right downtown," Rachel said, still looking at the screen.

"We have to try. It's going to be hard. Sounds like there're infected all over the place and the survivors are going to be in a panic. I'll get us there, but I don't expect to be able to just drive up and park at the station. Max said the last one leaves at midnight. If we're not there and on that train by then, we back out and try to come up with something else."

Dirk Patton

Rachel had listened closely as I talked, her hand drifting to rest on top of Dog's head. He closed his eyes and enjoyed the contact. Not for the first time in my life I thought I'd want to come back as a dog if there really was such a thing as reincarnation. Sleep, eat and get your head rubbed. How bad can that be? Then I remembered the whole neutering thing and decided being a human wasn't so bad.

It didn't take long to reach the road for Gallatin, the disembodied voice warning me the turn was coming a mile before we got there. Slowing, I steered us onto the new highway as the first drops of rain splattered on the truck's windshield. The leading edge of the storm was here and blocked out the evening light from the setting sun. We drove on through the gloom, the intensity of the storm increasing with every mile and the wind picking up enough to occasionally push the truck around on the rain-slicked pavement.

The Dodge had good headlights and I was running with them on high as we approached Gallatin. We started passing the occasional house and double wide trailer, then a small gas station. Everything was dark and felt abandoned. Nothing was moving, survivor or infected, and the rain intensified as we rolled into town and passed an empty Walmart.

"Where did everyone go?" Rachel asked in a low voice that sounded like she was just musing out loud, so I didn't bother to answer with what would only have been a theory.

Quickly the number of buildings along the road increased and we were soon passing dark fast food joints, bars, strip malls and the omnipresent Starbucks. What I wouldn't give right now for an iced mocha and a cigarette. Daydreaming about past vices nearly ended our day early when I was slow to react to a vehicle that barreled out of a side street.

I wrenched the wheel to the left and jammed the brakes as the car scraped along the passenger side of the truck. Rain was pouring, the road was slick and we went into a skid. I lost the battle for control as the big truck slid off the pavement and into the grassy median that divided the highway. We came to a stop without any further incident and the car roared off into the distance. Clouds of water thrown up by its tires hung in the air, obscuring the red taillights.

Rachel had a death grip on a grab bar on her side of the cab. Dog wound up on his back somewhere behind me, grunting as he scrambled back to his feet. What the hell was that about? Then a bad thought hit me and I turned to look out the back window of the truck at the road the car had emerged from.

A dozen figures were visible, sprinting toward us through the rain. Infected females. The other driver had been in a panic, running for his life. They were still a hundred yards away and weren't an immediate threat, so I gently pressed on the throttle to get us back on the pavement and out of there. The engine got louder and a moment later I heard the high pitched whine of tires spinning on wet grass. Shit!

Letting off the accelerator, I shifted into reverse and fed in a little power but got the same results. The truck was two-wheel drive, so I couldn't just pull a lever and go into four by four and drive us out. We weren't going anywhere without a little assistance to get back onto the pavement. Rachel and Dog were getting antsy and I glanced over my shoulder at the approaching females. They had cut the distance in half and were still sprinting.

"Time to fight," I said to Rachel, popped my door open and stepped out into the rain.

Dog followed and Rachel scrambled across the cab. She slipped on the wet running board as she started to step out, ending up face down in a large puddle of water. I yanked her onto her feet and turned my attention to the fast-approaching females.

The truck was sideways in the median and between us and the infected. I raised my rifle and rested my arm on the bed rail, acquiring my first target and firing. The body dropped and I started picking off the other running figures. Two of them from the back of the pack changed direction and ran perpendicular to me as soon as I started shooting. Fuck me, but here were more smart ones. I had hoped the ones I'd encountered in the woods south of Murfreesboro had been an anomaly. Apparently not.

Right now, I didn't have time to worry about them. Of the original pack, there were still five of them sprinting at us and they were all inside twenty yards. Shooting one, I shifted aim and noted that Rachel was now standing next to me. Her rifle fired at the same instant as mine and two more dropped. Then we ran out of time.

The two that were still charging leapt, both landing in the back of the truck. One of them came down on the fifth wheel hitch and I clearly heard her leg break over the pounding rain. The other leapt again, directly at me. I had already backpedaled and drawn my pistol. She hit the ground three feet in front of me and started to gather herself for another leap. Before she could launch herself into the air, she was tackled to the ground by Dog.

Knowing he would finish her off, I looked for the other female and saw Rachel struggling with her at the side of the truck. She hadn't moved back as quickly as I had and even with a broken leg, the female had managed to lunge forward and get a grip on her rifle. The infected was trying to pull it out of the way as Rachel used it to fend her off.

Stepping forward, I shot the female in the head with my pistol then spun around to check on Dog. He stood in the rain, looking drenched and unhappy. The female he had tackled lay dead on the ground a few feet away with most of her throat missing.

Holstering the pistol, I brought the rifle up and scanned in the direction the two smart females had run. Nothing. Turning a full three sixty, I still couldn't find them, but there were plenty of buildings they could be hiding in or behind. Keeping the rifle up and continuing my scan, I paused when I thought I detected movement at the edge of a burger place. It was only trash blowing in the wind.

Rachel moved a few feet away from me and started scanning with her rifle. I was happy to note that she was careful to lower the muzzle as she rotated through the direction I was standing. Dog moved between us, nose slightly raised.

We stood there watching for a couple of minutes but neither of us spotted anything. Knowing we were burning time we didn't have, I told Rachel and Dog to keep watch. Lowering my rifle, I looked over the situation the truck was in.

The median sloped slightly away from the pavement on each side, the center being about two feet lower than the edge of the road. This was done to drain water. The grass the truck was sitting on was dense and rain slick. Slippery even under the soles of my boots. The truck was perpendicular to the pavement with the rear tires sitting in the lowest part of the median.

I thought about trying to get it moving again but quickly dismissed the impulse. All that would be accomplished would be to dig through the grass, into the mud. Then we'd really be screwed, with no way to get it out other than a tow truck. I didn't think AAA was going to answer their phone.

Checking on Rachel, who was still scanning for threats, I started looking at the businesses up and down the highway. Through the limited visibility, I saw what I thought looked like a local hardware store about half a mile down the road. Hoping they'd have what I needed, I closed up the cab of the truck, hit the lock button on the key and dropped it in my pocket.

Calling Rachel and Dog onto the pavement, I pointed out our destination and told Rachel to lead the way. I would normally take point, or be the one in front, but with two females running around in the quickly darkening evening I was more worried about our rear and flanks. Rachel was learning the skills she needed but I knew I was the one to keep an eye on three directions at once as we moved.

Setting off through the rain, Dog trailed Rachel. I stepped off behind him, maintaining about twenty feet of separation. We moved as fast as we could, but when you're trying to watch every direction at once, you don't move too fast.

Ten minutes later we reached the business I'd seen. It was as I suspected, a local hardware store, and if it matters it was called

Rolling Thunder

Mick's. The front of the business was all glass and either the power was out, or the proprietor had turned off all the lights when he left. Either way, the interior was dark as a tomb.

Having Rachel watch our backs, I tried the door and wasn't surprised to find it locked. Using the muzzle of my rifle, I tapped hard on the glass a few times, hoping if there were any infected inside they would come to investigate so I could shoot them. Giving it a long minute with no response, I stepped back and fired half a dozen rounds from my suppressed rifle through the glass.

This was safety glass and didn't shatter and drop out of the doorframe. Instead, six neat holes were punched through, each surrounded by a spider web of cracks. The holes were in the same general area, and I kicked the weakened glass out of the frame without making a lot of racket.

Telling Rachel and Dog to stay put, I stepped through the opening and had to click on the flashlight attached to my rifle to see. I walked the width of the front of the store, aiming down each aisle as I came to it just in case there were infected that hadn't been attracted to my tapping. When all seemed clear, I carefully moved to the back of the building.

At the very back, a large section had been devoted to lumber. Heavy duty, steel shelving held all different dimensions of boards and I quickly located what I was looking for. I pulled two, twelve-foot-long 2x8 pine boards off a shelf and leaned them against the stack on end so I could get a shoulder underneath.

A sudden banging from above sent a fresh surge of adrenalin pumping through my system and I snapped the rifle up, seeking the source of the noise. A set of windows in the wall a dozen feet above floor level looked over the store. Probably the manager's office. Shining the light through one of them, I could see an infected male pressed against the glass and pounding with both fists.

Lowering the rifle and ignoring him, I squatted, got my shoulder under the two boards and stood. Taking a moment to get the load balanced, I turned in place, swinging around to head for the front of the store. As I completed my turn, I heard a crack then the sound of shattering glass from behind. A moment later there was the heavy thud of a body impacting the painted concrete floor.

Rolling Thunder

Dropping the boards off my shoulder, I pivoted, rifle coming up and spotlighting the male I had seen in the office window. He was dead, having fallen on his head. His neck was bent at an angle so unnatural it could only mean that it was broken. I let out a breath and lowered my rifle, turning back to pick up the lumber I had dropped and was tackled to the floor.

10

The female that tackled me hadn't screamed or done anything else to alert me to her presence. I didn't know if she had come out of the office with the male, or had been skulking around the store waiting for an opportunity to attack. Regardless, she was obviously one of the smart ones and had hit me hard in the side. Most of the wind had been knocked out of me and my head bounced off the concrete floor when I went down, stars popping to life in the darkness before my eyes.

I felt hands grasping for my throat and I pushed everything else aside and started fighting. I got a grip on her hands, but she was strong and moved with a frightening speed. Every time I shifted my weight to try and gain some leverage, she responded before I could take advantage of the new position.

She was trying to reach my face and throat with her teeth while she struggled to break her arms free. I was having trouble maintaining control. Shifting again, I was prepared for her move and turned with her, succeeding in rolling her underneath me where I could use my greater body weight to my advantage.

Rolling Thunder

Forcing her arms into a cross, I locked in the leverage and used the weight of my upper body to press forward. I was rewarded with a snap as her right arm broke. A normal human would have reacted to the injury but she kept fighting like she hadn't felt a thing.

She squirmed under me, bucking and twisting and nearly succeeded in throwing me off as we scrambled on the floor. Finally getting around her broken arm, I pressed my forearm onto her throat and leaned into it as hard as I could while trying to draw my knife. She fought harder, trying to twist her head to get away from the pressure I was applying but couldn't overcome my strength.

I couldn't get a grip on my knife, needing my free hand to fend off the slashing nails that were aimed at my eyes. We kept struggling and after close to a minute she began weakening from lack of air. I was compressing her throat so hard there was no way she was breathing. From that point, she went quickly.

Less than another minute later, she went from fighting to twitching as her brain died from lack of oxygen. Finally, she lay still underneath me and I wasted no time in flipping the body over, drawing my knife and stabbing into her brain to make sure she stayed down. Not having time to celebrate my victory, I climbed back to my feet, grabbed the boards and headed for the exit.

Rachel and Dog were still on watch and fell in on either side of me as I walked out the front of the store and headed for our stuck vehicle. It was raining harder and the sun was long gone, making it about as dark as could be. The only respite were the widely spaced street lights that ran down each side of the road. So, the power was still on.

The bad thing was the street lights were set so far apart that the light one shed didn't meet up with the light from the next one. Dark areas were left between each pair of poles. The unlit areas seemed to be all the darker because of the contrasting light on either side.

"Watch the dark spots between the lights," I said to Rachel as we walked.

"Got it."

I walked with the two boards on my left shoulder, pistol ready in my right hand. With the extra, ungainly weight, I wouldn't be winning any pistol shooting competitions, but I knew I'd be able to hit anything within forty feet or so. We covered the distance to the truck slightly slower than we had made it to the store, but we made it without encountering any more infected.

I stopped fifty feet from the truck, lowered the boards to the ground, raised my rifle and flicked the flashlight on. First, I checked under the truck to make sure there weren't any surprises waiting for us, then slowly worked my way forward and checked the bed. All clear.

Scooping up the boards, I put one in place on each side, jamming an end under the front edge of each set of rear tires. As long as I could drive the truck up and onto the boards, we'd have a solid path to the pavement. But if I gave it too much throttle, the tires would just grab the boards and spit them out behind us without moving an inch. Ready to go, we all climbed into the cab and I started the engine and shifted into drive.

I pressed on the accelerator like I had an egg under my foot, applying just enough pressure to change the engine note. We didn't move and I didn't hear any indication of the rear tires spinning. I gave it a fraction more throttle, then we were moving.

Slowly at first as the tires came up off the grass and onto the lumber, then faster as we rolled up the hill. I pressed a little harder to get some speed and momentum so we didn't bog down when we came off the front edge of the boards. We bumped off the end and the truck kept going until we were back on asphalt and heading deeper into town.

"Everything ok in the store? I heard some noise."

Rachel was drying her rain soaked hair with a towel she had taken from the house we'd stayed at earlier.

"I won't be going back there. They have a lousy approach to customer service."

Rachel looked at me, grinned and shook her head then went back to blotting the water out of her hair.

"Actually, I think one of the smart females I told you about was in there. She was absolutely silent until she attacked. I can't say for sure. She may have been in an office with a male that broke through a window and let her out, but I think she was stalking me from the moment I entered the store."

The grin on Rachel's face disappeared. She well understood the impact of female infected having enough intelligence to actually hunt the survivors rather than just scream and attack. Up to now we'd been able to count on any infected attack being announced in advance by a scream, but it didn't seem we had that luxury any longer. Survival had gotten a lot tougher.

I glanced at the dash and noted the time on the clock. We'd lost nearly an hour due to our little mishap. Four hours left and we still had to get into downtown Nashville. By nature I'm fairly optimistic, but I was having a hard time thinking we were going to make the last train out before the herd arrived.

I pressed harder with my foot and pushed our speed to eighty. Driving this fast in the dark and rain was risky, but I didn't think it was as risky as not making the last train. With no other way to cross the Mississippi, we'd be stuck between the three herds that were converging on the state.

"So what's Plan B? What do we do if we can't get to the train, or get there too late?"

"We do what the pioneers did. We use a boat to get across. Of course, they had time to build rafts, time we won't have, and I'm having a hard time imagining we'll have much luck finding a boat. Anyone that can get their hands on one has probably already done so. Also, we cross on a boat, we're on foot when we get to the western shore. We can always steal another car or truck, but..." I trailed off, not really sure where my train of thought was going.

We blasted through Gallatin without seeing any other people, infected or healthy, and quickly reached the highway where the GPS voice told me to turn. State Highway 386 turned us to the southwest and would connect with I-65 in a few miles. I kept our speed up, wipers on high.

The rain was falling even harder. Torrential best describes it, and the wipers did their best, but couldn't keep up with the volume of water that was falling out of the sky. The headlights barely pierced the gloom and I had to jam on the brakes and make some fancy maneuvers to avoid a pile up of cars that appeared when we crested a small rise. After much skidding on the wet pavement, I got us back under control and decided to lower our speed a bit.

Reaching I-65 we turned due south towards Nashville and started seeing an occasional car speeding away from the city in the northbound lanes.

"Where do you suppose they're going?" Rachel asked.

Rolling Thunder

"I don't know. This freeway goes up to Kentucky and from what we've heard, things aren't any better up there."

We watched as two more SUVs passed us going north. Both were heavily loaded with people and supplies. One of them was flashing his lights and honking his horn. I didn't know if this was for the other SUV, or if he was trying to warn me about something. It definitely didn't give me a warm fuzzy. I checked the time and our speed and turned the radio on, scanning AM, hoping for an update from Max, but he was off the air.

As we continued south, we started seeing more businesses along the interstate. After only about fifteen minutes of driving, we merged with I-24 that also fed into the city and I had to slow more as we started regularly encountering wrecked or abandoned vehicles. With the darkness and rain, I couldn't see them sitting there until we were almost on top of them and wasn't happy that I had to hold our speed under forty.

Some of the areas we passed through still had power. Most didn't, but there were some that were brightly lit as we drove past. Every one we passed that had light also had large groups of infected stumbling around. I suspected the dark ones did too. We just couldn't see them. The navigation screen showed the freeway we were on splitting a short distance ahead, and the voice told me to stay on I-24.

Approaching the interchange where the road split, I stepped on the brakes and came to a stop. Ahead were two lanes that swept up onto a ramp and was the direction the GPS wanted me to go. But the ramp was jammed with tangled wrecks. Looking at the screen it appeared that I-65 could get us where we were going, it just dipped farther south before getting there.

All three of us jumped when a female slammed into my door, beating on the glass with bloody fists. A second later, two more were pounding on Rachel's window and I stepped on the throttle and started us moving forward again. We quickly left them behind, but as we slalomed our way through the wreckage on the pavement we encountered more infected.

We were running many of them down, crushing their bodies under the heavy tires. There was no power in this area and they would just suddenly appear out of the rain, right in front of us. Even if I had wanted to avoid them, I couldn't have.

Rolling Thunder

"Is this a good idea? Going into the city, I mean," Rachel asked.

I kept my eyes glued to the road ahead and a tight grip on the steering wheel as I answered.

"If I said I wasn't having second thoughts, I'd be lying, but the situation hasn't changed. We need to try and get to that train."

Rachel didn't say anything, just stared ahead as intently as I was. Dog might have had a different opinion but he kept it to himself. We drove like this for another mile. Then the wrecks thinned out and I was able to put on a little more speed. I still didn't want to be going too fast and damage the truck by crashing into a large group of infected.

Directly ahead was a pale glow that strengthened as we approached. When we crested a rise, I hit the brakes, bringing us to a complete stop. Less than a mile away, a defensive barricade had been set up. It looked much like the wall I'd built in Murfreesboro and it was lit like Christmas morning. Pressed against the base were thousands, if not tens of thousands, of infected. They were trying to get to the men on top of the barricade that blocked our route.

11

For the moment, there weren't any infected in our immediate vicinity. Shutting off the headlights so we didn't draw attention, I sat and stared at the barricade. Rachel was mumbling something I couldn't understand and I didn't bother to ask her to repeat it.

We could either turn around and try to find our way to the river and hope there would be a boat we could steal, or we could find a way around this and get to the train. The existence of the barricade encouraged me. Gave me a little hope that if we could get around it, we could make it to the train. Forward.

I messed with the navigation screen and found an exit a mile behind us that looked like our best option. We were eight miles from the train station and while I fully expected to have to cover some of that on foot, I didn't want to walk any farther than absolutely necessary. The more time we spent outside the protection of a vehicle, the greater the chances of a lethal encounter with a group of infected. Or survivors, I reminded myself. Shifting into reverse, I backed up until the crest hid us from the barricade before turning the lights back on.

Rolling Thunder

"What are we doing?" Rachel asked.

"There's an exit a mile back. We're going to get off the freeway and work our way to the train station on surface streets. This looks like an industrial area and I'm hoping there won't be that many infected roaming around. If we're lucky, all of them in the area have been drawn to the barricade."

I got the truck turned around and started driving north in the southbound lanes. I wasn't particularly worried about running into anyone as we had only seen a very few vehicles moving and they were all going away from Nashville. Reaching the exit, I swung wide and made the turn onto the ramp which quickly took us below the level of the elevated freeway.

At the bottom of the ramp, two pickups and a police car were smashed into each other. The metal was so mangled that it was all but impossible to tell where one vehicle ended and the other began. Bouncing over the concrete median, I slowly drove around it, moving under the cover of the freeway and out of the rain. The sudden absence of what had become an incessant pounding on the sheet metal roof was a physical relief. The wipers finally caught up with the rain and quickly started squeaking their way across the glass.

Glancing at the navigation screen, I made a left, splashing through several inches of water that had accumulated on the road. All too quickly, we left the protection of the overpass and the wipers stopped squeaking as they were once again overwhelmed by the deluge. Driving slowly down a wide road, I tried to watch for any threats, but it was too dark and visibility was only a dozen or so yards. Driving between rows of gigantic, two-story warehouses we were making good time, but I wasn't about to push our speed and get us into trouble.

All the warehouses had massive parking lots to accommodate the eighteen wheelers that routinely visited them. The lots were surrounded with tall, sturdy chain link fencing. The truck's headlights spilled enough illumination to the side that I could see through into many of the lots. Infected pressed up against the barrier, trying to reach us.

Rachel stared at them out of her window as we slowly drove past. After several minutes, she reached for the dash and turned on the heat to drive off a chill. I run hot by nature and wasn't chilly, but didn't protest.

Rolling Thunder

We had covered almost two miles and according to the navigation system had less than six to go when the road forked at a river. We needed to turn south, but the path was blocked with trailers, stacked five high. The barricade ran from the river bank to the brick wall of a warehouse and it looked like whoever had built it had the time to do it right.

Stopping the truck with a curse, I turned my attention to the navigation screen, looking for a side road that might get us around. There were plenty of smaller streets we had crossed since leaving the freeway, but all of them dead-ended. Not particularly good news. I looked at the screen some more, trying to memorize the layout of streets we needed to follow to get to the train station.

"We're on foot from here, aren't we?" Rachel asked, also looking at the screen.

"Looks that way," I answered in a distracted voice. Breaking my attention from the display, I checked the clock. "We've got about three and a half hours left to cover just under six miles."

I started to finish that sentence with something upbeat and positive about how easy it was going to be, but bit back the thought for fear of jinxing us. Gathering up our gear, we stepped out into the rain, both of us soaked to the skin in moments. Dog stood next to me, looking absolutely miserable, squinting his eyes against the falling water. After a moment, he shook and if I hadn't already been drenched he would have corrected that oversight.

Closing the truck up tight, I hit the lock button on the key before pocketing it. I didn't expect to ever see it again, but if we couldn't make it to the train we would need it to head west.

Raising my rifle, I looked through the night vision scope and scanned a three-hundred-and-sixty-degree circle. I didn't see any immediate threats, but then night vision doesn't let you see any further through the rain than normal vision. Rachel had moved to stand next to me and Dog, and after I finished a second scan of the area I led the way towards the river. My hope was that the barricade didn't go far into the water and we could wade around the end, or at the worst, swim. As we approached, I had to discard that idea.

From the edge of the pavement to the river was a forty-yard swath of grass and as soon as I stepped off the pavement, my feet sank into the saturated ground. Halfway across and the water was over the tops of my boots. I didn't need to take any more steps to realize the swollen water was running fast. Way too fast for any of us to risk going in.

There was an occasional banging noise coming from the barricade and I peered through the scope to try and identify the source. Eventually, I happened to be looking at the right spot when the noise sounded. The rushing river was carrying bodies along with tree limbs and other debris. I watched as a corpse slammed into the metal barricade before whirling away on the current. OK, definitely not going that way!

Turning, I was happy to see Rachel with her rifle up and watching our rear. I stepped next to her and filled her in on what I had seen.

"Could you tell if it was infected or not?" She asked.

"No. All I could see were lots of bodies being carried by the flood. Couldn't even make a guess."

"Couple of males crossing the road near the truck."

She kept her rifle up and aimed as she spoke. I spotted them easily enough but decided to conserve ammo since they were moving parallel to us and seemed to be unaware of our presence.

"I think the only option we have left is to try and go through the warehouse this barricade butts up against. I'm sure there will be doors on the far side, and hopefully, they aren't welded shut."

Rachel nodded and I headed back toward the pavement with her on one side and Dog on the other. He was completely soaked by now and walked with his head hanging down, a constant stream of water running off the end of his muzzle to the ground. I tried to feel sorry for him, but I was just as wet.

The warehouse we needed to get through was one of the largest buildings I had ever seen that wasn't a sports stadium. It was built from red brick and as tall as the barricade. The wall that faced the river was at least six hundred feet long, but the wall that fronted the road was well over a thousand.

The longer side was fitted with a loading dock that ran its entire length and had more roll-up doors than I could count. Every hundred feet,

Rolling Thunder

there was a ramp up from the parking lot with a metal access door at the top. None of these had a handle on the exterior and had most likely been put there to meet the local fire code for emergency exits.

Our first obstacle was a twenty-foot-high chain link fence that surrounded the parking lot. There were also a couple of dozen infected males shambling around, bumping into parked trucks or trailers as they moved. The lot itself was a maze, semi-trucks parked all over.

There were probably a thousand hiding places for the infected and we'd have to be very careful as we moved through. But first, we had to get over or through the fence. Over was out. There was no good way to get Dog big furry ass that high into the air. That meant through or under. We walked the perimeter, looking for a gate.

We finally found it at the far end of the parking lot. The gate was actually a large guard shack with motorized sections of fence that rolled out of the way for incoming and outgoing trucks. The shack was wooden construction for the first four-feet off the pavement, then rows of windows above that to give the guards a good view of the area.

Dirk Patton

It was dark inside the building, but using the night vision scope I spotted three infected males wearing security uniforms. They were all just standing there as if still on duty. I also spotted two doors in the shack. One on the outside of the gate, the other inside so the guards could move in and out without having to open it. Here was our way in, we just had to deal with the infected.

Moving quietly, I stepped up to the exterior door and gingerly tried the knob. It was locked tight. The door was heavy steel with a mesh reinforced window in the top half. I didn't have anything that could force it. I checked the windows and wasn't pleased to note they were marked as ballistic, or bullet resistant. That meant they were very tough and very hard to get through without making enough noise to attract every infected in the state.

I was startled and took an involuntary step back when one of the guards slammed against the inside of the glass right next to me. Soon the other two joined him and all three were pounding away. The sounds of their blows were muted and hardly audible, which was another indication of the strength and thickness of the glass. Well, there's always a way.

Rolling Thunder

Moving Rachel and Dog under a small overhang to give them some protection from the rain, I told them to stay put and jogged the short distance back to where we'd left the truck. The Dodge started up as soon as I turned the key and I quickly had it back to the guard shack, front bumper within a few feet of the locked door.

Digging through the tool box in the bed of the truck, I found the sturdy canvas tow strap I had seen when I'd first inspected the vehicle. I wrapped the strap around the door knob a few turns, tying it off tightly. Hooking the other end to one of the tow hooks hanging below the truck's front bumper, I turned to Rachel.

"OK, hop in. When I signal you, put it in reverse, hit the throttle and don't let off until it either yanks the door off the hinges or the knob out of the door."

She nodded and stepped forward.

"Just watch your ass. I don't need you getting taken out by a flying door," Rachel said as she climbed behind the wheel.

I made a face at her back which she somehow saw, turning and sticking her tongue out at me. A moment later the note of the engine changed slightly when she shifted into reverse and held the big truck in place with the brakes. I moved to the side away from the hinges, made sure Dog was clear and raised my rifle to cover the door.

Looking over at Rachel, I saw her watching me and nodded my head before quickly turning my attention back to the door. The diesel engine roared and the four rear tires momentarily spun on the wet pavement before grabbing the asphalt and sending the truck backwards. The tow strap uncoiled to its full length in a fraction of a second, went taut, then the door popped open with a screeching protest of metal. Rachel did exactly what I told her and the truck continued on to tear the door off its hinges and drag it thirty feet across the pavement.

The males wedged themselves into the opening and I gave them a moment to get outside so I wouldn't have to drag the bodies out of the way after I shot them. The first one stumbled out and when he was in the open, I shot him in the head. I quickly brought down numbers two and three as they emerged into the rain. I was about to step forward to clear the shack when Rachel sounded the truck's horn. I snapped my head in her direction just as I was tackled from behind and knocked to the wet pavement.

12

It was so dark, and raining so hard, that neither Dog nor I had detected the three females that attacked us. When the one in the lead tackled me, I flew forward and landed hard on the asphalt. My rifle was between my body and the ground, adding a few bruises. My face hit hard and I was reasonably sure my nose broke. Not the first time and probably won't be the last.

I heard Dog go into his *savage* mode and I pushed off the ground, trying to roll over and pin the female beneath me. I was halfway there, almost to the tipping point, when another female slammed into us and slid in front of me. She screamed in my face, fetid breath turning my stomach, and lunged at my throat with her teeth.

I managed to get the rifle barrel between us, which prevented her from biting into me, but didn't stop her from pressing her putrid lips against my skin. While I battled with her, the one on my back was frantically tearing at my vest and clothing, raking the back of my head and neck with her nails as she ripped into me. I tried to reach my Ka-Bar, but the female in front was pressed too tightly against my body for me to draw the blade.

Unexpectedly, the female on my back was gone, and I was able to apply enough force to the one in front to clear space. I drew the knife and buried it in her throat, twisting up until I hit her brain. Rolling the corpse to the side and getting my feet under me, ready to battle the second one, I was momentarily confused when I saw Rachel and Dog standing there looking at me. Dog had killed the first female. Rachel had dashed over and yanked the second one off my back, allowing Dog to have the honor of finishing her off. I grinned my thanks, wiped the blade clean and sheathed it.

These three had attacked silently. So far, I had only seen a very few female infected that attacked without mindless screaming. Unfortunately, it seemed as if we were starting to encounter more and more of them. Raising the rifle, I scanned the area, spotting a small group of males shambling in our direction from a neighboring warehouse. They were still a safe distance away, but we didn't have time to be messing around.

"In the shack!"

I gestured to Rachel and Dog. Disconnecting the tow strap, I hopped behind the wheel of the Dodge. When they were safely

Rolling Thunder

inside, I pulled the truck tight against the wall of the small building, front bumper pushing against the chain link gate and driver side door lined up with the empty doorframe. This effectively blocked any infected from being able to enter the building and I could open the truck's door and step out of it and step directly into the guard shack.

There was nothing notable inside, so I quickly moved to the steel door that let out into the parking lot side of the gate. Rifle at the ready, I reached forward to turn the knob but had to pause a moment to change my grip on the rifle. The latest anesthetic that Rachel had injected me with a few hours ago was wearing off and my hands were hurting. Rachel noticed me pause and shake them in the air, giving me a concerned look.

"Bad?" She asked.

"They're fine. Just a little tender," I lied.

"Bullshit. Come over here and sit down."

"No time. Later," I said, getting ready to open the door.

Rachel stepped close and grabbed my arm, pulling me away from the door.

"Like I said, bullshit! You're hurting, and if you're hurting it's going to affect you. This will take five minutes at the most. We have that much time if we don't waste any more of it arguing."

Not releasing my arm, she guided me over to a vacant chair and forcefully pushed me down. Digging through her pack, she found the necessary supplies and set about working on my hands. While she was busy, the males I'd seen approaching, arrived. They tried to squeeze between the truck and wall to get to the doorway, but I'd parked the truck with only a few inches of space left. They couldn't get to us. Dog walked over to the door and sat down with a low growl to watch them. Just in case.

"Looks like your nose is broken." Rachel leaned sideways and shone a small flashlight on my face. "Actually, I think it's an improvement. It's straight now."

She finished treating my wounds and quickly bandaged me up, took a moment to pack gauze into my nostrils to stop the bleeding then re-stowed the supplies. I thought about saying something smart-ass in response, but remembered she always found a way to get even, so I settled for thanking her for treating me.

Rolling Thunder

The treatment really hadn't taken all that long and, though I wouldn't admit it, I was glad she had insisted. The numbness in my hands was welcome after the sharp, burning pain that had been growing worse by the second. Ready to go, I looked out the windows into the lot and saw a few males shambling toward us. They were probably coming to investigate the noise the ones outside the gate were making as they repeatedly bumped into the truck.

Glancing at Rachel and Dog to make sure they were ready, I opened the door, pushing it wide in case there was a surprise hiding behind it. The closest male was twenty-yards away, and I didn't waste any time putting him down with a shot to the head. Scanning the expansive lot, I spotted several more, most of them stumbling towards us. Thankfully, I didn't see any females.

That could be a good thing or a bad thing. I much preferred the ones that screamed and ran at you, giving you time to shoot them before they could attack. Unlocking the knob, I closed the door behind us. I still hadn't seen any sign that even the smart female infected could operate a doorknob and I wanted to leave an escape route that was free of infected.

Dirk Patton

There must have been fifty trucks parked in the lot. If I had tried, I couldn't have created a better maze we had to work through to get to the warehouse.

"Do you think the lot goes around the far side of the building? Maybe we don't have to go through."

I mentally kicked myself. Rachel was right. If the lot went around the building, it would be a much safer path than wandering through a dark, cavernous warehouse with who knew how many infected inside. I nodded at her and led the way across the lot, frequently bending to look under parked trailers. I didn't want any surprises. I shot seven more males as we made our way through the dark.

The rain still poured down, drumming on the roofs of all the trailers and pounding the pavement. My hearing had shrunk to a small radius immediately around me and the only way I was finding threats was by seeing them through the night vision rifle scope. Try walking around a large open area with a cardboard toilet paper tube held up to one eye. Close your other eye so all you can see is what is in the field of vision of the tube. Now, try to spot and deal with random threats as you walk. It's not easy, and I was as tense as a bowstring.

We finally reached the far side of the lot where I shot two more infected before they noticed us. The fence here separated the paved lot from a large, weed-choked field where dozens of males shambled around. Occasionally, one would bump into the fence, causing it to rattle against the steel support posts. Following the perimeter with the scope, I saw where it connected to the corner of the building. It didn't go around.

"Good idea, but it looks like we're going inside," I said to Rachel.

She nodded and turned to look at the warehouse. The back corner was where the offices were located, the roll up doors beginning fifty feet to our left. Concrete steps led to a narrow platform with another heavy, steel door that was next to a bank of windows that looked out onto the lot.

This was probably where the dispatchers worked, keeping an eye on the traffic in and out of the yard. Weaving around two more trucks, we reached the steps and climbed up onto the platform. Stepping in front of the windows, I looked through the scope and saw a typical office.

A body covered in what looked like dried blood was lying half under a desk.

"Is it clear?"

Rachel was keeping an eye on the lot to our backs while I checked the office space.

"One body on the floor, which means there's probably at least one infected running around in there."

At the door, I pressed my ear against the steel in a vain attempt to detect any danger from the other side. All I could hear was the roar of the rain. Checking to make sure Rachel and Dog were ready, I tried the knob, quite surprised when it turned freely in my hand. Holding it fully turned, I took a deep breath. Stepping back, I pulled the door open and aimed my rifle into the dark interior.

I could see shelves stacked with boxes, but nothing was moving. Dog stood slightly back from the doorway, nose twitching as he sampled the air. After a moment, he took a step forward to the threshold and growled very quietly. He smelled infected, but I didn't think they were close.

Rolling Thunder

Stepping through the door, I kept the rifle up and ready. Dog, then Rachel, followed, and she pulled the door closed behind us, locking the knob. She must have had the same thought as me. No reason to leave an easy, open path at our rear.

Moving the rifle around so I could scan with the scope; I checked the long aisle we were standing in. Empty. Next, I looked down the open row in front of us as well as scanning up and along the shelving. Nothing moved or seemed to present a threat.

There were hundreds of skylights in the roof, probably enough to turn off all the lights and save a lot of electricity on sunny days. It was pitch dark outside, however. The only light they let in was when lightning flashed and everything in the warehouse lit up for a fraction of a second. Like being caught in a single flash of a strobe light.

There were also a few weak lights attached to the ceiling. They provided enough illumination for us to see well enough to avoid objects on the floor. The amount of light was comparable to navigating a house after dark with only night lights.

To our right, parked next to the door that led to the office area, were two electric golf carts.

That made sense in a building this size if you wanted your employees to spend time doing anything other than just walking from point A to B. I was sorely tempted to hop into one of them. We'd be across the warehouse in just a few minutes, but with speed also comes noise. They might have been electric, but their motors would whine and I suspected the tires would squeak and squirm on the painted concrete floor.

Reluctantly passing on the opportunity, I started us moving forward. The aisle was so long I couldn't see the far end of it, even in the night vision scope. And we were moving across the short side of the rectangle that comprised the building. At least the aisle was wide, a necessity to get forklifts in and out.

To either side, heavy gauge steel racks soared above us. Every shelf was full of boxes of whatever it was that moved through this warehouse. I was stepping carefully to make as little noise as possible. Behind me, I could just hear Rachel's soft footfalls. Dog's nails, on the other hand, clicked loudly with every step he took. I stopped us and turned to look at Dog, contemplating the possibility of tying rags on his feet.

Rolling Thunder

While I stood there looking at him, he turned his head slightly to the side and squeezed his eyes shut before letting out an explosive sneeze. It was so loud that both Rachel and I jumped as it echoed through the building. Dog shook his head, then sneezed again. The second one was nearly as loud, then he sniffed and was over it.

He stood there looking at us, waiting to see what we were going to do next. After the first sneeze, I'd held my breath. A moment after the second one, a chorus of screams from infected females sounded from deep within the warehouse.

13

The screams echoed, which made it impossible to tell what direction they were coming from. There were too many to identify individual voices and get a count of the number of females. Not good. We were still relatively close to the door we had come in and I thought about retreating, but that didn't really present a good option. Time to catch the train was running out and the only reason we were in the warehouse in the first place was because we hadn't found a better way forward.

Deciding to push on, I started moving but only covered a few feet before stopping. We needed to be stealthy and Dog's nails were making way too much noise on the hard floor. I didn't know what we were going to do. The females would be able to zero in on the noise and the confines of the warehouse worked to their advantage. If I'd had a suppressor for my pistol, I would have had that in my hand as it was better suited for the tight quarters of the aisle, but I didn't, so I kept the rifle up and ready.

From what I thought was only a few aisles to our left, I could hear running feet, again too many to identify individuals. Rachel and Dog heard it too, Dog raising his nose in the air and sniffing. I hoped his sneezes had echoed as badly as the screams and the females hadn't been able to locate us. Watching him sniff the air, I *really* hoped he didn't sneeze again. Rachel had been peering around in the darkness, and she leaned in to whisper in my ear.

"Let's use that," she mumbled.

I looked down the aisle where she pointed, not seeing anything at first, then spotted what she was talking about. A low, flat, four-wheeled cart was neatly tucked underneath a shelf thirty feet behind us. It had probably been used by warehouse workers who had to go around and pull items to fill orders that were less than an entire pallet of merchandise.

The cart sat on four small, rubber tires and should move easily and silently across the warehouse floor. Telling Dog to stay, I rushed back down the aisle, grabbed the handle and pulled it back to where he and Rachel waited. I was right. It rolled smoothly and with almost no sound.

Parking it right next to Dog, I bent, scooped him into my arms and set him down on the flat surface of the cart. I don't think he understood what was going on, giving me one of his hurt looks, but he didn't protest or try to jump off. Rachel stepped in and grabbed the handle, gesturing for me to take the lead.

Not wasting any more time, I started us moving again. We had only gone a dozen feet when three females entered the aisle a couple of rows to our front. Freezing in place, I watched them through the scope, only needing another half-pound of pressure on the trigger to fire. They stood there, heads moving more like an animal than a human as they looked, listened and sniffed. Not finding us in the dark, they continued in their original direction which was at a ninety-degree angle to our path.

Slowly letting out a quiet breath, I glanced behind to make sure Rachel was ready and started moving again, stepping slow and quiet. She was moving as quietly as I was, but there was a faint rubbing sound coming from one of the cart's axles. It was just at the threshold of hearing and I didn't think it would alert the females to our location. I hoped.

I froze the instant I heard a clatter of objects falling to the floor to our rear, turning quickly and stepping so that I was shoulder to shoulder with Rachel. She had frozen in place also and I muttered in her ear for her to keep an eye on our front. Behind us, two females stood in the intersection of our aisle and the closest cross row we had just passed. One of them must have bumped into a workstation and knocked a cup of pens and some other items to the floor. They checked the area and once again I noted the animalistic way they moved their heads.

After what seemed like hours, they turned and started moving down our aisle in the direction we had come from. I stayed rooted in place until they reached another intersection and disappeared. Turning, I started us moving forward again.

Another crash a couple of aisles over made me catch my breath, but I didn't pause this time. I still didn't have a good feel for how many females were hunting us, but I did know I had seen two separate groups and there was at least a total of five. The bad news was it seemed like they were working their way through all the aisles in the area and would probably find us soon.

We passed a couple more rows. I had taken to stopping just before each intersection. I would stand and listen for a few moments, then carefully lean out and check both directions with the scope. This was slowing us down, but I know my luck and didn't want to risk bumping into one of the search parties.

We passed another row and I slowed and glanced back at Rachel, thinking it was her footsteps I was hearing. When I looked back, she stopped, but the footsteps continued for a moment. Shit. We'd been found and were being stalked. Where was the bitch?

The path to our front and rear was completely clear when I checked it with the scope. That left one of the parallel ones. The steel racks that towered over our heads like canyon walls was four feet deep to accommodate standard shipping pallets. The shelves were set up back to back. That meant an eight-foot-thick barrier between each aisle, but there were plenty of gaps in the stacked inventory to let sound pass through.

It seemed like I had been hearing the steps with my right ear, so I suspected that the female was in the next aisle to that side. Was she alone? She was obviously one of the smart ones that would stalk us rather than just scream and charge, and if there was one smart one, there were probably more.

We were mid-way between intersections and I started moving back towards our rear as quietly as I could after motioning for Rachel and Dog to stay put. I strained to hear as I moved, trying to tell if the female knew I was hunting her and was retracing her steps to meet me. All I could hear was the drumming of the rain on the roof several stories over my head and the sound of my own heart pounding in the quiet.

Lightning flashed and, for a heartbeat, everything lit up in an electric white strobe. I reached the intersection, paused to check both ways then stepped out and around the shelving, losing sight of Rachel and Dog. I spent nearly a full minute to move the eight feet that comprised the depth of the shelving. With exaggerated caution, I peeked the rifle around the corner to check the aisle.

To my right was clear. To my left, at the mid-point of the aisle, I saw two females standing close to the shelving. They were facing Rachel's position and appeared to be intently listening as they waited.

With no other good option, I slipped my finger inside the trigger guard, steadied my aim on one of them and squeezed. The rifle popped, loud in the quiet warehouse despite being suppressed, but still nowhere near as shattering as it would have been without the suppressor.

The female's head snapped to the side and she dropped to the floor, dead. I shifted aim as the other reacted. She tried to dash away, but I had her caught in an aisle and she could only run towards or away from me. She chose to attack and, with the element of surprise gone, let out an ear-piercing scream.

I fired my second round, saw the bullet tear her cheek open and rip away a portion of her face. She ignored the injury and kept coming. Snapping off a second shot, the warehouse lit up again with a strobe of lightning. I watched her head snap back then the trick of the light made her appear to freeze-frame for an instant.

Her body was off balance, seemingly suspended in mid-air with blood spraying out behind. I blinked and she unfroze, tumbling dead to the floor. Even before her body came to a stop, there were screams sounding all around me in the dark. There was no time now to do anything other than run.

I dashed back around into the aisle where Rachel and Dog waited, the skin on my back crawling as more screams sounded, way too close. I covered the distance to where they waited, Dog now standing up on the cart with hackles stiff. Not slowing as I approached, I

Rolling Thunder

hissed at them to move and Dog leapt to the floor, leading the way towards the back of the building.

He was ahead by a few paces, Rachel falling in to run at my side when three females rushed into the next intersection in front of us. I had been running with the rifle up and shot one the instant I saw her, popping off a round at the second but hitting her in the shoulder. Dog sped up and launched himself into the air, impacting the wounded female on the chest and riding her to the floor.

Rachel and I fired at the third female simultaneously, both bullets impacting her head and nearly decapitating the body. Not used to shooting while running, Rachel had slowed to take the shot and I skidded and slipped on the floor when I heard her fall. Turning, I saw her face down with a female astride her back.

The infected had locked both hands into Rachel's long hair and was pulling her head back to bite into the side of her throat. Reversing direction, I drew my Kukri and slashed at the infected. Normally I would have at least managed to bury the blade in her brain, if not remove all the head above her mouth, but my hands weren't at their usual strength.

As the blade bit in, I was unable to maintain the grip needed to force through the tissue and bone and only succeeded in lodging a couple of inches of it into the female's face. This got her attention but didn't stop her from attacking Rachel. Cursing, I swung the rifle and clubbed her to the floor. Rachel wasted no time scrambling away from the fight.

Stepping in, I kicked the female as hard as I could in the temple and her body went limp. I couldn't tell if I'd killed her or only knocked her unconscious, but she was down and not moving. Gripping the Kukri's handle, I yanked it free and stabbed through the throat, cutting into her spine. After wiping it clean on her clothing, I sheathed the blade at the small of my back. I spent a quick moment to scan our rear, which was free of females for the moment, then turned and ran after Rachel and Dog.

14

Dog had killed the female I had wounded with my rifle. He was waiting at the intersection. Not pausing to check the row we were crossing, I ran harder. Rachel kept pace at my side. Dog ran on the other side of her. More screams sounded, some behind and some to our left, but it sounded like only a few voices.

The thought occurred to me that the females were using the screams to communicate with each other. Or at least maybe the smart ones were. I wasn't really sure how that theory might help at the moment, so I filed it away to think about later when I had the opportunity.

We were almost to the next row when two more females charged into the intersection only feet in front of us. I couldn't have stopped if I'd tried, so I didn't. Instead, I changed my direction slightly and blasted into them. I was running with my rifle up and as I made contact, I shoved the barrel into the throat of the one to my right and pulled the trigger in burst mode. The three rounds blew out the back of her neck and head.

Dirk Patton

I had lowered my left shoulder and rammed it into the face of the one directly in front of me as I shot the other. I had at least a hundred pounds on her and was moving fast when I delivered the hit. She was lifted into the air, landing flat on her back a few feet down the aisle. Her head hit the concrete floor with a loud, meaty smack and she didn't immediately try to bounce back to her feet. Swinging the rifle, I fired three rounds into her heart as I ran past.

Behind us, I heard a lone scream and glanced back but couldn't see anything. When we reached the mid-point between intersections, I slid to a stop, turned to our rear and dropped to a knee as I raised the rifle. A single female was charging, leaping over the two I'd killed at the last intersection. I took a moment to steady my aim, then fired. The bullet struck her on the bridge of the nose, instantly destroying her brain. The body flopped forward to the floor and her momentum continued as a slide for another half a dozen feet.

Aisle to our rear clear, I was standing when Rachel gasped. A female landed on her, knocking her to the floor and trying to tear into her throat. I was stepping forward to help when I was knocked down as well, another female on my back. When I hit the floor, I rolled, and we wound up coming to a stop against the bottom cross piece of the shelving that created the aisle.

The female on me was strong and fast and I struggled to get a grip on her. Finally, I was able to wrap my hands into her long, thick hair. Controlling her head, I slammed it into the edge of the steel shelving once, twice then a third time. On the final impact, she quit struggling and her eyes rolled up in their sockets. Yanking my right hand free of her hair, I drew my knife and stabbed up through her mouth into her brain. Kicking the body away, I rolled over to help Rachel.

She had been attacked by a female that was larger than she was and wasn't faring very well. Scrambling across the floor on my hands and knees, I pivoted on my hip and used the momentum to kick the infected in the side. She was knocked off Rachel and rolled a couple of times before snapping to her feet and leaping at us. I met her in mid-leap with the blade extended and ended her night.

Dog was a dozen feet away, engaged with two females. He had torn the Achilles tendon out of one of them and she squirmed around on the floor, unable to walk. She was trying to reach Rachel, who hadn't gotten back to her feet. The other female was a big woman, not fat, but big like a man. She was fighting with Dog and he was wearing her down with his speed and power.

He had broken both of her forearms with his jaws and she was bleeding heavily from deep bite wounds in her sides and thighs where he'd taken chunks bigger than my fist out of her. She might have been infected and in a rage, but her body still had to obey basic biological principles. No amount of adrenaline is going to overcome blood loss, and she was bleeding out.

Moving slower, she lunged at Dog, her arms flopping uselessly. He took the opportunity to leap at her chest and knock her to the floor. He had her throat in his jaws as she came to a stop on her back. He tore her open and locked his jaws on her head until she stopped moving.

While he fought, I finished off the other female before dashing to Rachel's side to check on her. Her face, chest, and arms were all bleeding from furrows torn into her skin by the infected, but I didn't see anything that looked too serious. She was moving slightly but didn't respond when I called her name.

Running my hands over her body, I checked for broken bones or other injuries I couldn't see under her clothing, not finding anything. Pausing my examination, I raised my rifle and checked to make sure we weren't about to be overrun with infected. First, I looked up, but there weren't any more females waiting to drop down on us. The aisle was clear in both directions.

Blood dripping from his muzzle, Dog trotted over and stood on the other side of Rachel, watching down the aisle. With his superior eyes keeping watch, I turned my attention back to Rachel and was dismayed to find her unconscious. That was when I remembered the medic who had checked her out just after our escape from Murfreesboro. He'd warned me to keep her from hitting her head again for a few days.

With a sense of dread in my gut, I unclipped the small flashlight from my rifle, pried Rachel's right eye open and flicked the light across it. Her pupil responded, but very sluggishly. I repeated the process with her left eye. The pupil responded normally. Shit!

I didn't know what this meant, medically, but I sure as hell knew it wasn't good. Carefully, I slipped my hands under Rachel's head and felt a swelling just a few centimeters from the bump she had gotten from being knocked out in Murfreesboro.

Dog's growl warned me and I spun, snapping my rifle up and sighting in on four shambling males that had just rounded the corner into our aisle. I dropped all four, scanned beyond them then turned to check in the direction we needed to move. Clear for the moment. I scanned the upper shelves again, which were thankfully still clear.

We needed to move before more of them found us. The problem was, how was I going to move Rachel? The cart we had used for Dog would have worked, but it was several intersections behind us and I wasn't about to leave her unprotected to go get it. Dog was a ferocious fighter, but he couldn't fend off a group of infected by himself.

Clipping the light back onto my rifle, I turned it on and scanned the aisle section we were in. I was hoping to see another cart, but there wasn't one in sight. Extinguishing the light, I said a couple of curses under my breath as I removed Rachel's rifle sling and looped it over my neck. Next to come off was her pack. I knew there were items in there we needed.

Rolling Thunder

Taking a moment, I salvaged all her spare magazines and ammunition before shoving the pack out of the way against the bottom of a shelf. Swapping for a fresh magazine in my rifle, I moved into a squat, straddling Rachel's hips. Gathering her upper body in my arms, I pulled her to me, held tight and stood up.

Using one arm to hold her limp form, I turned and slid down her body until my shoulder was just above her belt. Pulling her upper body onto my back, I straightened with her draped over my left shoulder. My left arm was raised and over her hips and the best grip I could get to balance her weight was by grabbing onto her ass. Hard. I made a mental note not to mention this to her when she woke up.

I took a couple of steps, bouncing her weight to a more comfortable position, then started staggering forward. I still had my pack on, coming in at over a hundred pounds, had both of our rifles plus Rachel's weight. Not my idea of a pleasant stroll, but there wasn't an alternative.

I walked with my pistol in my right hand, unable to handle the rifle and keep Rachel's weight balanced on my shoulder. I had no peripheral vision to my left due to her body pressed up against my head and moved Dog to that side to keep watch. I almost paused when there was another clatter of objects hitting the floor to our rear, but I could tell that whatever had made the noise was far enough away that it was out of pistol range.

Lightning flashed again, freeze framing the aisle and the five males that stood in a loose group at the upcoming intersection. I paused to check the shelves in front of us and didn't see any females lying in wait, so continued forward. I hoped I was only dealing with warehouse employees who had turned and become trapped in the massive building.

Never having worked in a warehouse, I assumed that one this size would have half a dozen or so clerical employees, which are typically women. Most, if not all, of the laborers and forklift drivers would be men. If my hopes and assumptions were correct, then I might get out without encountering any more females. Small groups of males didn't particularly concern me as long as I had room to maneuver and a weapon to put them down.

I reminded myself to not get complacent or overconfident when it came to the males. They might not have the speed and agility of the females, but what they lacked in those areas they made up for in sheer strength. They could also bunch up quickly and if I got cornered by even a small group, I could be in serious trouble.

Turning my upper body enough to see Dog, I verified there wasn't anything else in the immediate vicinity that was presenting a threat. Telling Dog to stay beside me, I walked forward and came to a stop ten feet from the group of males. They had heard his nails clicking on the floor and were turning their heads trying to locate the source of the sound. None of them could tell what direction it was coming from and almost looked comical the way they moved.

Raising my right arm, I shot the closest one to me in the back of the head. The pistol was shockingly loud after the suppressed rifle, all the hard surfaces in the warehouse reflecting and amplifying the noise. As soon as I fired the shot, the other four males snapped their heads in my direction, snarled almost as one and moved towards me.

Standing fast, I methodically fired four more shots, dropping each in turn. When I could hear again after the crash of the pistol fire, Dog was growling, and there were snarls from behind. Turning carefully, so I didn't unbalance myself and drop Rachel on her head, which was about the last thing she needed right now, I saw seven more males shambling down the aisle towards us.

The leader of the group was twenty yards away and I decided to give him another few seconds so I would have an easier shot. Hey, you try shooting accurately with a hundred-pound pack on your back and a full-grown woman balanced on your shoulder!

He had closed almost half the distance and my finger was tightening on the trigger when there was a sound from above my head. I didn't hesitate or look to see what the noise was, just moved backwards as fast as I could with my burden. An instant later, a female landed on the floor in the spot I had been standing.

Before I could shoot, Dog was in motion, taking her to the ground, and I refocused on the closest male and shot him from five feet away. OK, maybe I didn't need to let them get so close. His buddies were right on his heels and I worked my way through the group with headshots until there was only one still standing.

I had shot him and seen the bullet strike his forehead, but he was still coming. What the hell? He stumbled over one of the bodies on the floor as he came towards me, falling flat on his face. Taking advantage of his bad luck, I stepped up and shot him in the back of the head at point blank range. The body spasmed then lay still.

Dog had killed the female, and I took a moment to satisfy my curiosity. Using the toe of my boot, I hooked the body under a shoulder and flipped it over. There was a long tear in the skin of the forehead from my first bullet. That didn't make sense. Bullets only do that to flesh if they're traveling at an angle. I had shot him straight on and the round should have penetrated directly into his head.

While I was standing there looking down at him, lightning flashed again and in that instant of brilliant white light I saw a metallic glint inside the wound. Son of a bitch! He had a metal plate in his head. All the first round had done was ring his bell. Probably quite literally.

Screams from deep within the warehouse snapped me back to action, but first things first. Shifting Rachel's weight, I leaned her against a shelf so I could let go of her body without dropping her. With two hands in action, I changed the magazine in the pistol and pulled my rifle around to the front of my body. With females on the way I wanted to be ready.

Grabbing on to Rachel again, I turned and headed off, stepping carefully over the infected bodies in the intersection. Lightning flashed again and four intersections ahead I could see the back wall of the warehouse. Unfortunately, the screams were getting closer, fast, and I was running out of time.

Looking around, I found a shelf at waist level that was only partially full. Sidling up to it, I worked Rachel off my shoulder and onto the shelf, shoving her arms and legs back into the darkness. I took ten seconds to pile boxes in front of her, so she was hidden from view before stepping out into the middle of the aisle. Without her weight, I felt light on my feet, and Dog and I stood in place waiting for the females.

Screams to my right and in front of me, all of them sounding close but they weren't visible in my rifle scope yet. Keeping the upper shelves as a part of my scanning, I paused when I spotted movement fifteen feet off the floor and halfway between my position and the last intersection.

There were more screams from the same positions as before, but I kept my attention on the two females I had spotted. They were working their way down the face of the racking, moving sideways towards me. Others were screaming but didn't sound any closer.

Rolling Thunder

Suddenly, I realized they were distracting me while these hunters were sneaking up. Not hesitating any longer, I shot the closest one that was clinging onto the shelves. The second one reacted immediately and started climbing, going for the top, and she was fast. So fast she nearly made it before my bullet knocked her off and she crashed to the floor with the sound of breaking bones.

I'm not bragging when I say there aren't many shooters in the world that would have gotten the second one. I know how fast I can acquire and engage new targets, faster than anyone I've ever worked with, and I barely got her before she would have disappeared over the top. Pushing that thought down, I re-scanned the shelves and didn't see any more movement.

Dog growled and I glanced down to see him looking in the opposite direction. I spun in place and scanned, shooting another female that was on the very top of the shelving and working her way to a position where she could have dropped right on top of me.

No more screams. I kept scanning the shelves in both directions without seeing any threats. I knew there were a few more females, but they had gone quiet. Cursing whatever had allowed them to start thinking and working together, I kept scanning and kept an eye on Dog.

Normally, I would have moved to force their hand, but I wasn't going to leave Rachel. I had hastily hidden her, and while she wasn't obvious to a casual inspection, I didn't want to trust they wouldn't sniff her out. Or that she wouldn't wake up and make noise that would attract them. Thinking about her, I glanced at the hiding spot and paused. I wasn't exactly sure I hadn't left a box partially sticking out beyond the front of the shelf, but I didn't think I had.

I made a quick scan, then moved to where I'd hidden Rachel and pushed the box aside. At first, I didn't understand what I was, or wasn't, seeing, then I was frantically shoving boxes out of my way and reaching into the area behind them. All the boxes from the far side had been removed, leaving the shelf clear and open into the adjacent aisle. Rachel was gone.

15

Cursing, I stepped back into the aisle and did a quick scan to make sure there weren't any females scaling the shelves on their way to attack me while I had been distracted. Nothing moved. I trotted to the closest intersection and scanned again as I stepped into the adjacent aisle.

I kept scanning as I advanced toward the pile of boxes on the floor that marked where Rachel had been taken. There were no more screams and I didn't see any females moving. Dog growled as two males moved into the intersection on the far side of our destination. I snapped off a couple of rounds and dropped them without breaking stride.

Reaching the location, I looked at the boxes on the floor and the empty space on the shelf. Reaching out with my foot, I pushed on one of the boxes with the toe of my boot and was mildly surprised at how heavy it felt. Whoever, or whatever, had moved them had done so silently. Not even Dog had detected them.

They had picked up and moved several very heavy objects, then lifted Rachel across a good six feet of shelving and presumably carried her away. Without any sound. The skin on my back puckered and crawled as I thought about the strength this would require. Were the females capable? They were strong as hell when enraged and attacking, but what about to do something like this? And when the hell did they start capturing survivors rather than killing them?

These were questions I needed to know the answers to, but right now the priority was to get Rachel back before something really bad happened to her. Kneeling, I called Dog over and started tapping the floor in the middle of the piled boxes. He lowered his nose and sniffed the whole area then looked at me.

"Find them, boy," I said, standing back up.

I had no idea if this would work. Dog was smart and certainly had the ability, but would he know what I wanted him to do? After a long moment, he lowered his nose back to the floor and sniffed. He moved through the boxes and started trotting in the direction we had come from with his nose less than an inch above the smooth concrete.

I followed, rifle up and head on a swivel. At the intersection we had come from, he turned right and headed deeper into the length of the warehouse. I counted intersections as we went, Dog pausing as we approached number eleven.

We were now deep in the warehouse, equidistant between the front and back walls and not too far from the longitudinal center. Every alarm bell in my head was telling me this was a trap. It had to be the infected that had taken Rachel as survivors would almost certainly have made a beeline for an exit. I scanned all around us, aisles and shelves, but nothing moved. Nothing had moved since we had started following the scent and it had been too long since I'd heard a scream.

Dog was still paused and the fur along the ridge of his back was stiff as he lowered his head below shoulder level to growl deep in his chest. I scanned in the direction he was looking but couldn't find anything. After a second negative scan, I stepped forward to the corner of the next intersection, Dog tight by my side, and peered around the shelf.

One hundred feet down and to our left was a body lying on the floor. I was almost certain it was Rachel but verified with the rifle scope. Moving carefully, I scanned the entire aisle, up and down the shelves, along the top of the racks, but saw nothing. Turning to my right, I repeated the scan and came up with the same results. What the hell? They had set up a perfect trap, using Rachel as bait, but where were they?

Pulling back so I was hidden from the aisle, I focused on calming my breathing and lowering my heart rate. After a minute, I could hear more than the blood pounding in my ears, and I stood stock still and listened. Dog was absolutely silent, standing next to me, and I concentrated on identifying the normal sounds of the environment so I could pick out anything that didn't belong.

I could hear the rain on the roof far above my head. Two distinctly different sounds depending on whether the water was hitting the metal roof or the plastic skylights. There was a moaning of wind as it rushed over the exterior of the building. Other than that, there was nothing making any noise. After five minutes, I decided I had to move even though I knew it was a set-up.

Back at the edge of the intersection, I did another careful scan of the aisle in both directions, again seeing nothing of concern. Rachel was still lying where I'd first seen her. I was worried about getting her up and on my shoulder. The maneuver was difficult under good circumstances and both of us would be completely vulnerable to attack while I was performing it. I needed Rachel awake and able to move under her own power if I hoped to get us out of there alive.

Pulling back, I shrugged out of my pack and dug for the medical kit. It took some searching, but I finally found a small tube of ammonia inhalant, or smelling salts. I had no doubt that any doctor would tell me it was bad to force Rachel awake with an obviously severe concussion, but the risk I was going to take was better than being torn open and eaten by a pack of infected females.

Another scan and I was ready to move. My rifle was up and ready and the small inhalant was safely tucked into a pouch on the front of my vest. Stepping carefully down the aisle, I paused when lightning flashed and lit up the interior. I gave my eyes a moment to re-adjust to the gloom before continuing.

I was moving down the left side of the aisle, shoulder nearly brushing the shelves so I could keep an eye on the opposite side. Dog moved down the right and I trusted him to alert me if he detected anything on the shelving above my head.

Dirk Patton

In short order, we reached the point where Rachel was lying. She was on her side, long hair covering her face. If she had been dropped where she was, I only hoped she hadn't hit her head on the hard floor again. Scanning in every direction, I slowly moved to her side, let the rifle hang down my back and drew my pistol.

Kneeling in front of her, I looked up at the shelves then checked on Dog. I didn't see anything, looking down and brushing Rachel's hair off her face. Pulling the inhalant out of the pouch, I squeezed the thin plastic until it snapped and was immediately hit by the sharp odor of ammonia. Before I could put the ampule under Rachel's nose, a scream sounded from above and to my right, instantly answered by more screams from all around.

Snapping my head up, I saw boxes tumble off a shelf high in the air, followed by a female who had hidden behind them. She leapt off the edge and I fell to the floor on my back, dropping the inhalant as I raised the pistol and fired three quick rounds. There was no time to aim for her head, just blast away at center mass and hope.

Luck was with me, one of my rounds finding the infected's heart and killing her. I tried to roll out of the way of the falling body but didn't make it. The woman crashed onto me with enough force to knock some of the wind out of my lungs.

Behind me, Dog was fighting with a female that had leapt out of the shelves on the far side of the aisle. As I was scrambling out from under the body on top of me, another infected landed on her feet directly in front of my face. I swung the pistol towards her, but she was too close and attacked before I could bring it to bear, knocking it out of my hand to skitter across the floor. She fell on me, hands grasping for my throat, her knees on my chest.

I managed to kick free of the body, then raised my legs and locked them in a scissor hold around her neck, pulling her off me. Controlling the momentum, I spun up onto the side of my hip then onto my feet in a crouch, drawing the Ka-Bar. She had already recovered and lunged without any hesitation. I stabbed as I slipped to the side of her attack, the blade going into the side of her neck to the hilt. Holding tight, I let her momentum tear the blade across her throat, opening both carotid arteries.

I looked around and saw Dog finishing off a female, another one lying dead in a spreading pool of blood to his rear. Checking the area, I saw at least a dozen males at the far intersection shambling in our direction. Sheathing the knife, I pulled my rifle up and scanned the shelves around us. I froze and stared when I spotted a female standing on the very top, looking back at me.

We stood that way for a few heartbeats, just staring at each other, then she turned and disappeared. I wished I had shot her when I had the chance. I had no doubt that she was dangerously smart and had somehow gotten the other females to work together to set up this ambush. Thinking about that level of cunning from an infected made my blood run cold, but I was out of time to think about it.

Turning back to the approaching males, I started dropping them with head shots, the last one falling within six feet of Rachel. Another scan and we were clear for the moment unless there were more surprises hiding behind boxes. With no imminent attack, I moved back to Rachel. Picking up the inhalant, I held it to my nose when Rachel didn't react. They evaporate very quickly once broken open, and it was dry. Digging out another, I broke it open and immediately thrust it under Rachel's nose.

Rolling Thunder

She coughed, sputtered and tried to bat my hand aside, but I held it in place, moving it along with her as she tried to turn away. She finally opened her eyes, squinted at me then quickly turned her head and threw up. Keeping my eyes on the aisle, I reached out and gathered her hair and held it behind her head while the waves of nausea from the concussion rolled through her.

Rachel heaved until nothing was left in her stomach, then stayed in the same position, gasping for air. I wanted to give her time to recover, but time was a luxury we didn't have. Tucking her hair inside the back of her shirt, I stood, glanced at Dog to make sure he wasn't sensing any threats, then leaned over Rachel.

"I'm sorry, but we have to go. Now," I said in a low voice.

Rachel was on her hands and knees, head hanging down as she fought the sickness. She nodded her understanding and sat up on her knees and looked at me. She looked like hell, pale and drawn with sunken eyes, but she raised a shaking hand for my help. Taking it, I pulled her to her feet and had to steady her when she wobbled and nearly crashed back to the floor. Once she was standing on her own, I looked around for my pistol and retrieved it from where it had fallen in the scuffle.

"Can you handle your rifle?" I asked her.

"Give it here. I'm fine."

Her weak voice told me she was anything but. Regardless, I pulled her rifle's sling over my head and handed the weapon to her. She worked it onto her shoulders and performed a quick check to make sure it was ready to fire if needed.

I was impressed with her toughness. I've had bad concussions. The kind where you get completely knocked out, and I knew how she was feeling right now. Dog came over to walk beside her, and we started moving towards the back of the warehouse.

16

We turned right at the first intersection, my intention to go pick up Rachel's pack. She carried all our food plus the large field medic kit. I wasn't too worried about food. We could always scavenge when we needed to eat, but I wanted that kit. It held the anesthetic for my hands, and I had a lot of healing to go before I could do without.

I knew I could handle the pain. That wasn't it. Just because I could handle the pain didn't mean the pain wouldn't affect my ability to fight. If I couldn't fight, well, we might as well just sit down and wait for the infected to find us. My, I was in a cheery mood.

Moving quickly, I wasn't worried about females stalking us. I didn't know if we had killed all of them except for the one I had seen on top of the shelves, but for some reason I read into her look that she was letting us win this engagement and was backing off. Maybe it was just optimism, which was in pretty short supply right now, but I didn't think we'd have to deal with any more attacks while in the warehouse. Female attacks, I clarified for myself as a small group of males wandered into an intersection ahead of us. I put them down quickly and kept us moving.

A couple of times I had to stop and put a hand on Rachel's arm to keep her upright, but she kept moving without complaint. I knew she was hurting, dizzy, weak and disoriented, but there wasn't a damn thing I could do about it. She would get better, but only with time. Ideally, that would be with time and rest. But we had a way to go before we could think about resting.

Reaching the aisle where I had left her pack, I moved quickly to it and scooped it up. Turning to help her put it on, I saw her sway slightly just standing there and realized there was no way I could put the weight on her back. While I was trying to think of a solution, Dog growled, and I turned to look down the aisle towards the front of the warehouse. A large group of males, more than twenty and I quit counting, were shambling directly towards us. I turned and looked at the back of the warehouse and for the moment the aisle was clear.

Dropping Rachel's pack to the floor, I extended the shoulder straps to their full length, stood and swung it over my left arm and on top of my pack. The extra weight made me shuffle sideways. I caught my balance and got my right arm through its strap and secured the pack in place. In the scheme of things, her pack wasn't that much extra weight, only about sixty-five pounds, but it felt like two hundred.

Sucking it up, I got us walking again. Rachel swayed as she moved and I felt like I was barely plodding along with the extra weight. The result was that we couldn't outpace the males following us. We were just barely able to maintain our distance. I thought about turning and eliminating the threat, but ammunition isn't endless. I had already expended a lot getting us this far. I didn't know when we'd be able to resupply, so it was definitely time for conservation.

We kept moving and I was splitting my attention between the aisle ahead, the males pursuing and Rachel's progress. She was keeping pace with me but walked like a drunk, seemingly unable to travel in a straight line. I was worried about her, worried about the concussion, but knew there was nothing I could do other than get her to safety so she could heal.

Sensing our urgency, Dog moved ahead and was checking each intersection before we arrived so we could keep pushing. He was fifty feet in front of me when he reached the rearmost row in the warehouse, a solid wall ahead of him. I watched him check the area visually, then raise his nose in the air for a moment before he turned to look at me. The row was clear. Reaching Dog, I paused to look for an exit. Rachel took the opportunity to lean her shoulder against the wall as I looked around.

The back of the warehouse was piled with broken and empty pallets, forklift parts, giant rolls of plastic shrink wrap and several other items I didn't bother to try and identify. What I didn't see was an exit, but I knew one had to be there. Modern fire codes would require them, and this looked like a busy enterprise that wouldn't want to risk getting shut down by the fire marshal. Glancing back at the approaching males, I grabbed Rachel's arm and got us moving along the wall in search of a door.

We had to pick our way through the junk that had been stacked against the wall and spilled out across the floor. Dog moved with little effort, seeming too nimble for an animal his size. Rachel struggled and I was worried about turning or breaking an ankle with all the weight on my back. The only positive news was the infected males would be slowed down at least as much since they were walking blind. Looking behind us, I saw the first one round the corner and start bumping along the wall in our wake. Soon the rest of his buddies stumbled into sight and followed.

Several spools of shrink wrap were leaned against the wall, the four-foot-long empty cardboard tubes that had held the plastic lying on the floor. Rachel stepped over one of these tubes but didn't lift her foot high enough. She brought her weight down too early, on top of the cardboard. The round tube rolled out from under her and she tumbled to the floor.

As she was falling, I reached out to grab her, but only succeeded in falling with her as I overbalanced the load I was carrying. We made a lot of racket and the approaching males got excited and started snarling and growling in anticipation of a meal. They were still far enough away that I didn't want to start expending ammo, but soon I wouldn't have a choice.

I clambered back to my feet, pulled Rachel up with me and started moving again. This time, I shuffled my feet, kicking the tubes out of the way so Rachel had clear footing as she followed me. I was holding my rifle by the pistol grip with my right hand and had a firm grip on her with my left hand as we moved. If we stumbled and fell again, I'd have no choice but to start thinning the herd that was in pursuit.

There was another lightning flash and ahead I could see three figures standing at the end of an intersection, frozen in place by the strobe of light. More males. Bad news. The good news was they were standing next to what looked like a roll up door.

Pushing myself, I picked up the pace, dragging Rachel to keep her with me. Dog stayed slightly to our front, still clearing each intersection as we came to it. Two intersections remaining before we reached the roll-up door, Dog suddenly growled and leapt to the side into an aisle. I lost sight of him but could hear him fighting. Wanting to run forward to help in case he was in trouble, I glanced back to see how Rachel was doing and barely had time to react.

The female I had seen on top of the shelves earlier was charging directly at us from behind and was no more than a dozen feet away. Leaping distance. Yanking Rachel to the side, I spun as the female launched herself into the air. I have fast reactions and would normally have been able to complete the turn to meet her attack, but all the weight of the packs was dragging me down and I didn't make it.

I managed to get Rachel out of the way, noting she fell into a pile of packing material a split second before the female slammed into my side. She knocked me over and I landed on my right shoulder. My rifle popped free from my grip and slid to the end of the sling that was around my upper body.

On my side, with the two packs preventing me from rolling, I knew I was in trouble. My right arm was pinned beneath my body and I couldn't get it free as the female levered my left hand aside and lunged for my throat. Seeing the bite coming I tucked my chin to my chest as hard as I could and fought to get my arms into action.

Despite my best efforts, she succeeded in getting her teeth locked on the side of my neck. I can't say it hurt that bad when she bit in and tore a piece of flesh out of me, but like any other combat wound that was because of all the adrenaline in my system. After the fight, if there was an after, it would hurt like a bitch.

Feeling part of my body being bitten off sent an additional surge of adrenaline into my blood and frankly, pissed me off. With a roar, I lifted my chin and smashed the side of my head into the female's face, feeling her nose and one of her eye orbits shatter from the blow. Her grip didn't falter, but she didn't try to immediately bite again. I slammed my head into the same spot on her face a second time then levered with my left arm.

I thought I was about to get an advantage when she shifted her grip and lunged at the side of my face with her teeth. Jerking my head around I avoided the worst of the bite, but not all of it. Her teeth broke through the skin on my scalp and tore long furrows down the side of my head. She shifted again in preparation for attempting another bite.

Before she could lunge there was the sound of a suppressed rifle right next to my ear. Her head deformed for a heartbeat before the side of it blew out and sprayed the floor with blood and brains. The skin on the side of my head was burning from spent gunpowder, and I didn't have to look to know that Rachel had shot the infected with her rifle. The muzzle had only been inches from my head when she pulled the trigger. Thankful she hadn't had a wave of dizziness at the moment she had fired, I shoved the corpse off of me and got to my feet as fast as I could.

The males that had been following us had closed most of the ground while I was occupied with the female and I had to bring my rifle up and start dropping bodies. Half way through, I changed magazines and noted that I was down to five spares. 150 rounds. When the last male fell, I reached down and pulled Rachel to her feet. She seemed steadier and looked marginally better, giving me a wan smile when she saw my wounds.

"You're bleeding like a stuck pig," she said, gesturing at my head.

"We'll worry about that later."

I turned and looked for Dog. Not seeing him right away, a thrill of concern passed over me and I headed for the aisle I had seen him enter. Before I got there, he came walking into the intersection, covered in blood and gore.

He looked OK. Then I noticed the last few inches of his tail were missing. He trotted up and nuzzled my hand for petting. Rubbing his blood-soaked head, I quickly checked him for other injuries, finding nothing wrong other than the missing part of his tail. Blood was flowing freely, but no worse than my injuries and we had to get moving.

The males that had been standing near the door were coming our way, drawn by the sounds of fighting. Even though I was uncomfortably low on ammo, I didn't think any of us needed another hand to hand fight at the moment. I shot each of them as we approached. Passing the bodies, I turned to make sure Rachel didn't stumble over them. I was pleased to see that she seemed even more alert and steadier on her feet. I still kept half an eye on her.

Reaching the door, I cursed when I found a heavy chain and padlock had been used to secure it. This was a large, commercial duty padlock made from case hardened steel and I didn't even bother to try shooting it off with my rifle. It would have been a waste of bullets. However, the frame on the door the chain was looped through was only made of the same rolled metal as the door. Not surprising, really.

Reminded me of a friend who, after a burglary, had installed two massive, high-security deadbolts on his front door. The only problem was the door was made of wood. The next time his house was broken into, the burglars used a cordless saw and cut the door around the expensive dead bolts.

I wished for that saw but settled for pressing the muzzle of the rifle against the thin metal and firing three rounds in burst mode. The frame tore apart and with some force, I was able to rip the heavy chain completely free. Quickly slapping the two security pegs to the open position, I raised the door a foot and knelt to look through the opening. Dark and rain. No infected in sight. Back on my feet, I shoved the door the rest of the way up and waved Dog and Rachel through. I followed them and lowered the door, taking a big breath of fresh air.

Surveying the area, I raised my rifle when a small pickup pulled to a stop facing the elevated dock where we were standing. Two men wearing police uniforms stepped out, but stayed behind the open doors of the truck. Dog growled, holding his position next to Rachel.

The one on the passenger side moved into the open with his hand held away from his holstered pistol and took a couple of steps towards us. He was dressed in riot gear, right down to a helmet with a face guard which was lowered into place, completely masking his features.

"It's OK, folks. We're here to rescue you."

He shouted to be heard over the rain.

"Aren't you a little short for a stormtrooper?" Rachel asked.

I just stared at her as she appeared to be trying very hard to not look at me and laugh. Bitch.

17

Rachel's comment distracted me, but I didn't lower the rifle. Something didn't feel right here. Assuming the cops were actually out looking for survivors, which I doubted this close to the time of the departure of the last train, I sure didn't think they would be driving around in anything other than police issue vehicles. Maybe I was wrong, but I wasn't ready to bet our lives on it. Maintaining my aim at the man who had stepped forward, I moved my eyes around, scanning the area.

We were facing a medium sized parking area that I guessed was where the warehouse employees parked. Over forty vehicles were in the lot and all looked like they'd been sitting in the same place for a while. Trash had blown against and been trapped by a few of the tires and even during a heavy downpour of rain, the glass looked dirty and streaked.

To the right, a tall, chain-link fence guarded the pavement from the other side of the weedy lot we had seen when we were looking for a way around the warehouse. The river was to our left and directly ahead was an exit to the road where the tall barricade sat. Nothing was moving other than the males banging up against the fence in the lot to my right.

"How did you know we were here?" I shouted.

I had my full attention back on the two men. Rachel picked up the tone in my voice and took a couple of steps back to stand next to me, adjusting the grip on her rifle as she moved.

"We need to go," he shouted back, shooting a quick glance at his partner who was still mostly concealed behind the driver's side door. "The train is leaving soon and we need to get you to the station so you can get seats."

I wasn't certain enough to start shooting, but everything about these guys felt wrong.

"We're fine walking," I shouted back. "I'm sure there're other people that need your help more than us."

They exchanged glances again. Then the driver made his move. He had been standing close to the door and stepped back to raise a shotgun he had kept hidden. In my world, the time it takes to move a step and try to bring a cumbersome weapon up and into play is an eternity. I shifted aim and shot him through the face shield before the muzzle of the shotgun cleared the door, then snapped my aim back to the other man.

When I'd shot his partner, he'd grabbed for his pistol but hadn't even gotten it out of the holster before the muzzle of my rifle was once again steady on his head. He froze in a partial crouch, right arm back and bent at the elbow with his hand on the butt of the pistol. I thought about just shooting him, taking the truck and getting on with our evening, but was curious what they had wanted with us.

"Go down there, take Dog with you, and get his weapons. Be sure you circle behind him and never get in my line of fire. Approach him from the side, so you're in the clear if I have to shoot," I said to Rachel, then remembered her concussion. "You up to it? Feeling OK?"

"I'm fine," she answered, called Dog and headed to a set of steps a few yards away that led down into the parking lot.

Rachel stayed well to my right, the man's left, as she circled around with Dog right at her side. She paused at the pickup to take a look at the man I'd shot before continuing on behind the truck. Clear of the vehicle, she crossed to his right before approaching.

"She's going to disarm you," I called out. "If you so much as blink I'll blow your fucking head off. If I miss, that dog will tear your throat out. Now stand very still."

He didn't even nod, just remained frozen as Rachel approached. When she was still four feet away, Dog moved directly in front of him, his muzzle less than a foot from the man's crotch. He stood staring up at him, lips curled off his bloody teeth.

Leaning in, Rachel extended her arm, moved his hand off the pistol and pulled it out of the holster. Weapon secured in her waistband at the small of her back, she moved several feet away and glanced up at me. I walked down the stairs and to them, rifle never wavering off the man's head. Stopping ten feet in front of him, I made him lay face down in the parking lot so I could search him.

Dog moved to stand with his jaws just inches from his head and I slung my rifle before stepping in and kneeling on the man's lower back. I swiftly ran my hands over his body to check for other weapons. He had a small .380 automatic pistol in his left cargo pocket, a four-inch knife in a sheath on his right forearm hidden under the uniform and another knife inside his left boot.

Rolling Thunder

Slipping the pistol into my pocket, I handed the knives to Rachel and flipped him over to search his front, but he wasn't carrying anything else.

I released the chin strap for the riot helmet and pulled it off his head. Handing that to Rachel, I thought it might be good for her to wear to protect her head.

"So, you're not a cop. How did you know we were here and what did you want with us?"

He was still on his back and I had my left knee applying pressure on his chest. Dog stood with his muzzle only inches above the man's face. As the rain washed the blood out of his fur, the red-tinged water fell on the man's forehead and ran into his eyes. Rachel stood a dozen feet away, rifle in her hands as she kept an eye out for any threats.

"We were just trying to help you! Why did you shoot..."

I hit him hard with the side of my hand, directly onto the bridge of his nose which broke from the blow. Thank God for the anesthetic Rachel had shot me up with or I would probably have hurt myself worse than I did him. He groaned and turned his head to the side as blood started pouring out of his nose. He began to raise his hands to his face but froze when Dog growled.

"This is the last time I'm going to ask you," I said in a low, even voice. "How did you know and why did you want us?"

"We saw you break into the warehouse and waited. We didn't want you," he sputtered and turned his head to spit blood out of his mouth. "We were here for her."

I have to say I wasn't terribly surprised at his answer. Out of the corner of my eye, I saw Rachel turn her head and look at him for a moment before resuming watch on the area.

"What did you want with her?" I doubted I would be surprised by his answer.

"There's a bunch of us that are getting ready to head up into the hills. We need women. Someone's got to keep the human race going."

He said the last like a mantra he'd heard repeated over and over. Looking away in disgust, I met Rachel's eyes. I knew what she was thinking without even having to ask because I was thinking the same thing.

"How many women has your group taken?"

Rolling Thunder

I leaned in, the top of my head brushing Dog's. The man gulped, choosing to swallow the blood still pouring from his nose rather than risk moving his hands.

"About ten," he stammered.

"Where are they?"

"Man, I can't tell you… whoa, hold on dude!"

I had drawn my Ka-Bar and pressed the point into the soft tissue under his jaw. His eyes were as big as saucers as he looked into mine, probably trying to decide if I would really kill him if he didn't talk.

"There's a warehouse. About a mile down this road right here. That's where we're gettin' things ready to move out. That's where they are, now don't hurt me again!"

Right choice.

"You really a cop?" I asked.

He hesitated, eyes sliding away as he tried to decide how to answer. That told me more than anything he could have said. Grabbing his arm, I looked at the cheap digital watch he was wearing. It was 2215. We had less than two hours to get to the train. Pulling the watch off his wrist, I slipped it onto mine, sheathed the blade and stood up. Dog took a couple of steps back and the man felt safe enough to raise his hands to feel his broken nose.

I looked around as Rachel stepped up on the other side of him. She shooed Dog away, clicked the rifle's safety off with her thumb and fired a single round into his head. She stood staring down at him for a few moments before clicking her rifle back onto safe and letting it hang on its sling.

"We don't need people like this in the world anymore."

She gave me a challenging look, perhaps expecting me to argue with her or exclaim that she'd just shot a defenseless man. I thought she knew me better than that.

"No argument here. You beat me to it," I said, walking over to check the pickup the two dead men had arrived in.

18

The man I'd shot lay in a crumpled heap in the rain. The face shield was shattered where my bullet had gone through before scrambling his brains. The shotgun was still gripped in his right hand and I pried it loose to check the load. Seven shells with 00 buckshot were ready to go and he'd been close enough to blow a hole the size of a trash can lid right through us. Making sure the safety was on, I stowed the shotgun in the small Nissan pickup.

I waved Dog into the tight space behind the seats and shouted to Rachel to strip the body armor off the man she had shot. I started doing the same with mine. I was going to try and get to the women these guys and their friends had kidnapped and I felt it was a pretty safe assumption that if these guys were decked out in riot gear, then so were their buddies.

Pulling the last of it off the body, I shrugged out of the packs and deposited them in the bed of the truck. I started adjusting the armor to fit my much larger frame. After a degree of frustration, and cursing, I had it all on and went to help Rachel get the unfamiliar gear strapped on and fitting reasonably well.

The body armor was police issue and of decent quality. It would certainly stop most handgun rounds as well as rifle rounds if the distance was great enough, but it didn't make us invincible by a long shot. I spent a couple of minutes explaining this to Rachel and making sure she understood.

I was also paying close attention to her as I spoke and was relieved to see her grasping what I was saying and responding appropriately. I had no doubt the concussion was still affecting her, and she probably had one hell of a headache, but at least she was functioning again.

Armor in place, I ripped the broken face shield off the helmet and tried to fit it over my head. It was about two sizes too small. Oh, well, I wanted it for appearances more than protection as it wouldn't stop a bullet. Tossing it away, I started to turn to climb in the truck, but Rachel stopped me with a hand on my arm.

"You're still bleeding."

She squinted at my head and neck in the dark. I reached up to touch my wounds, and my hand came away with fresh blood that was quickly washed off by the rain.

Rolling Thunder

"It's just the rain. Keeping it from clotting. No big veins or arteries. If there had been, I'd be gone by now."

"We need to bandage you up."

"Later," I said, moving her to the passenger side of the truck and holding the door for her. "When we're safely on the train. Time is short and if we're going to help those women we have to get moving."

Rachel nodded and climbed into the cab. I walked around the hood and got behind the wheel, slammed the door, put the truck in gear and headed for the road. I was glad the warehouse where the women were being held was close, as well as on our way to the train. It was now 2231 and I was getting a little nervous about making it in time.

I drove slowly, without any lights showing. I didn't want anyone at the warehouse to see us coming. The rain and dark shrank the world around us. I could only see a few yards beyond the front of the truck, which forced me to keep our speed just above an idle. There were a couple of wrecks I had to steer around, then hopped the median to get around a utility pole that had fallen across the roadway.

I shifted into neutral and let the truck roll to a stop without touching the brakes when we came around a curve. Several vehicles, with their running lights on, were parked next to a medium sized warehouse. The warehouse itself was lit and light spilled out through open doors into the parking lot. Several men were loading boxes into the back of a large pickup.

I pulled out my knife and used the pommel to shatter the dome light so I could open the door without giving away our presence. Setting the parking brake, I popped my door open and stepped out, bringing my rifle up to use the night scope. A slow scan of the area, to include the roof of the warehouse, didn't spot any lookouts. More amateurs. They were in a group and they were armed, probably accustomed to pushing people around. They didn't think someone would come along and mess with them.

The warehouse was only a couple of hundred yards away from our position and I decided not to risk driving any closer. Shutting the vehicle off, I put the keys on top of the rear tire and made sure Rachel knew where they were. I waved her and Dog out of the truck and made another scan of our target. All clear. I checked three hundred and sixty degrees around

Rolling Thunder

us, still not seeing anyone on sentry duty and no threats to our rear.

Shrugging into our packs, we went over to the sidewalk on the opposite side of the street and started moving towards the building. As we walked, I frequently used the scope to check the area. I was trying to get a feel for the movement patterns of the men. As we closed the distance, I started picking up the sounds of idling engines. The low rumbles had been masked by the sizzling sound the rain made when it hit the asphalt.

These guys were getting ready to leave. Between our time constraint of trying to catch the train and their imminent departure, this was not a good tactical situation. In fact, it was piss poor. There was no time to get a headcount, find out what types of weapons we would be facing or any of the number of other things I would have liked to know before going in. We didn't even know where they were keeping the women.

The fickle little gods of war must have decided to take pity on me for once. As soon as I had the thought about the women, I spotted them. An Army surplus deuce-and-a-half with a canvas cover over the cargo area was idling in the parking lot. I happened to be looking right at it when one of the men walked up and shined a flashlight in the back. The light was only on for a few seconds, but that was long enough.

I clearly saw several women with terrified expressions on their faces and the lone guard sitting at the back. He was armed with what looked like some sort of civilian assault rifle but was handling it sloppily, holding it by the barrel just a couple of inches below the muzzle. The man with the flashlight had a brief conversation with the guard before putting the canvas flap back in place and going into the warehouse.

I spent a couple of minutes outlining for Rachel what I had in mind and she eagerly agreed. Rushing into a situation with absolutely no intel and with a clock ticking in the back of your head is never good. But it was go now, or watch them drive away any minute. We headed directly for the back of the truck. I stayed to Rachel's left and moved Dog to my left.

As we drew closer, I could hear male voices shouting back and forth inside the warehouse. Pausing Rachel with my hand, I made another scan of the area with my scope. This time, I spotted a lone figure at the far end of the parking lot. He was sheltering from the rain under a shallow overhang and staring off into space. I could make out a holstered pistol and a bolt action hunting rifle slung over his slumped shoulders.

He hadn't been there the last time I'd scanned, I was sure of that, but didn't bother dwelling on it. He had probably been around the corner taking a piss. Or just looking for a different view. Few things in life are as mind-numbingly boring as sentry duty.

"This is about to get bloody," I said to Rachel, maintaining my aim on the sentry. "Are you sure you're in?"

"I have had it with men thinking because the world is falling apart that they can just take a woman and do whatever they want to her. Fuck them! They made their choice. Now they've got to pay the price."

Rachel's voice was harder than I'd ever heard it. I suppose if I was a psychologist or psychiatrist, whatever the difference is, I would have been able to articulate how Rachel's trauma in Georgia was affecting her now. But I'm not. I am, however, smart enough to understand the connection.

Besides, I happened to agree with her. Every time I thought about my wife in Arizona, I said a little silent prayer that she hadn't fallen victim to some assholes like these.

"OK, here we go."

I squeezed the rifle's trigger. The sentry dropped like I'd cut the strings that were holding him up when my bullet shattered his skull. The heavy rain masked any sounds the body made falling to the ground. I scanned again, re-checked the roof and finding nothing started us moving. We walked straight to the back of the truck and I positioned myself to the side, Dog behind me. Rachel stepped up to the canvas flap and pulled it open.

"Please, help me. Can you help me?"

She was good, putting just the right note of *helpless woman* in her voice.

"What the hell?"

I heard scrambling from inside, then the guard stuck his head out of the opening to look at Rachel. He hadn't bothered to raise his rifle to protect himself and I didn't hesitate to strike. Lunging forward, I buried all eight inches of the Ka-Bar into his throat, grabbed his collar with my other hand and yanked the body out of the truck. I maintained my grip on him all the way to the ground, the steel blade in his throat ensuring he couldn't call out for help.

Withdrawing the knife, I changed its angle and stabbed up into his head, slicing into his brain. Cleaning the blade on his jacket, I sheathed it and checked the area again with my rifle. Three men with boxes loaded in their arms were coming out of the warehouse, headed for one of the parked pickups.

"Get in there and make sure they stay quiet. We may have a problem here," I said to Rachel as I tracked the three men.

I heard her scramble up into the cargo area and start talking to the women in a low voice. Dog was at my side, shoulder pressed to my hip and ready to run or fight, whatever I needed him to do.

The three men had come out of the warehouse door and turned to their left. There were three trucks parked in that direction. If they were going to the closest one, I probably had nothing to worry about. But if they went to the second or third, they would very likely spot the body of the sentry I had shot.

They were laughing and talking as they walked, not paying attention to their surroundings and going right past the first truck. They passed the second one and stepped up to the third where they set the boxes down in the bed and packed them in place. The sentry's body was ten feet behind them. Fortunately, they were so absorbed in their conversation they hadn't noticed it. Yet.

Finishing what they were doing, all three turned to go back into the warehouse. As one, they froze when they saw the body and I didn't wait to engage. Pulling the trigger, I shot the one on the left in the back of the head, sending his body pitching forward onto the pavement. I had already shifted aim and fired my second round before the first body hit the ground. The second man went down without even having a chance to start moving.

Unfortunately, the third guy had better reflexes and was throwing himself to the side when I fired. My bullet hit him, but I was pretty sure it wasn't a kill shot. He disappeared behind one of the pickups and began screaming for help. A heartbeat later there were shouts from within the warehouse. It sounded like a lot of men.

19

I quickly moved to the front corner of the idling truck, resting my rifle across the hood and sighting in on the open warehouse door. It didn't take long for running figures, weapons in hand, to appear. I started dropping them as fast as I could acquire them in my scope. Three went down, permanently, before the rest realized what was happening and scrambled for cover.

They settled for sticking rifles and pistols around the door frame and firing. Their shots weren't aimed and my odds of winning the lottery were probably better than their odds of hitting me. One guy kept sticking his whole arm around the doorway at the same spot to fire a pistol. After his third shot, I was ready for him and drilled a round through his forearm as soon as it appeared. The pistol fell to the ground and I could hear his screams over the shouts and firing coming from the rest.

I was trying to decide the best way to break off from the firefight and get out of there with the truck when Rachel and another woman appeared beside me. Rachel was holding her rifle and the woman had the dead guard's weapon in her hands. I glanced at her and recognized the pants and shoes she was wearing as most likely being part of a law enforcement uniform. She saw me look, met my eyes and nodded her head.

"Who's your friend?" I asked, involuntarily doing a double take at the woman.

She was shorter than Rachel. More compact with long blonde hair, but even disheveled and dirty she was a stunning beauty.

"Eyes on the target, big boy," the woman said. "I'm Melanie Fitzgerald, Tennessee State Police."

"What do you want us to do?" Rachel asked, frost evident in her tone.

She had her back against the truck's door, rifle held high across her body. Even in the midst of a firefight, she managed to convey her displeasure that I had noticed another woman. Melanie, ignoring her, looked pissed off and ready to kill anything.

"Is that a full mag in that AK?" I was referring to the guard's rifle.

"Yes. 30 with another 30 taped to it."

I hadn't noticed the spare magazine.

Rolling Thunder

"Will it go full auto or is it legal?"

"Full. What do you have in mind?"

She moved in front of Rachel so we could talk while I kept the assholes in the warehouse occupied. Rachel looked ready to shoot her. What is it with women? I wasn't even involved with Rachel. Was married to someone else. Yet, here she was, acting like I was betraying her or something. I put her problems out of my mind and focused on the task at hand.

"We need to keep these guys occupied long enough to get out of here. You two in the cab with Dog. Get him on the floor. I want that AK out the passenger window and when I get behind the wheel, you need to keep their heads down so we can get the hell out of here."

"You got it," Melanie said and wasted no time in climbing up. She scooted all the way across the bench seat, Rachel and Dog piling in right behind her. "Ready!"

I fired two more rounds at body parts I could see, smiling when one of them blasted a knee cap that had been carelessly stuck into the open. The owner fell across the opening and I followed up with a round to his head. Dropping my rifle to hang on its sling, I jumped into the cab.

Slapping off the parking brake, I pressed in the clutch and rammed the truck into reverse.

No sooner had I started us moving than Melanie opened up with the AK on full auto. She was leaning out the passenger window and expertly controlling her rate of fire. With enough room in front, I slammed on the brakes, jammed the gear shift into first and floored the throttle. The big diesel engine spooled up and we shot forward. The turbo whistled as it reached full speed before I slammed us into second and bounced across a curb and into the street.

Melanie was leaning way out of the window and firing directly behind us at this point. She paused to change magazines before pulling the trigger and holding it as she hosed down the front of the building. It didn't take long for the AK to run out of ammo and she sat back in her seat and leaned forward to look in the mirror bolted to the outside of her door. She watched for a bit then ducked.

"Incoming!" She shouted to be heard over the roar of the engine.

Rachel instantly ducked and leaned into me. Bullets started slamming into the cab of the truck. There were screams from the women in back, one of them most likely taking a round. The mirror in the middle of the windshield shattered when a bullet came through the cab and struck it. Then two more holes appeared in the windshield. I started swerving the truck as much as I could, but these things aren't exactly sports cars and it takes a lot of wheel turn to get a little movement.

I did the best I could and it must have been good enough because no more rounds hit us. By now I was in fourth gear and stayed on the throttle when an abandoned Toyota loomed in the dark, directly in our path. The heavy steel bumper smashed it to the side, the truck barely shuddering and not slowing from the impact. God, I love military vehicles!

We roared around a curve in the road and Melanie leaned way out her window to look behind us.

"No signs of pursuit."

She pulled herself back into the cab.

"Do you know how to get to the train station?" I shouted over the noise from the rain, wind and roar of the engine.

"Stay on this road. I'll tell you where to turn when we get there," she shouted back.

Dirk Patton

I wanted to talk to her and get her story, but it was just too loud in the truck. Besides, all we had to do was make the train and there would be plenty of time for talking once we were aboard. I looked over quickly to make sure everyone was OK with no bullet holes and didn't see anything to worry me.

Dog was squeezed into the passenger side foot-well and Rachel had her legs tucked behind mine to give him room and not interfere with me shifting gears. Dog sat up, looked at us and raised a paw onto Rachel's leg. There was enough light from the dash to see the blood that started soaking into her pants.

Rachel reached over and grabbed the flashlight off my rifle, clicked it on and leaned forward to check him. I had to focus on my driving, smashing through a couple more abandoned vehicles and keeping an eye on my side mirror for signs of pursuit from the guys at the warehouse. I had just been starting to think we were free and clear when two sets of lights bounced over a rise in the road a half a mile behind us. Rachel clicked the light off and snapped it back onto my rifle, telling me Dog had lost a nail and part of a toe, but was OK otherwise. I didn't have time to worry about him right now.

Rolling Thunder

"We've got company! Half a mile back and closing," I shouted. "How far to the turn?"

I pressed harder on the throttle, but it was already on the floor. The truck was maxed out at a blistering 60 miles per hour. These things weren't built for speed.

Melanie looked around quickly before answering.

"Two miles. I think."

Shit. They'd catch us before we got to the turn. They couldn't run us off the road with the light pickups they had, but they could sure as hell pull alongside and start pumping bullets into us or our tires. I glanced over my shoulder and confirmed there was an opening behind the seat into the cargo area. Shouting for Rachel to drive, I let off the throttle long enough for her to slide across my lap and take the wheel. As soon as she had control, I clambered up and over the seat back and into the cargo area.

The women in back were sprawled across the floor, bracing themselves as best they could. I couldn't help but step on arms and legs as I made my way to the back of the truck. Yanking the flap of canvas out of the way, I handed it to the woman closest to me and told her to hold on to it so it didn't get in my way. On my knees, I looked out at the quickly approaching trucks and raised my rifle, taking aim at the lead truck's windshield.

I couldn't see the driver behind the glass, but that didn't matter. Rifle in burst mode, I pulled the trigger twice in quick succession and sent six rounds into the cab. At first, I didn't think my shots had done any good. But the truck slowly started to drift to its left, moving faster and faster until it slammed head-on into a steel street light pole at an intersection. The pole didn't move and the truck disintegrated when it hit.

The other truck swerved around the wreckage and kept coming. The driver began weaving at random times to try and prevent me from getting a shot. I had his rhythm figured out and was starting to pull the trigger when Rachel hit the brakes and skidded into a turn. I was thrown off balance and tumbled across the floor, ending up in a pile with three of the women who had also been thrown by the unexpected change in direction.

Fighting my way free of the tangle of limbs, I crawled to the back of the cargo area and looked out. The second truck that had been pursuing was stopped at an angle in the intersection we had just passed through. As I watched, it reversed, turned and disappeared back the way we had come from. What the hell?

That question was asked again a moment later when Rachel hit the brakes. Too hard. I wound up in another pile of women at the front of the cargo area. There was a point in my life when this would have been a fantasy come true. Now, it was just a pain in the ass.

"Why are you stopping?" I shouted to Rachel, grimacing as one of the women stepped on my left hand as she climbed out of the pile.

"Roadblock," she answered.

Now, I'm as chivalrous as the next guy. Probably more so, or my dad would have kicked my ass when I was growing up. But, that news got me moving and pushing struggling women out of my way. Reaching the back of the truck, I swung a leg over the short tailgate and dropped to the ground. Moving around to the cab, I was surprised to see the mob of people filling the street right in front of the truck.

The road we were on wasn't wide. It only had a single traffic lane in each direction with a narrow turn lane down the middle, and it was clogged with bodies. I couldn't see far enough to tell how deep the mob was and hopped up on the driver's side running board to talk to Rachel and Melanie.

Dog had moved onto the seat when I'd climbed into the back. When I appeared at the open window, he stepped into Rachel's lap to greet me. With a grunt, she pushed him away, looked at me and pointed through the windshield.

From the higher vantage point the truck provided, I could see over the heads of the crowd and spotted the bottleneck. No more than two blocks in front of us were a couple of cops with half a dozen men in civilian clothing standing behind them. They had blocked the road and seemed to be looking for someone as they would occasionally pull a person out of the crowd and send them to stand in a fenced and guarded parking lot next to the road. Was this really the right time to be doing this?

"Notice anything wrong with this picture?" Rachel asked.

I looked at the crowd, the cops and their helpers, but didn't see anything.

"Look at the parking lot," Rachel said, pointing, exasperation clear in her voice.

Rolling Thunder

I looked where she indicated and got pissed off all over again. Every person in the parking lot was female, and from here they all looked young and attractive. You've got to be kidding me. These guys were that brazen?

Movement at the roadblock drew my attention and I watched as the second pickup that had chased us pulled to a stop behind the small group. Two men got out and ran to the ones dressed as police. They began having an animated conversation with lots of arm waving, then one of the new arrivals pointed in our direction.

There're two ways to deal with people like this. You can try to avoid them and get on with your day. Or you can confront them head-on and hurt them bad enough that they decide to run away. Avoiding bullies isn't in my DNA. I don't like them and, quite honestly, in my day I've had a few occasions where I enjoyed putting them in their place.

"I'm going to put a stop to this. Are you with us?" I asked Melanie.

"Yes," she answered with a frown on her face. "But I don't think it's going to work to try to arrest them."

"Arresting isn't what I have in mind."

I had Rachel give her one of the pistols taken off the men we'd killed outside the warehouse. I was kicking myself for not having brought the shotgun, but it got left behind when we traded the Nissan for the deuce-and-a-half.

"Melanie, the days of civil obedience to the law are over. Not only do we need to get past these guys to get to the train, I don't like what they're doing. You're right about arresting them not working. You know what the alternative is, but let me be very clear. If they aren't willing to just walk away, there's going to be blood. There's going to be bodies on the ground. Are you OK with that, or do you want to get out here?"

I looked across the cab at her, Rachel turning to gauge her reaction as well. She looked back at us for a moment, turned to look at what was going on at the road block then made up her mind.

"I'm in. Let's stop these fuckers."

20

I had Rachel and Mel, she liked the shortened version of her name, climb into the back of the truck while I slipped behind the wheel. A quick check of my weapons and I was ready to go. Sounding the truck's air horn, I revved the big diesel and let the clutch out just enough to start it moving. Slowly the crowd parted, frightened and angry faces looking up at me as I pushed through. It took a couple of minutes to make it to the roadblock.

Arriving, I intentionally kept the truck rolling when the two uniformed cops stepped in front of it with their hands raised for me to stop. There was a moment when I thought they were actually going to keep standing there until the massive front bumper bulled them aside, but at the last second they both jumped clear with angry shouts.

Introduction complete, I knocked the shifter into neutral, set the parking brake and hopped to the ground with Dog on my heels. The two cops were already striding towards the driver's side of the truck where I stood waiting for them, anger obvious on their faces. My rifle was slung on the front of my body, my right hand resting on the pistol grip.

They came charging around the front of the truck and saw me standing there with Dog. One of them faltered when he saw us, but the other kept right on coming. He had his baton in his left hand, gripping it tightly as he advanced.

"What the hell is going on here, officer?" I barked out in my best military growl. I was going to give them a chance to get out of this in one piece.

"You're under arrest," he answered, face florid from his anger. "Take those weapons off and get on your knees."

He was an arm's length in front of me and had come to a stop. He was big and beefy, and probably fairly strong, but he was used to his size and the uniform intimidating people. I was going to have to disappoint him.

"Officer, I know what you're doing here. Now this can go two ways. You and your buddies get into your vehicles and drive away, without those women you've pulled out of the crowd."

Rolling Thunder

He stood staring at me and I could see the wheels turning. We stayed like that, frozen, staring each other down for nearly half a minute.

"You said two ways."

I knew he would have to ask.

"You won't like the second option. It involves pain, and probably not very many of you living for more than the next couple of minutes."

Now I'm not one of those guys that likes to threaten. It's always seemed like a waste of time to me to talk about what I'm going to do before I do it. But I was playing to my audience and had a goal in mind. I saw a flicker of uncertainty pass across his face. Then he looked around to make sure the other men still had his back.

Just as I'd hoped, they'd moved in tighter to be able to hear the conversation. They had bunched up when they should have spread farther out. I let a smile spread across my face. I had no doubt that I must have looked rather fearsome with blood still running down the side of my head from the wounds I had taken fighting the female in the warehouse.

Some people, however, have either lost the inner lizard brain that tells them they are in mortal danger, or they choose to ignore it. Whatever the case was with him, he made the final mistake of his life when he reached forward to grab my vest. Instead of pulling away, I stepped into his reach, grasped his hand, twisted his arm until his palm was facing him and snapped his wrist.

I didn't let go, hanging on tight as I drew my pistol, jammed the muzzle to his forehead and pulled the trigger. If I still had the .45 I'd acquired in Atlanta, the round would have blown a hole out of the back of his head and hit one of his friends, but the lower powered 9 mm hollow point stayed inside his skull. Either way, he was just as dead, the body dropping to the ground.

After I pulled the trigger, there was a moment of absolute silence from his buddies as well as the crowd at my back. I kept the pistol up and pointed at the face of the second cop who was less than ten feet away. The silence stretched until one of the men at the edge of the group started to reach for his pistol. I caught the movement out of the corner of my eye, but before I could react Dog snarled and attacked.

Rolling Thunder

They fell to the ground, the man screaming as Dog clamped down on his wrist. The man next to him turned and started to raise his shotgun in Dog's direction, but a shot from behind me sounded and he spun around and fell to the ground with a gout of blood from a bullet hole in his neck. Everyone else froze again, staring over my shoulder. I knew they were looking at Rachel as the shot I'd heard had been her suppressed rifle, not the pistol Mel was carrying.

I called Dog off, figuring the man was now too chewed up to use that hand for anything. Dog gave another snarl, then released his hold and trotted over to stand a couple of feet to my side. He faced the group with bloody fangs showing. None of them moved.

"Last chance," I said. "Lay your weapons on the ground and leave, or more of you are going to die."

The group stood and stared at me, some of them frightened and some angry. It was the angry ones I had to watch. A moment later there was movement at the back of the group as one of them who had been staring at me with clenched teeth raised his rifle in my direction. I didn't have a shot, but a loud pistol spoke from the right side of the truck and he dropped dead into a large puddle of water.

That was enough for the rest. At first, one of them bent forward to lay his rifle on the ground, but that was like a dam breaking and soon they all disarmed themselves and backed away towards their vehicles with hands up and empty. As the distance opened, I quickly holstered my pistol and raised the rifle to cover their retreat.

In less than a minute, all of them had piled into their vehicles and sped off with lots of tire spinning on the wet asphalt. When the last vehicle turned a corner and drove out of sight, I lowered my rifle and looked around. Meeting Mel's eyes, I nodded my thanks. She looked a little green around the gills.

"That's the first time I've ever shot another person," she said in a slightly shaky voice.

"You didn't shoot a person, you saved me," I said.

I remembered the first time I had killed another man and knew there wasn't anything more I could say to help her work through the emotions she was dealing with right now. Looking around for Rachel, I found her at the back of the truck with a large portion of the crowd surrounding her. She was explaining to the people what was going on. The women in the back of the truck had pulled the canvas flaps open and were looking out at the crowd as Rachel spoke.

This was all nice, but we had a train to catch. I turned to ask Mel where the station was, but she had already walked over to the women in the parking lot. Several of them were crying and hugging her.

Glancing at my new watch, I wasn't happy to see it was 2300. We had an hour. Assuming the train actually waited until midnight to leave. Assuming it could. What if the infected were moving faster than expected? It had been hours since I'd heard the midnight timeframe on the radio and as much as anyone I knew how fluid things could get when trying to evacuate ahead of a battle. For all I knew, the last train could have pulled out already and we were about to be royally screwed by a few million pissed off infected. Time to move.

Shouting for Rachel and Mel, I waved Dog into the cab, turning my head when a hand grabbed my arm. It was a young boy, still in his early teens.

Dirk Patton

"Please help me. My brothers and I are trying to get my dad to the train, but I don't think we're gonna make it."

I looked down at him and initially thought about telling him I had other responsibilities and couldn't help everyone, but something made me rethink. I don't know why. I generally have a pretty hard heart, or at least I think I do. Katie, my wife, tells me I'm just a big, dangerous teddy bear that wouldn't hurt a fly unless it pissed me off first. Maybe she's right. She usually is.

"Where's your dad, son?" I asked as Rachel walked up and stood there listening.

"He's at the back of the crowd with my two brothers. Thank you!"

The look of relief on the boy's face was obvious as he turned to lead me to his dad. Mel walked up, leading the group of women that had been pulled aside and I told her to stay with the truck. It was sitting there idling and in this situation would tempt even the Pope to hop in and take off. She nodded and Rachel and I set off through the crowd that was now starting to flow forward towards the train station.

I followed the boy, pushing through the crowd as people rushed forward with whatever possessions they couldn't leave behind. They had them piled in shopping carts, garden wagons, and wheelbarrows. Anything that would roll. I wasn't sure, but I doubted any of them would be allowed to bring their stuff with them onto the train. This wasn't a pleasure trip.

As the crowd began to thin towards the rear, I could see two larger boys, both in their late teens, standing to either side of a man close to my age who was sitting in a wheelchair. Next to them a tall pile of hard-sided equipment cases was strapped to a two-wheeled cart.

The man was shifting side to side in the chair, trying to see through the crowd. His face lit up in a smile when he saw his son. Rachel and I trotted towards the small group, arriving a moment after the boy who'd asked me for help.

"Your boy asked for help," I said by way of introduction. "We've got a truck and can get you in it for the rest of the way to the train."

I waved for them to follow me but skidded to a stop when the man spoke.

"Thank you for your help. I was ready to send my boys on without me so they could get out."

I knew that voice and the way Rachel stopped, she did too.

"You're Max!" Rachel exclaimed.

He grinned at her and nodded.

"Yes I am, pretty lady. I take it you've heard one of my broadcasts."

"More than one, and thank you for doing that. Now, we've got to haul ass!" I spoke up before Rachel could start a conversation that we didn't have time for.

Turning, I started jogging back to the truck. Most of the crowd had moved on and the road was fairly open. One of the older boys pushed Max in his chair, matching my pace. The youngest one dragged the wheeled cart of cases, which I now assumed was Max's radio setup. The other boy was armed with a rifle and he stayed behind them, keeping the rear safe.

We made it to the truck quickly, Mel standing by the open driver's door waiting for us with the pistol in her hand. I ran to the back, unhooking and dropping the tailgate. With it down, the floor of the cargo area was four feet off the ground and it took me helping Max's two

Rolling Thunder

older boys to lift him, in his chair, high enough to clear the lip.

Several of the women who had stayed in the truck reached out and helped pull Max safely into the cargo area. The radio equipment was lifted next, Then the three boys scrambled aboard. Tailgate secured, Rachel and I joined Mel at the cab and moments later we were rolling again.

We drove for nearly four more miles, passing everyone that had been in the crowd. They were now jogging or walking as fast as they could to the station. We passed a couple of families and I slowed at tearful pleas from two mothers who ran alongside and handed small children up to the women in the back of the truck. Fuck me, this sucked.

21

The station was a madhouse. Portable, generator-powered floodlights cast a stark, white light across the area and two trains sat on the tracks with every conceivable type of car hooked to them. Cattle cars, freight cars, open ore cars, flat cars, Amtrak passenger cars, even tanker cars.

National Guard soldiers and Nashville police, real police, were attempting to control and direct the throng of people, but it was like trying to hold back the tide. There must have been ten thousand bodies jammed into the small area. All of them were pressing forward to get to the safety promised by the trains, ignoring the instructions being shouted over a loudspeaker. This wasn't good. There were too many people and they were too disorganized to possibly get loaded before the trains left in less than an hour.

There was also the problem of how were we going to get on. I didn't like the idea of forcing my way through the crowd to board a train that would take me to safety, but leave the people behind that I had bulled my way ahead of. Altruistic? Foolish? Probably yes to both, but I am what I am.

Rolling Thunder

I was looking around and weighing our options when there was a loud shout to my left. I turned my head and saw a National Guard Sergeant leading a small squad of soldiers in my direction. Rachel noticed them too and reached up to tap my body armor. I had already forgotten I was wearing it and glancing down saw that it was covering my uniform and rank. I set the parking brake, shrugged out of the upper body armor, which I handed to Mel and told her to put on, then popped the door and stepped down to meet the Sergeant.

He was a young man, but I recognized the look in his eyes. Eyes that have already seen more death and destruction than the owner had ever imagined possible. When he was a few feet away, he checked out my uniform, eyes momentarily pausing on my oak leaf, then came to a modified form of attention. We weren't on a parade ground and the last thing he needed to do was stand there as rigid as the Queen's Guard at Buckingham Palace.

"What's the situation, Sergeant?"

I preempted him asking me any questions about what I was doing there with a truckload of civilians. His eyes squinted for a brief moment, but he held his questions.

Dirk Patton

"Sir, we've got more evacuees than we have room on the trains. Word just came down that we're pulling out at 2330 – 11:30 PM or in less than twenty minutes – and I damn well expect a riot any minute."

He looked around at the crush of frightened humanity trying to reach the trains.

"Why early? I had heard midnight?"

"The infected are close. Less than three miles and there's a shitload of them. Sir."

Like every good NCO that curses in an officer's presence, he protected himself by adding 'Sir' to the end of his sentence. I used to be quite good at that little trick.

"So what's the plan? Load people until the last second and whoever isn't on a train when it pulls out, they get left behind?"

I knew what the answer was, what the only viable solution was, but couldn't stop myself from asking for clarification.

"Yes, sir. That's about the size of it."

He spoke in a quiet voice and I could tell he wasn't happy about it. I looked around at all the faces and flashed back to the defenders in

Rolling Thunder

Murfreesboro that had stayed behind and lost their lives to buy time for a hasty evacuation. It was going to be the same here. Only these weren't defenders that had accepted their fate. These were families with children in tow that had always been able to more or less depend on the authorities to take care of them in a crisis. Change wasn't always good.

"Who's the on-scene commander?"

"That would be Colonel Crawford. He's on the balcony at the station."

The Sergeant turned and pointed at a small balcony high on the wall of the train station that must have given a commanding view of the entire rail yard. I could see three figures standing at the railing, looking down at the crowd, but they were too far away for me to make out individual features.

Making a decision that I knew Rachel wouldn't be happy with, I turned back to the Sergeant.

"OK, I know the Colonel. I'm going to report to him. While I'm doing that, I want you and your squad to get all the civilians in this truck onto one of those trains. There's a man in the back in a wheelchair that also has some equipment cases with him and it is very important that they get on the train with him. Am I clear?"

"You're clear sir, but I'm going to have to bump some of these civilians to find room for that equipment."

His words weren't arguing with my order, but I could tell by the tone of his voice that he didn't like the privilege of rank that I was using. Too bad. I didn't have time to explain.

"Sergeant, I understand what you're not saying, and believe it or not I agree with you. But there's more here than meets the eye. Just get it done."

I turned when he acknowledged my order and almost ran into Rachel. I hadn't realized she had stepped down out of the cab and had been standing behind me while I talked with the Sergeant.

"What the hell do you think you're doing?" She asked, arms crossed across her chest.

"Getting all of you on the train," I said, finding it hard to meet her accusing eyes.

"And then what? What the hell do you think you're going to be able to do? You heard

Rolling Thunder

the man. The infected are less than three miles away. This city is lost, and most of these people are going to die. Do you want to die with them? Are you giving up? Have you given up on your wife? On me?"

I was taken aback when tears started rolling down her cheeks. I had to look away from her, glancing up at the truck where I met Dog's eyes. He was lying across the seat, head hanging over the edge and watching me intently. I looked back at Rachel. Tears streamed down her face, being washed away by the steady rain. She wasn't making any attempt to cover up her emotions.

"Rachel, look..." I started to say but didn't know what to say.

If I told her I couldn't take a seat on the train that would result in one of these people losing their lives, she'd insist on staying with me and I couldn't live with that either. I had told myself that I was going to get them on the train, go see the Colonel, find some more ammo and hop back in the deuce-and-a-half and get the hell out of there ahead of the infected. Maybe not the best plan in the world, but it was all I had at the moment.

After nearly a minute of staring me down, Rachel shook her head, grabbed me in a tight embrace, kissed me and turned away. She called Dog out of the truck and they went to join the group at the back as Max was being gently lowered to the ground by two of the soldiers.

Rachel didn't look back and, after a moment, I turned and started pushing my way laterally through the crowd towards the station. Just before I lost sight of them, I looked back to see Dog watching me, Rachel with her back stiff and a firm grip on his neck. I felt like shit. To tell the truth, I had a lump in my throat.

Rolling Thunder

22

The lower level of the train station was empty and echoing, and it was nice to get out of the rain. At the back of the large waiting area was a set of stairs and I headed for them. Pausing when I found the pile of crates I expected to be there, I took a minute to drop all my empty rifle magazines and load up with full ones. I added a half dozen grenades to my arsenal while I was at it. Restocked, I climbed the stairs and wandered around the low-ceilinged upper floor offices until I found the balcony.

There were three men standing on it and I recognized the one in the center as the Army Colonel that I had met at Arnold Air Force Base. He was also the man who had given me the news that I was back in the Army, softening the blow with a big promotion to Major. Not that I would ever see the pay or benefits of the rank, but at least I could get things done like I just had with the Sergeant.

"Colonel Crawford," I said, stepping out behind him.

He turned, took half a second to recognize me, then broke into a big grin and stuck his hand out. I held my bandaged hand up and grinned, remembering his bone crushing grip and not about to experience it with my damaged paw.

"You made it out alive! Not really surprised after reading your file. You were quite the bad ass in your day."

"Thank you, sir. But, in my day? That really hurts, sir."

I smiled at him and he returned the smile before introducing me to the Captain and Master Sergeant that were standing next to him. The Master Sergeant, Darius Jackson, was a short, black man that was built like a fireplug and wore a Special Forces tab on his shoulder. I suspected he was one of Crawford's men from the 5th SOG.

"You probably don't remember me, but you were an instructor at Bragg when I went through selection," he said after looking closely at me for a few seconds.

I looked at him, but that was too many years and too many faces ago.

"Sorry, but I don't. Was I a prick?"

"Oh, yes sir. You were a gold plated one!"

Rolling Thunder

He grinned before turning back to look at the crowd below, shifting his head when raised voices caught his attention. A small squabble had broken out between some civilians. Cops and soldiers were quickly converging on the spot, pushing their way through the crowd. Before they could arrive, there were a couple of gunshots and one of the men who had been arguing fell to the ground.

The surrounding people screamed and surged away from the fight, hampering the progress of the authorities, but one of the cops pushed through. The shooter turned in his direction, pistol raised, and the cop shot him several times. A woman with a group of kids screamed loud enough for us to hear her clearly, falling to the ground to hold the wounded man.

The crowd stopped moving away and several men suddenly grabbed the cop and dragged him down where they started kicking him. Other police and soldiers arrived, one of them firing a burst into the air on full auto. This broke up the melee long enough for them to pick up the injured cop and carry him to safety.

Checking the watch, I noted the time was 2325. As if I had caused it by looking, first one train then both started sounding their whistles.

The five-minute warning. The crowd gasped, then surged forward with shouts and screams, quickly becoming a mob.

I looked for the small squad that I had tasked with getting Rachel and the other people on the train, but couldn't spot any of them. I hoped this meant they were already safely boarded. Fights were now breaking out in the crowd, more gunfire and screams accompanying them.

This was now a riot and I could see the cops and soldiers on the perimeter starting to melt back and run for the front of the train closest to the station. At a cattle car, directly behind the locomotives, a squad of soldiers was set up with machine guns, apparently holding a safe zone for the crowd controllers to pile into when it was time to go.

I would have liked to hear what happened at Fort Campbell and how the Colonel had wound up here in Nashville, but time was not on our side.

"What's the plan, Colonel? From what I hear the infected are going to be joining the party any minute."

Rolling Thunder

I moved up to the rail and stood between Crawford and the Captain, who was talking quietly into a satellite phone.

"Captain Blanchard over there is calling in our ride right now. We're going to join a flight of Apaches and Black Hawks to give some air cover for these trains. It's a little wild to the west and they're going to need our help. Besides, the Air Force has a package waiting for the infected and we don't want to be here when they deliver it."

I just nodded, relieved that I wasn't going to die here today. Well, at least it looked like I wasn't going to. Then I thought about what he'd just said. Package? Oh, shit. In military speak, that most likely meant a nuke.

The running cops and soldiers made it to the waiting railroad car and started piling in. Nearly a hundred people had followed and when they saw the squad with machine guns they knew their fate was sealed. Some of them stopped and just stood, staring at the train. Others kept running, ignoring a soldier that was ordering them to not come any closer over a hand held loud hailer. One of the civilians started firing and soon others joined in as they rushed the defensive position.

"Goddamn it!" Crawford growled.

A moment later the Master Sergeant turned and spoke to the Colonel. The Lieutenant in charge of the squad was requesting permission to open fire on the civilians to defend his position. Crawford gripped the balcony rail so hard I expected it to snap, but only took a second to nod his head with permission.

The order was relayed and almost immediately two machine guns and half a dozen rifles started firing at the swiftly approaching mob. The attackers were quickly cut down. The larger crowd went almost silent as every head turned in that direction to see what was going on. With the immediate threat neutralized, I watched the squad grab their weapons and equipment. They piled into the waiting car where they set up two of the machine guns pointing out the open side door.

"Get them rolling," Crawford ordered just before screams started coming from the far-left area of the crowd.

Looking for the source of the commotion, I could hear the Master Sergeant relay the order into his radio. For a moment, the screams of the crowd were drowned out by the two train whistles and the bass roar of the locomotives throttling up. By the time the engineers let off

Rolling Thunder

the whistles, the trains were moving. Slowly at first, but they visibly gained speed as the four locomotives at the front of each train belched dense clouds of black diesel smoke into the air. Now the crowd screamed as one, some voices in terror and pain, others in anger and dismay as the trains continued to accelerate.

At the edge of the illumination cast by the floodlights, I could see a growing commotion. Infected started appearing, their front ranks slamming into the milling crowd. Taking the binoculars offered by the Master Sergeant, I focused on the area and watched as thousands of females sprinted forward and started taking down the evacuees.

Many of the civilians were armed and got off several shots before falling to the unstoppable surge. Watching from my elevated position, it reminded me of watching tsunami footage on TV. An unstoppable wall of destruction just rolled over everything in its path. Not caring to see any more, I handed the glasses back and checked on the trains.

Each train was very long. Longer than I could estimate. It looked like they had hooked up every car that had wheels. The rear of the train hadn't cleared the station yet and as the wave of infected kept rolling over the crowd, they began grabbing onto the passing cars and hitching a ride.

Taking the glasses back, I nudged the Colonel, pointing out what was happening and handing them to him. He raised them and looked at the situation, then growled an order to the Master Sergeant without taking his attention off the trains. More radio calls, then a moment later two Apaches flared into a hover over the trains.

The Army's Apache helicopter is probably the most lethal rotor wing aircraft ever built. I'm sure there's some Russians that would argue the point, but they would be wrong. On the nose of the Apache is an electrically operated chain gun that fires thirty millimeter explosive shells that can pierce up to two inches of military grade armor.

Against flesh and bone, each shell will absolutely destroy anything within a ten-foot radius of where it strikes. The gunners didn't have to worry too much about accuracy. Their only real concern was to not shoot up the train, or shoot too close to it and send shrapnel into the cars packed with evacuees.

A moment after arriving on station, both Apaches opened up with their chain guns. Each directed their fire to the side of the train that was closest to the infected. The ground erupted and everything that was hit disintegrated. I could make out the occasional body part fly through the air, mostly arms and legs. But the problem with the infected, as I had learned, is that they don't stop coming just because the ones in front of them are blown into a cloud of pink mist.

The only way to stop them was to keep shooting until there weren't any left. Apaches carry up to twelve hundred rounds of ammo for the chain gun, but at a rate of fire greater than three hundred rounds per minute that's less than a four-minute supply. Of course, they don't fire continuously. The gunners having to let the guns cool, but they still burned through their full load of ammo before the rear of the trains passed out of the station.

They bought the necessary time, however, as the trains were both now moving too fast for any of the infected to grab on and climb aboard. I watched several females make leaps at the passing train, all but one failing to get a grip and bouncing off to tumble on the ground. The one that did manage to grasp a guard rail at the rear of a passenger car had her arm yanked completely free from her body. She tumbled to the ground and wound up under the big, steel wheels which cut her into pieces. I could still see the arm hanging from the rail. The hand had locked in a grip; the last position her brain had told it to take.

"Sir, our ride's here."

The Captain's voice drew my attention from the battle, and I looked up as a Black Hawk hove into view, hanging in the air over the roof of the station.

"Let's go, gentlemen. There's nothing more we can do here."

Crawford turned and marched inside the building, not looking to see if we were following.

23

The Colonel led the way to a janitor's closet that had a steel ladder going straight up to a hatch set into the ceiling. Climbing easily, he paused at the top to work the release mechanism before shoving the hatch all the way open. A blast of wind from the Black Hawk's rotor drove gusts of rain into our faces as we climbed.

The roof was steep and gabled, slippery from the rain. All of us moved in a crouch with one hand also touching to help with balance and grip. The Black Hawk moved into a hover with the side door adjacent to a high point and we scrambled up and into the helicopter the way only men accustomed to unusual boardings could. Once we were on board, with safety tethers attached, the pilot spun us around and brought us over the rear of the trains, about three hundred feet in the air.

The two trains were running parallel to each other, the one on the right maintaining a steady speed as the one on the left accelerated. I worked a set of headphones over my ears so I could communicate on the intercom.

"Hey, Master Sergeant. How far before those tracks converge?"

They might be running parallel now, but that's because we were in an urban area. In rural areas the railroads would generally only have one track that would branch out as it came into cities.

"About twenty miles. The switchgear is already set and we've got a couple of Apaches on station to make sure no one screws with it."

Sometimes, I absolutely loved the Army.

I still wanted to hear the story of Fort Campbell but when I looked around, Crawford and Blanchard were in a deep conversation over a tablet computer the Captain held in his lap. Not feeling like trying to insert myself into their tete-a-tete, I moved closer to the open side door. I stayed back enough to avoid the worst of the wind-whipped rain and looked down at the train. Lightning flashed, momentarily lighting the world and I didn't like what I saw. I called the pilot on the intercom and had him turn on a spotlight and focus it on the train below.

Dozens of infected females were clinging to the sides of many of the cars. A fairly large group of them had made it onto the roofs of several and were roaming about looking for a way into the smorgasbord beneath their feet. As I watched, one of them lay down and leaned over the side, finding an open window that she quickly slithered through. Shit. A lot of these people weren't going to be armed and wouldn't have a good way of fighting off the females. Before I could say or do anything, another one followed and disappeared inside the train.

"We've got infected on the train, going in windows," I called out over the intercom.

A moment later Crawford was next to me, looking out the open door. Moving back into the cabin, I checked a couple of equipment lockers and found a coiled fast rope. Fast roping is normally only done out of a stable, hovering helicopter. Trying to do it out of one in motion, onto a moving platform that's slick from rain is downright insane. But that's what I was going to do. Those people in the train needed someone down there that could help in a fight.

"What the hell do you think you're doing?" Crawford asked, looking at the rope I was busily securing to the helicopter.

"I'm going down there, sir."

I checked the connection of the rope and tugged as hard as my weakened hands would allow to test it. Weakened hands. I'd forgotten about my injuries. Oh, well, if I let go I'd just get down that much faster.

"Are you crazy? No, you are crazy. We're moving at thirty knots. You can't control the rope and your descent at this speed!"

"I've done it before," I lied. "It's not easy, but it can be done. Unless you're ordering me not to go down there and help those people, sir."

I paused and looked Crawford in the eye. He stared right back. Jaw set as he probably debated hitting me over the head and handcuffing me.

"You're a crazy son of a bitch. You know that?"

"Been told that a time or two, sir."

I grinned, slipping on the heavy leather gloves that had been in the locker with the rope. Over the intercom, I filled the pilot in on what I was doing and he said something similar to Crawford, then wished me luck as he started bringing us down closer to the train. Looking around to make sure everyone was clear of the rope, I pushed it out the door where it uncoiled smoothly and started flapping in our wake.

Rolling Thunder

I would have much preferred to have the pilot fly low enough for me to just step out the door and onto the train. But trains create a lot of turbulence as they move and it was also pretty dark out there. If the train went into a tunnel or under an overpass, the pilot wouldn't have time to pull up. For that matter, the same could happen to me dangling from a rope like a moron.

"Hold on," I heard Master Sergeant Jackson say over the intercom.

Looking around, I saw him slipping on a pair of gloves. Crawford was shaking his head but moved to the edge of the open door to assist. Pulling off the headset, I gave Crawford a wink and a thumbs up as I stepped backwards to the edge of the door, rope in hand.

Looking down, I didn't like how the rope was whipping all over the place. In theory, when my weight came on it would straighten out. While I might be blown a little behind the helicopter, I should still come straight down onto the train. In theory. Of course, there's probably a reason why no one does this.

Watching Crawford, I could tell he was communicating with the pilot, waiting for word that we were as stable as we were going to get. Jackson moved in front of me, facing the door but ready to grab on and follow me down. I met his eyes and grinned when he mouthed "crazy motherfucker" at me. Yep. Couldn't argue with that assessment.

Colonel Crawford suddenly leaned towards me and flashed a thumbs up. I didn't hesitate. If I did, I'd never step out of this perfectly good aircraft.

Normally when you fast rope out of a helicopter, you go straight down. All you have to worry about is controlling your descent. Not unlike sliding down a brass pole in an old fashioned fire house. This was nothing like that.

As soon as my body exited the door and entered the air flow of the helicopter in flight, I was whipped back so severely that I nearly smashed into the belly of the Black Hawk. I started spinning like a top in the slipstream and my hands felt like they were being flayed open. But I gripped tighter, pulling the rope as close to my body as I could, using just my feet to control my speed.

I slid fast, and as I got further below the helicopter the wind steadied. I was only being pushed back a small amount, but still spun and was getting dizzy. Watching the swiftly approaching roof, I clamped as hard as I could

Rolling Thunder

with my boots, slowing a little, but the rope was wet and I barely controlled my slide.

Three seconds after I stepped out the door, my boots hit the roof of the train. Hard. I stumbled. If not for my grip on the rope, I would have fallen and gone over the side. Catching my balance, I kneeled, maintained my grip on the line, looked up and signaled for Jackson.

It's not unusual for multiple guys to be on a rope at the same time, following each other out the door with minimal spacing. This way you get a lot of boots on the ground in a hurry. I was glad Jackson had the experience and forethought to wait for me to make it down in these conditions before he started.

He arrived quickly, boots hitting hard when he landed. They hit too hard and his feet went out from under him, legs flailing in the air as he started sliding towards the edge of the roof. He still had one hand wrapped around the rope, but it was slipping through his grip as he skidded across the slick metal.

I lunged for him, landing on top of his legs. They were pinned with my body weight, and his slide stopped with his upper body hanging over the edge. I was reaching for his hand when an infected female screamed from only a few feet away.

24

The son of a bitch! How could he abandon her like that?

Rachel's emotions threatened to overwhelm her and she squeezed tighter on Dog. Part of her thought she should let Dog go with John, but at the moment, he was all that was keeping her from having a complete breakdown. Confused and angry, she tried to deal with her emotions.

She'd never been one to fall in love easily, or even get infatuated with whatever man happened to come along and smile at her. For the past several years she'd been too busy with work and medical school to even entertain the idea of a relationship. That didn't mean she hadn't dated occasionally, though never any of the guys from the strip club she had worked in. A couple of doctors and one fellow medical student.

The doctors had both been looking for trophy wives, one of them actually proposing on their third date. He had offered to pay for the rest of her schooling and make sure she got into a good teaching program when she was ready to start her residency. Their third date was their last. The classmate had been an immature, narcissistic jerk and, to this day, she couldn't understand why she'd slept with him on their first and only date.

Now, she finally met a man that treated her like an equal. A partner. Taking charge when needed, yet willing to listen to her ideas and suggestions. He wasn't exactly the most handsome man she'd ever met. Way too battered and rugged, but that was part of his charm. Had she fallen in love with him? With a married man, that was only thinking of finding his wife?

"Let's go!"

Melanie was grabbing her arm and Rachel snapped out of her reverie, realizing that the group had already started moving off with the small squad of soldiers escorting them. Pulling her arm out of Melanie's grip, she called Dog and rushed to catch up. She'd seen the way John had noticed the smaller woman's looks and wasn't feeling very friendly towards her at the moment. Melanie fell in opposite of Dog and tried to match the pace Rachel was setting with her longer legs.

"You have a problem with me?" She asked as they strode towards the back of the group.

Rolling Thunder

"I don't even know you. How could I have a problem with you?" Rachel answered without looking at the woman.

They caught up with the group and Rachel positioned herself next to Max as one of his older boys pushed the wheelchair. At the head of the group, the soldiers on point were pushing the crowd aside to create a path for them. There were grumblings from the people and a few shouts of anger. One man refused to step aside and two of the soldiers knocked him out of their path and pointed their rifles at the surrounding bodies to make sure no one decided it would be a good idea to retaliate. No one was happy, but then no one was foolish enough to test their determination.

Rachel was dismayed to see what was happening. The thought of American military personnel forcing their way through a frightened crowd of American citizens that were only trying to escape certain death was a sobering one. Modern Americans, despite isolated terrorist attacks like the World Trade Center, had never had to deal with conflict and strife in person, in their own cities.

Evacuations, refugees and military interventions that wound up killing civilians were something that happened elsewhere and was watched on the evening news while one was comfortable in their nice, warm home. This was still surreal to Rachel. And to everyone else around her, she suspected.

"You understand why he left, don't you?" Melanie's question re-focused her on the here and now.

"What do you mean?"

"What I mean is, I don't know what there is between the two of you, but he didn't leave *you*. He left because he saw all these people and wasn't going to take even a single seat on that train so he could be safe. If he did that, then someone else would get left behind and die."

Rachel came to a full stop, but the soldier behind her put a hand in the middle of her back and kept her moving with the group. Tears started flowing down Rachel's cheeks again as she walked. She cursed herself for letting stupid emotions affect her this much.

The group reached the entrance to a passenger car and came to a halt as the soldiers cleared more civilians out of the way. A narrow path opened and the Sergeant waved Max and his equipment forward. When he was loaded, the

Rolling Thunder

Sergeant started moving the women up and onto the small access platform at the rear of the car.

It must have been crowded inside already as the boarding process was slow. Rachel jumped when both trains sounded their whistles. Anxious voices in the crowd were raised as bodies started pushing in. Looking over her shoulder at the train station, Rachel could see the balcony and there were now four figures standing on it watching over the loading of the trains. There were more shouts and gunfire started erupting all around them. She started to turn, but Melanie grabbed her arm.

"Where do you think you're going?"

Rachel whirled on her and roughly pulled her arm away. "Look, I know you mean well, but..."

"But nothing," Melanie stepped forward and shoved her face at Rachel. With their different heights, it was more like she shoved it at Rachel's chest, but her mouth was set and her eyes as intense as her voice. "Don't be stupid. I've known him for all of twenty minutes, and I can already tell he's a survivor. You really think the Army doesn't have a plan to get their people out of here? I guarantee you they do, and he'll be right there with them. Unless some stupid woman causes him to have to try and rescue her and they both wind up getting killed."

Rachel stared back at the big, blue eyes that were looking up at her. She wanted to punch the perfect little nose. Smash the cheerleader white smile. Kick the perky little ass all over the parking lot and leave the woman lying in the rain.

Dog, picking up on the tension, forced his body between the two women. He repeatedly shoved his nose against Rachel's balled fist until she relaxed and opened her hand. Automatically, she started rubbing his ears and the tension suddenly bled out of her, leaving her feeling exhausted.

"Let's get on the fucking train," she said in resignation and turned back to the queue of women waiting to board.

There was more firing from the far side of the other train, then Rachel heard at least two machine guns join the fight. They fell silent after no more than fifteen seconds, the crowd quickly disintegrating into a mob. From behind her, two of the soldiers that were providing rear guard started firing their rifles at panicked civilians who were charging their position.

Rolling Thunder

Rachel thought about turning to help, but just then the queue started moving. She followed Melanie up the steps and into the back of the car with Dog on her heels. The soldiers pressed in behind her. They stepped up to guard the platform, still firing occasional shots at the angry mob.

The inside of the car was packed with humanity and was oppressively hot and humid. The people crammed up against the walls were opening windows to get some ventilation. Rachel was pushed farther into the car as the remainder of the squad boarded. It was standing room only and she wound up face to face with Melanie, Dog jammed in between their legs.

Face to face wasn't exactly accurate. Melanie turned her head back and forth, trying to find a position where her's wasn't pressed against Rachel's breasts. Rachel wasn't happy with the arrangement either, but they finally shifted their bodies around until Melanie's face was against her shoulder.

"If you can see the pervert that just grabbed my ass, would you be kind enough to shoot him?"

Melanie was trying to turn and see who had groped her, but they were jammed in too tight by now and she could hardly move. Rachel tried and failed to stifle a laugh.

"What's so funny?"

"The world has ended. The apocalypse is here and men are still grabbing ass whenever the opportunity presents itself. Some things will never change."

Melanie looked up at her for a moment and started laughing, too. The mirth didn't last long. New screams from outside the train floated through the open windows, silencing every conversation in the car. The infected were here.

The train lurched hard, then it started rolling. People towards the rear of the car shouted and complained as everyone was thrown back by the sudden start. For a moment, there was so much weight on her body that Rachel couldn't breathe, then as people regained their balance, the pressure lessened. The train slowly picked up speed, more screams and now gunfire right outside the windows.

Rachel craned her neck around to try and see, but there were too many heads in the way. They were still gaining speed, slowly, and she was worried that the infected could overwhelm the train. No sooner had she had that thought than

Rolling Thunder

there was the bass pulsing of rotor blades from above the roof. Moments later, some kind of very large gun started firing into the ground right outside the train.

The firing and explosions seemed to go on forever. All too frequently there was the sound of shrapnel striking the metal sides of the train car. Once, a round must have been almost right on top of them and shrapnel shattered a couple of windows and elicited screams of pain from injured passengers.

Speed continued to build and eventually, either the firing ceased or they moved away from the battle, Rachel couldn't tell which. She tried to relax. Tried not to think about John and get herself upset and angry all over again. Instead, thought about why the shorter woman managed to rub her the wrong way.

"So, what is the story with you two?" Melanie asked, speaking into Rachel's right shoulder.

"We met the day of the attacks in Atlanta and have been together since. I can hardly believe that was less than three weeks ago. It feels like we've been fighting and running together forever."

"That's not what I meant."

"I know it's not what you meant and it's none of your goddamn business!"

Rachel could feel Melanie nod her head.

"So you wouldn't mind if I made a run at him?"

Rachel couldn't believe what she had just heard. Was this woman a psycho? One of those that had to have a man just because another woman had him or might want him? She was half a second from going off when she felt Melanie start shaking. It took her another second to realize it was laughter.

"You're real funny. Did anyone ever tell you that?" Rachel said, no longer angry, but not amused either.

"Sorry, but you just answered my question. And maybe your own question too."

Rachel thought about it and was opening her mouth to say, "Bitch" when a chorus of screams erupted from the front of the car. She snapped her head towards the commotion, banging her chin on the top of Melanie's head.

Rolling Thunder

The car was poorly lit by a dim string of lights attached to the center of the ceiling and running from front to rear. They gave enough illumination for Rachel to see an infected female wreaking havoc amongst the tightly packed evacuees near the front. Before she could react, another one came through an open window and immediately fell on the people jammed against the wall.

"Close the windows! They're coming in the windows!" Rachel screamed.

A couple of people heard her and started closing their windows, but another female slithered in just across from Rachel and latched on to a tall man. The evacuees were packed in so tight there was no room for them to move away from the danger. No room to fight. Of the ones that were being attacked, most couldn't even get their arms free of the crush to defend themselves. The females took full advantage, slashing and biting as they scrambled across the sea of heads.

The stench of hot blood and other bodily fluids being released flooded the car. Panicked screams erupted as people frantically shoved on their neighbors as they tried to get away from the threats. There was a shot and a scream. Then more guns fired. None of the gunfire seemed to have any impact on the females and another came in one of the front windows and added her fury to the attacks.

Rachel was wedged tight between Melanie and the soldier behind her. The front of the car was getting the worst of the attacks and the panicked people were pressing towards the rear as hard as they could. Their fellow riders were being so compressed that most of them couldn't breathe.

Rachel wanted to get her arms free. Get her rifle up and into the fight. But she was stuck as tight as if a heavy blanket had been wrapped around her and chained in place. She could barely even draw a breath and nearly peed her pants when another female came through the window directly across from her.

25

Both of us snapped our heads in the direction of the scream. A female advanced on us, crawling on all fours to better maintain her balance and grip on the roof of the train. Crawford had said we were moving at thirty knots, which is about thirty-five miles an hour. That's a strong wind to try and hold on to a slippery metal surface in the rain, but she was managing to do it. The good news was the conditions were slowing her down dramatically, or we'd both already be dead.

My rifle was somewhere behind my back, dangling from its sling and I was at completely the wrong angle to reach my pistol. Drawing my knife, I was preparing to use one hand to pull Jackson back onto the roof before engaging the female, but was preempted by a single pistol shot.

The female collapsed, then slid to the side of the roof and disappeared over the side. I looked at Jackson, still with his entire upper body hanging out into space. Only my weight on his legs was keeping him from falling head first off the train. A pistol was in his right hand and a grimace of exertion on his face as he held himself into a half sit-up, stable enough to make the shot.

"Show off," I shouted to him, sheathing the Ka-Bar before dragging him onto the roof.

He grinned as he got his feet under him, holstered the pistol and raised his rifle. I had mine in my hands by now and we moved so that our backs were touching, he facing the front of the train, me the rear. I started scanning with the night scope, identifying females clinging to the skin of the car we were on and shooting them. Jackson was also apparently finding targets as I could feel the gentle bump of his back against mine as his body absorbed the recoil of the rifle.

It didn't take us long to clear the roof of infected, but there were still the sides of the cars. I was turning to tell Jackson to go to the left when he suddenly spun and knocked me flat to the roof. A second later the train roared into a tunnel with only a couple of feet of clearance between the roof of the car and the concrete ceiling.

It was pitch black in the tunnel. Lights from inside the cars spilled out windows and reflected on the walls, but it didn't help us see up on the roof. The noise was deafening and the stench of diesel exhaust was almost overpowering as it concentrated in the narrow space.

I was on my belly, still facing the rear and trying to make my body meld into the roof of the train. As I lay there, I had visions of something hanging down from the tunnel ceiling and what it would do to my body at this speed. Pushing the thought out of my head before I jinxed myself, I looked along the roof and could just make out another female crawling directly at me.

Moving my arm carefully, so I didn't raise any body part that would strike the ceiling, I drew my pistol and extended it. When she saw the weapon aimed at her, the female froze in place.

"What the fuck?" Jackson said after a long moment. "Is she infected or not?"

"She is. I can see her eyes. I've encountered a few of these smart ones."

We had to shout to hear each other. While I was distracted with the conversation, the female spun around and crawled away from us. She quickly reached the opening between cars and dropped out of sight. Shit. That's what I get for not staying focused.

Pistol still gripped in my hand, I started slithering along the roof after her. It didn't take long to reach the opening and, leading with the pistol, I poked my head over the edge and looked down. The female was nowhere to be seen. Had she gotten in a door into one of the cars? Fallen off? Nah, I never get that lucky.

Staying on the roof, I scooted sideways to peer down one of the sides of the train. The contrast between the lighted windows and darkness below prevented me from being able to see anything. Back in the middle, I pivoted in place without raising my body, then slid over the edge.

The platform rang hollowly when my boots landed on it. Squatting, I tried to see under the edges of the two cars I was between. It was too damn dark and the angle was too steep to try and use the scope on my rifle. Standing up, I looked around.

I was on a shallow platform that was little more than a steel grate attached to the back of the car I had roped onto. Folding stairs were attached to the edge, pulled up and secured with a short chain so they were out of the way while we were in motion. The car behind me was set up exactly the same. There was a couple of feet of gap between the platforms through which I could see the massive steel coupling that held them together. Below that, the tracks rushed by and I couldn't figure out where the bitch had gone.

The doors on each of the cars were solid metal without benefit of windows and appeared to be hydraulically operated. This was probably so they couldn't be opened while the train was in motion. The area between cars wasn't exactly safe.

To the right of the door was a large, red metal flap and there was just enough light for me to make out the stenciled lettering. *Emergency Door Release.* Hoping this was truly an emergency release and didn't require a special tool or key that only firemen carry, I lifted the flap. Behind was a small lever with a T handle on the end, pushed all the way in. On either side of it, two large arrows pointed down. I followed the instructions and pulled the lever.

The door in front of me wasn't large, no wider than an interior door in a normal house. When the lever clicked into place, it slid open and disappeared into the rear wall of the car. The stench that flowed out of the car was horrible.

Dirk Patton

Too many people packed into too tight of a space. Correction. Too many dead people.

For a moment, I stared in amazement as the horrible smells of death, blood, fear, sweat, bowels and bladders washed over me. I don't have a weak stomach, and I've been around the violently killed the majority of my adult life, but this wasn't like a battlefield. This was a charnel house. Oh, God, tell me Rachel wasn't in this car!

Dead bodies spilled out onto the platform when the door they were leaning against opened. I wanted to step away from them, but there was nowhere to go. The shock of the slaughter had distracted me from what had killed them until I saw movement at the far end of the car. A female infected was moving from one body to another, so slicked with blood that she looked like a red demon directly from hell.

I watched her for a moment, then started seeing more movement as other females shifted from one feast to another. Raising the pistol, I started firing, stopping only when I'd killed all eleven of the infected that were in the car. Shaking slightly, I changed the magazine and holstered the pistol. Turning, I was startled to see Jackson standing behind me on the other car's platform.

Rolling Thunder

I've never seen a black man turn pale before, but he did. For a moment, I thought he was going to have to lean over the edge and throw up, but he gulped some air and regained a degree of composure. He met my eyes and opened his mouth. He just looked at me, not saying anything.

"First time you've been up close?" I asked.

He nodded as he answered, "Yeah. I've shot plenty out in the open. And watched APCs – Armored Personnel Carriers – and helicopters take them out, but... fuck me. Fuck me."

He shook his head, staring at the stream of blood that was running out of the open door and dripping off the edge of the platform onto the tracks below. I pointed at the door behind him, and he took a deep breath and turned. Reaching up to the side of the door, Jackson pulled the release lever, and the door slid open.

We were at the front end of the car, and there was a little open space, no more than three feet. Every person in the car was screaming. A female infected was standing in the open area, her hands wrapped in a young girl's hair as she tore into her throat. She didn't hear the door open and had no idea we were there.

Jackson stepped behind her and yanked her off the girl. He lifted the female into the air, twisted and tossed her towards me. She landed on her back on the platform, head dangling over the edge and I stomped down on her forehead hard enough to snap her neck and nearly tear her head off. I kicked the body off the platform and followed Jackson inside.

There were too many people crammed too tightly together, so neither of us drew a pistol or raised a rifle. Instead, we each pulled out our Ka-Bars and started working our way through the car. We roughly pushed evacuees out of the way so we could reach the females that were attacking.

The order of the day was stabs to the heads, hearts or brain stems. Anywhere we could use the knife to put them down swiftly and permanently. There were already a lot of dead people and we couldn't help but step on bodies as we worked our way deeper into the car.

We were both shouting for people to move to the next car as we slashed and stabbed. Even if that car was full of dead bodies, we needed room to fight. The panicked people didn't hesitate, surging forward and the car quickly started opening up. Ahead, I saw Jackson

Rolling Thunder

ram his knife into the skull of a female and I spun and pinned one to the floor with my boot as she lunged at an escaping child.

Before she could fight her way free, I killed her with a stab to the heart. I was looking for my next target, pausing and snapping my head around when I heard a familiar snarl. It had to be Dog! Ignoring everyone else, I bulled my way forward, killing another infected and brushed past Jackson's broad back.

On the floor, a few feet in front of me, Dog stood on the body of the infected he'd just killed. Rachel sat on the bloody floor with Melanie cradled in her arms, her hand pressed to Mel's throat. Blood pulsed between Rachel's fingers with a regularity that told me Mel's carotid artery had been torn open.

Her eyes were still open, and she was looking up at Rachel, her mouth moving. Rachel leaned down and put an ear to her mouth for a moment, then straightened up and removed her hand from Melanie's neck. The blood had stopped pulsing.

Carefully lowering the body to the floor Rachel, stood up and looked at me, tears streaming. I didn't know if she was happy to see me or was about to hit me. I stood my ground when she stepped forward, but instead of striking me she wrapped her bloody arms around my neck and pressed her body tightly to mine.

"I love you," she said, squeezing me as tightly as she could.

Rolling Thunder

26

The scream of a female infected saved me from having to immediately respond. Pushing Rachel away, I spun as a young infected girl squirmed her way into the car through an open window. She momentarily got hung up on the frame, screaming and reaching for a family that was frantically scrambling to get away from her. I shifted the knife to my left hand, drew my pistol and fired. The bullet took off the upper part of her skull, her body going limp and hanging down into the car.

"Everyone get these damn windows closed!" I shouted, scanning the rest of the car for any additional threats. Up and down the car men and women leapt to get them shut.

"We've got to clear all the cars," I said to Jackson.

He gave me a look that mirrored what I was thinking. As tightly packed in as the evacuees were, it would be a royal bitch to move through the train. A change in the light from outside the window caught my attention and I looked out the blood-smeared glass. It took me a moment to realize we had exited the tunnel and the change was because the light was no longer reflecting off a damp concrete wall.

"Together, or do we go in opposite directions?" Jackson asked, checking the load in his rifle magazine.

"We'd better split up. You got a preference?" I was referring to going forward or back.

Jackson nodded towards the front, turned and trotted off, waving a couple of the soldiers from the squad that had gotten Rachel onto the train to follow him. Motioning to the rest of the squad to follow me, I turned to head for the car behind us and came face to face with Rachel. I didn't know what to say. Hell, I didn't even know what I was feeling.

She couldn't have caught me any more off guard than she had. What I did know was now wasn't the time to have a heart to heart discussion about our feelings. Before I realized I was doing it, I reached out and placed my hand on the side of her face. Just like I would with Katie when I was getting ready to walk out the door on a business trip. Great. This was all I needed.

Rolling Thunder

Lowering my hand, I told Dog to stay with Rachel and trotted to the back of the car and hit the release for the door. I was distracted, thinking about Rachel and what she'd just said to me. Thinking about Katie and the emotions and fears that I had walled off so I could focus on staying alive and finding her.

All those feelings had been painfully released by Rachel's profession of love. Emotions distract us and most likely will get us killed. That's nearly what happened when the door opened.

A female infected was standing on the platform and launched herself forward like a missile, leading with snapping teeth. I felt her lips brush my throat as I fell backwards into the car, and if not for Dog I would have died. He reacted the instant she appeared and before the female could make another push for my unprotected throat, he slammed into her. The two of them rolled through the door and onto the narrow platform, then with a scream, they both disappeared in the opening between the two cars.

I scrambled off my back and dashed forward, Rachel right behind me, pushing soldiers out of the way as we both tried to get to the edge

Dog had fallen over. On my stomach when I reached the gap, I stuck my head into the open space and looked down. The female was gone, and it took me a moment to spot Dog in the darkness.

He was straddling the large coupling with his front legs, his rear swinging in open space just inches above the tracks that were rushing past. His eyes were the size of saucers as he held on and I cried out when he started slipping. Not thinking of my own safety, I surged forward until all my upper body was in the gap, the edge of the platform cutting into my stomach.

I had a bad moment when I felt myself continue to slip, thinking I was going under the train. Rachel dove across my legs and screamed for me to get Dog. Extending to the limit of my reach, I was just able to get a grip on his front legs at the shoulders. And not a moment too soon as he lost all traction on the coupling and slid into open space.

Dog is a big animal, over a hundred pounds, and my hands felt like they were being torn open and my shoulders pulled out of their sockets. But, I gritted my teeth and held on as Dog's rear feet swung just above the track like a pendulum. With a loud grunt of exertion, I pulled him up, paused and gave a second mighty pull which brought him far enough to get his front paws onto my shoulders.

Shifting my grip, I wrapped my arms around his body and pulled again as he scrambled to get purchase on my back. Then he was moving up and over me and into the car. Rachel grabbed the back of my belt and moved her weight off my legs as she dragged me across the platform and into the car. When I was fully aboard I rolled over onto my back, breathing hard and just lying there. Rachel collapsed next to me. Head pillowed on my shoulder and Dog came to stand over me and lick my face.

"OK, that's one for us to about a hundred for Dog," I said, referring to the number of times he had saved us versus us saving him.

Dog wouldn't stop licking, and I finally had to push him away. When I raised my hand to deflect another attempted lick, there was blood running down my arm from inside my glove. Pulling out from under Rachel, I looked at my other arm and saw more blood. She saw it too and sat up quickly.

"You must have torn them open. I've got my pack and the medical kit. Let's get you taken care of," she said, standing up and grabbing my forearm to pull me to my feet.

"After I clear the train," I said, but she was already shaking her head.

"There're three perfectly good soldiers standing right there," she gestured. "You don't have to do everything. Does he?"

She turned and looked at the Sergeant that led the squad.

"We've got this, sir," he said.

I looked at him for a moment and didn't see any of the resentment in his face that had been there when I'd told him to load my people on the train. Finally, I nodded my agreement. He turned and headed for the car behind us with the remainder of the squad on his heels.

Rachel directed me to an empty seat, keeping a hand on my arm like I was either an invalid or was going to dash off the moment she let go. Unslinging my rifle, I put it on the seat next to me and sat back while she gathered supplies. Conscripting one of Max's sons to carry her pack over, she opened it and rummaged through. Finding the med kit, she opened it and began spreading its contents across another

Rolling Thunder

empty seat. Taking the flashlight off my rifle, she handed it to the boy and told him to shine it on my hands while she worked.

I had already lost the heavy fast roping gloves, but was still wearing a pair made of thin leather that would help me grip my weapons in the rain. Pulling the Velcro closures at the wrists, Rachel carefully worked these off my hands. There was so much blood that the inside of the gloves had stuck to the gauze bandages. She had to pour water from her canteen into them until they released and could be removed without causing more damage. Gloves off, she cut through the bandages that were thoroughly saturated with blood, tossing them under the seat when they came free.

I had torn out the stitches on both palms and on the back of my right hand. The wounds from being nailed to the cross by The Reverend were open, raw and bleeding steadily. Rachel shook her head and set to work organizing the supplies. While she prepared, Max rolled over next to me and locked the wheels on his chair.

He produced a pack of cigarettes, shook one out and saw the look on my face. He grinned and held the pack out to me but Rachel slapped my arm when I started to raise my hand to take one. Max laughed a deep, throaty laugh, pulled one out of the pack and placed it between my lips. Lighting his first, he leaned forward and lit mine. The first drag was the most delicious thing I'd ever tasted. I grinned at the thought that I had a good idea how a heroin addict felt. Max mistook my grin for a thank you and nodded a welcome in response.

27

Maybe it was my imagination, maybe it was the cigarette, or maybe it was the distraction of talking to Max, but it seemed Rachel was being more gentle than normal as she treated me. Probably the smoke. I was savoring the cigarette with my head leaned back and Max had rolled another foot forward so we could talk easily. He had beat me to the punch of asking about our story, so I told him.

I made sure to include how his broadcasts had helped us, had certainly saved our lives, and left out certain parts that no one other than Rachel and I ever needed to know or think about. I skipped over a lot of details to do with the injuries that Rachel was treating, but she was happy to fill in the gaps. She made me sound like a military genius when she took over telling the tale about the defense of Murfreesboro. I wanted to downplay my role, never being one to trumpet what I do, but she wouldn't let me.

"OK, that's us. Now it's your turn," I said, grunting as Rachel started another stitch in the palm of my hand.

Dirk Patton

Max lit another cigarette and shifted his shoulders to a more comfortable position.

"I used to be in the Navy. Was a SEAL, in fact. Got hurt in Afghanistan and wound up in this chair. I spent a few years pissed off at the world, bored and angry as hell. Started drinking. A lot. And was generally a nasty prick. My wife finally had enough and left one night when I had drunk myself into oblivion. Took my boys with her. Even took the goddamn dog."

Dog raised his head from where he was lying by my feet. When no one gave him any attention, he relaxed with a sigh and put his chin back on my boot.

"Probably the best thing that happened to me. Suddenly, I didn't have anyone to cook for me, wash my clothes or do the shopping. I was on my own. It took a few months, but I got off the booze. Damn the world is a boring place when you're sober!

"Anyway, Ryan here started coming around to check on me. He was old enough to drive by then so my ex couldn't stop him. He was just starting to play around with ham radio. The next thing I knew I had a whole room devoted to it and was spending the majority of every day in there.

Rolling Thunder

"Kept me off the sauce and I got to talk to a lot of interesting people from all over the world. When this shit hit, my boys were spending the week with me while their mother was off with her new boyfriend. Anyways, I had stayed in touch with friends in the Navy and at the Pentagon, and while no one knew what was coming there had been talk for a couple of weeks that a big strike against us was in the works. I had been preparing. Weapons, food, water and medical supplies. And knowing our government the way I do, I also got my hands on an AM transmitter. Figured there might be some folks that could use some information when the shit hit the fan.

"My house was way back in the woods, well north of Atlanta, so we were OK for a bit. As the infection started spreading and the infected started moving, we had to hit the road. Had a hell of a nice one-ton van with a big push bar on the front courtesy of the VA and that got us out of Georgia and up to Nashville. Our luck had about run out when it broke down on the way to the train station and we got caught up in that crowd where you found us. I owe you more than I can tell you."

I waved off his thanks with the hand Rachel had finished, then used it to accept the fresh cigarette Max offered. Rachel straightened her back with a groan, pausing in her work and snatched it out of my hand. Sticking it in her mouth, she lit it with Max's zippo, took a couple of inhales then passed it to me.

"I never even tried a cigarette until I met you," she said, looking at me with an accusatory smile. "They taste like shit but make me feel relaxed."

"That's what I always said about gin!" Max said with a laugh.

"So how are you getting the information you're broadcasting?" I asked him, not rising to the challenge of being blamed for Rachel smoking.

"Satellite phone and friends in the Pentagon. Well, not in the Pentagon anymore, but they're at the secure site where the Pentagon has moved to. They talk to me when they can and tell me what they can. It's pretty chaotic. The White House and Congressional leaders have set up at a separate location and there's not a lot of leadership coming down the chain of command. Not that there ever was, but it's worse than usual."

Max leaned forward and continued in a low voice, "There're some generals that are about ready to seize control and cut the President and Congress out of the loop."

This didn't surprise me when I thought about it. Our current president was no friend of the military and the idea of a coup after the devastation of the country wasn't nearly as far-fetched as some might think.

"What have your friends told you about this secondary outbreak? What about the smart infected females that are popping up?"

Rachel had finished suturing both hands by now and was busily bandaging them. That meant the big needle of antibiotic was coming soon. I kind of hoped she'd forget.

"What I know is that it wasn't just nerve gas that was released in the attack. There was also a very contagious virus combined in the aerosol. This virus is what is keeping the infected alive, apparently helping them survive the biological changes the nerve gas causes. They've also learned that it has a secondary effect that takes about two weeks to incubate. It mimics the effects of the nerve gas, impacting brain chemistry, but it does it differently and doesn't completely destroy all of the higher brain functions."

"So anyone who turned from the second wave will still have some of their higher cognitive functions intact?" Rachel asked without pausing in her work.

"That's what I'm told, but I haven't seen it myself. Tell me about it."

I told Max about the females that I was calling smart. It all made sense, what he was saying. I hadn't seen any like that before the second wave.

"Do we know just how smart they are? And by the way, it only seems to be women that are retaining any intelligence. The males that are infected seem just as dumb as ever."

"I don't know," Max answered with a concerned look on his face. "But you can bet I'll pass on what you've told me and ask some more questions the next time I'm on the phone."

"What about those of us that haven't turned?" Rachel asked, holding a large vial up to the light and stabbing a syringe into its top.

"No one knows. Our researchers are stating that some of us, hopefully about ten percent of the population, are immune to the nerve agent and by extension the virus. How they know, I don't know. Don't even know if they're right, or if we're all going to wake up tomorrow morning with a hunger for human flesh."

That thought killed the conversation, plus it was time for my shot. Rachel waved me out of my seat, and I stood up with a sigh, turned around and unbuckled my belt and pants. Rachel pulled them down in back, swabbed an area with alcohol and jabbed the needle in. OK, forget what I said about her being gentler.

28

It's a little over two hundred miles from Nashville to Memphis. I estimated the trip would take about four and a half to five hours. We'd been rolling for close to an hour. The thunderstorms were behind us, but there was heavy cloud cover and the landscape outside the windows was completely dark.

I raised my rifle a few times to peer through the night vision scope, but there wasn't anything to see other than passing trees and pastures, so I sat back and relaxed. Max had rolled off to a row of seats where his boys had stretched out to get some rest. Rachel and I sat together with Dog at our feet.

"We should talk about the elephant in the room," Rachel said.

I didn't want to have this conversation, but she was right. Saying what she'd said was no different than firing a rifle. Once you pull the trigger, you can't take the bullet back.

"What did Mel say to you just before she died?" I asked, trying to delay the inevitable.

Rolling Thunder

"She told me to quit lying to myself and be honest." Rachel turned her head to look at me as she talked. "She saved my life, you know. A female came through the window right next to us and was coming straight at me. I was jammed in so tight I couldn't move and she jumped and put herself between us."

"Sounds like you two had quite a conversation about me," I said after a minute of silence.

"Don't flatter yourself. You're not that conversation worthy."

I grinned but didn't say anything.

"Actually, we almost came to blows a couple of times. Not over you, she was just one of those people that... well, she was just one of those people. But she was also right. I'm sorry if I've made you uncomfortable, or whatever it is, but we could die ten minutes from now. I just spoke my mind and my heart."

I sat there for a long time, digesting what she'd said. I knew she wanted me to tell her something. Anything. Opening your heart up to someone and then getting nothing in return is one of the loneliest feelings in the world.

"Rachel, you know my situation. What I may or may not feel for you doesn't enter into the mix right now. I'm married. I love my wife, and I'm going to find out what happened to her or die trying. That hasn't changed. Any feelings I have for you aren't going to stop me from doing that."

"Really?" She sounded pissed. "Is that *really* why you think I told you how I feel? You actually think I want you to stop, to just give up on her? You've seriously misjudged me if that's what you think."

"Then what?" I turned to meet her eyes. "What do you think can happen? Suppose I tell you I love you and we keep looking for her and find her alive and waiting for me. What then?"

Rachel looked back at me. Her eyes moving slightly, side to side, as she looked into each of mine.

"I don't know. All I know is how I feel about you and I haven't thought about any of the rest of it. My promise to help you find her is still good. If we find her alive and waiting, I'll be happy for you and wish you well. But that doesn't change anything about how I feel today. How I've been feeling for a while."

Rolling Thunder

Shit. My head was spinning, and I just wanted to crawl in a hole and pull the ground in behind me.

"Just tell me one thing," she continued after a long pause. "Do you love me too?"

I drew in a deep breath, held it and let it out in a long sigh.

"Honestly, I don't know what I feel. Do I have feelings for you? Yes. Am I in love with you? Maybe. I don't know. You remind me so much of her it's hard for me not to like many of the things I see in you that first attracted me to her. What I know is I'm glad we're together, and I'm truly sorry I can't give you what you want right now."

After a long moment, Rachel placed her hand on top of mine and gave me a weak smile.

"I can deal with honesty. Just let me know when you know."

I smiled back, grateful the conversation was over. One of the things I loved about Katie was that we never had to have these conversations about our feelings. I made up my mind right then and there that when I found her I was going to remind her that I fought my way across the entire country to be with her. Every time she started fishing for a compliment about her appearance, or reassurance that I loved her, I'd remind her.

Not that she did it often, but I'd just found the Holy Grail for married men everywhere. *'Honey, I fought my way across two thousand miles and millions of infected to come back to you, getting shot, bitten and generally having my ass kicked the entire way. Of course, you look good in that outfit!'*

I couldn't help but laugh at myself and fortunately, before Rachel could inquire into what was so amusing, I saw Jackson enter the front of the car. He was pushing his way through the evacuees, looking around then nodding when he spotted me. I didn't feel the need to stand up to greet him. I was just too damn tired and sat there watching him approach.

In his wake I could see a man in an Air Force Class A uniform, I think the Air Force calls them something like Service Dress or some such nonsense. This struck me as really odd, considering we were in a combat zone, not a conference room. Then I saw the single star the officer was wearing, said a curse to myself and climbed to my feet. What the hell was a Brigadier General doing here?

On my feet and stepping into the aisle, I looked up from the star to the face of the man and was momentarily confused. I knew the face. It didn't belong in a uniform with a star on it, or any uniform as far as I was concerned.

I lunged forward, pushing past Jackson, who spun when I moved, expecting to see an attacking infected. My right hand was up and a punch that would knock his head off was started when I remembered my damaged hand and modified my movement. Instead of striking the fake General's face with my fist, I connected solidly with my forearm, knocking him to his back on the bloody floor. I continued forward, drawing my Ka-Bar and landed on his body, pressing the tip of the knife to his throat.

"You gutless fucker! I should carve you up right here," I snarled, my face inches from his.

Jackson had been caught completely unprepared for my attack on the man he had accepted as a General. The soldiers that had accompanied him stood frozen, looks of shock on their faces. Recovering quickly, Jackson stepped to my side and placed a hand lightly on my shoulder.

"Major, take it easy."

From the corner of my eye, I could see his other hand held a pistol along the side of his leg, pointed at the floor.

"Fuck easy," I growled. "This piece of shit isn't a General. He's an Air Force Captain and a deserter."

"Sergeant, get this crazy man off me!" Captain Roach shouted, trying to bluff his way out of the problem he found himself in.

"He's telling the truth, Sergeant," Rachel spoke up from behind me. "That's an Air Force Security Forces Captain, not a General. He was with us when we were evacuating people at Arnold Air Force Base and was supposed to be guarding our rear, but he just disappeared. We thought the infected got him, but he must have abandoned us and run away."

Roach's eyes were looking all over the place, the momentary bluff and bravado gone.

"I didn't run away. I got knocked out and barely made it out alive."

I heard Jackson's pistol slide back into his holster a moment before he removed his hand from my shoulder.

Rolling Thunder

"What do you want to do with him, sir?"

I wanted to gut the son of a bitch and toss him off the train for the infected to feed on. I wanted to stand him up against the wall and shoot pieces of him off, one at a time. Desertion during time of war is a serious offense in the military and is punishable by either life at hard labor or execution.

Maybe we weren't fighting a declared war, but I didn't think anyone was going to give Roach an inch on that technicality. Half a second from ramming the blade into his head, I thought better of my actions. Sheathing the knife, I stood up and looked at the two soldiers standing on the other side of Roach.

"Search him and restrain him. I don't care how you tie him up, but you'll answer to me if he gets away!" One of them quickly bent down and started frisking Roach while the other covered him with his rifle. "And get that goddamn uniform off him! It's a fucking disgrace to all the good men and women who have died."

Turning, I took a deep breath and met Jackson's eyes.

"What are you going to do?" He asked. The look on his face told me he'd be fine with whatever I decided to do to Roach.

"I'm going to let the Colonel decide. He's the ranking officer," I growled, anger coarsening my voice.

Jackson nodded and watched as the soldiers finished searching Roach. They removed two pistols and a knife before yanking him to his feet and stripping the uniform off him. When he was undressed to his underwear, one of them used the knife they'd taken from him to cut his shirt into strips. The pieces of fabric were then used to tightly bind his hands behind his back before he was roughly shoved into a seat. More strips were employed to tie his ankles to the steel legs. He wasn't going anywhere.

"Can I use your radio to talk to the Colonel?" I asked Jackson.

He didn't hesitate to pull the small unit out of his vest, remove the earpiece and hand all of it to me.

"The Colonel is Bird Dog," he said before I could ask.

Rolling Thunder

Earpiece in place, I called for the Colonel and a moment later heard his voice answer. I filled him in on the situation with the infected first, then briefed him on Roach. He remembered Roach from Arnold.

"You didn't kill him on sight?"

"Damn near did, sir. If I was the ranking officer on scene, I wouldn't have hesitated."

"Not sure I would have shown the same restraint, but I appreciate you not finishing the piece of shit off right then and there. What's his status?"

"Restrained with a couple of guards on him. He's not going anywhere."

Crawford was silent for a bit, then asked me to put Jackson on the radio. I handed the equipment over and sat back down while Jackson spoke with the Colonel.

"What's going on?" Rachel asked. She was sitting next to me, leaning over to look at where Roach was secured to a seat.

"I don't know the Colonel well enough to guess what he's going to do. What Roach did, first deserting, then impersonating a General so he could get on the train and escape? Well, he's in deep, deep shit at a minimum. Desertion during time of war is enough under the UCMJ – Uniform Code of Military Justice – to stand him up against a wall and put a bullet in his head. I can't remember the last time the US executed a deserter, but it's been a very long time. If it was up to me, we'd restart the precedent with this prick."

Jackson wrapped up his conversation with Crawford and came over to stand next to me. I looked up and met his eyes.

"Would you really have shot me, Master Sergeant?"

"Let's just say I wouldn't have, and stay friends," he answered with a grin.

I nodded and grinned back. This guy was OK.

"What did the Colonel say?"

"He appointed me his advocate. I hear testimony from the two of you, then from the prisoner, and make the decision. If I find him guilty, the Colonel has already authorized execution."

"You and the Colonel must go back a ways," I said, not really surprised at the trust and responsibility Crawford was placing in Jackson.

"Lot of years, sir. We've eaten a lot of the same dirt."

I nodded. It's actually quite common in the Special Forces community, where differences between officer and enlisted are much less strictly adhered to than in the rest of the military, for officers and NCOs that have worked together for years to become friends and even trusted confidants.

"I'm not going to drag this out, and I don't think we have time to worry about niceties. Hell, he doesn't even have legal counsel. So, I've already heard Rachel. Tell me."

I did. Starting with when I arrived back at Arnold from rescuing Gwen in Atlanta and encountering Roach as he fought with an infected. I detailed how we had gone into flight ops and brought the people out. The fight across the tarmac to the ill-fated Globemaster flight and how Roach, who was in the rear, had disappeared as we started pressing into the herd of infected between us and the plane. We had all thought he'd been taken down and killed. In fact, had never had a reason to suspect otherwise. Until now.

Jackson listened intently and when I was finished, asked a couple of questions, then nodded and went over to stand in front of Roach. I was too far away to hear what he was asking and what answers he was getting, but I could see Roach's body language and tell he knew he was arguing for his life. The conversation lasted five minutes, then Jackson walked back over to me.

"He tells the same story you do, up to the point where you went out on the tarmac. Says that he was attacked by a female and knocked unconscious. When he came around, the plane was burning and all the infected were at the far end of the runway, so he got the hell out of there. Swears he didn't run off. Any chance he's telling the truth?"

Shit. Anything is possible, but I didn't believe Roach's story for a second.

"If he's telling the truth, what's with the uniform? I might be willing to give him the benefit of the doubt if it wasn't for him showing up impersonating a General."

"Yeah, that's where I have a problem too." Jackson nodded. "He says he had to hide in the

General's office during his escape from the base and needed to change clothes because his were covered with blood."

"Not the last time I saw him, they weren't," Rachel said. "And that was after we had made it onto the tarmac. He was dirty from a scuffle, but there wasn't blood on him then."

"And neither of you saw anything? He was there when you started out onto the flight line, then he was just gone?"

Both of us nodded. Jackson stared out the windows at the darkness, thinking. He stood like that for a long time before turning back to me.

"I don't believe him, sir. But I also don't like not having any hard evidence. He could be telling the truth, regardless of what I think. I can't put a bullet in a man's head just because his story *sounds* like bullshit."

"So what do we do with him?" I asked, a sour taste in my mouth.

"That's why officers make the big bucks. Sir." Jackson grinned as he spoke.

I would have been more than happy to pull the trigger based on what I knew about Roach. As I thought about it, what the hell had he been doing on the first floor close enough to an exit for me to rescue him from an infected outside the building? Flight operations had been on the opposite end of the building, on the second floor.

That's where he should have been, along with his Security Forces airmen. The son of a bitch had been running! Trying to sneak away while people were dying. With everything that had been happening at the time, I just hadn't put it all together in my head.

Rolling Thunder

29

Air Force Security Forces Captain Lee Roach slowly replaced the handset on the desk phone. It was early evening and he was the duty officer for the day, responsible for all Security Forces activities on Arnold Air Force Base. He had just received a call from the prissy little Major running flight operations. She was requesting armed Security Forces be stationed inside flight ops, claiming that an Army Major had just informed her that more people were becoming infected and she was concerned for her staff's safety.

He knew Major Masuka well, having pursued her romantically despite their difference in rank. It had taken him weeks, but he'd finally convinced her to have dinner with him. The date had seemed to go well. Dinner had been pleasant and he was sure he had charmed her with his stories of rousting drunk airmen out of local bars and brothels.

Driving to her quarters, he thought he'd picked up signals that he would be spending the night. But had been firmly rebuffed, when he put his hand on her shoulder and tried to kiss her outside her door. Not just rebuffed. Humiliated. The bitch!

Roach had not been a popular kid growing up in rural Washington State. He wasn't good at sports, didn't have a quick wit and wasn't anything special to look at. But he was very smart. He usually blended into the background unless being singled out by bullies for humiliation.

Raised by a single mother who only had time for herself and a parade of boyfriends, he hadn't had a nurturing family life to fall back on. Roach was not smart like the kids who scored high on their SATs and were destined for great lives, but smart like a predator. By the time he was a sophomore in high school, he realized that he fit the classic definition of a psychopath. And that thrilled him.

He fantasized regularly about raping and killing the popular, pretty girls that laughed at him when it was his turn to be publicly tortured by the bullies. His favorite fantasy was to picture himself standing in front of a classroom full of the worst bullies and the girls that laughed the loudest and longest. He wanted to see the fear on their faces as he raised a gun and one by one shot each of them in the face.

Rolling Thunder

But despite being a psychopath, Roach was practical and didn't want to spend his life in a state mental hospital or prison. Instead, he started searching for a path that would give him the power and authority to punish those that he felt had wronged him. And get away with it.

Mid-way through his senior year of high school, he was approached by an Air Force recruiter and immediately saw the opportunities the military offered to someone like him. He turned eighteen a month before graduation. The day after he didn't walk across the stage to get his diploma, he boarded a plane to Lackland Air Force Base in San Antonio, Texas to start basic military training. The pretty blonde cheerleader that he had raped and strangled the night before was never found in the rugged terrain of the Cascade Mountains.

Basic had just been more of the same for Roach. He looked on the instructors as bullies and used his well-honed survival skills to stay off their radar as much as possible. He had tested well when he took the ASVAB – Armed Services Vocational Ability Battery – and had been allowed to choose his MOS – Military Occupational Specialty. He had jumped to select Security Forces, the Air Force Military Police. What better way to be able to act on his need to punish others than to be one of those who were supposed to protect them.

Roach was a good cop as far as having the right instincts about the people he encountered in the line of duty. He regularly impressed his commanders with his abilities. He was also a brutal cop. Rarely did a suspect or detainee come into holding without having been subjected to some strategically placed blows from Roach's baton or steel toed boots.

He always managed to get away with it. Twice he went before review boards after complaints were filed, but always had a plausible justification for his actions. Roach was happy for a couple of years, but his anti-social behavior and reputation for brutality had estranged him from fellow enlisted who he grew to dislike and eventually despise as beneath him.

Night school paid for by the Air Force couple with a new six-year commitment, and Roach became an officer. He was now elevated above the enlisted personnel to whom he felt superior. No longer able to be the cop breaking up the fight or dragging in the drunks, he refocused his needs on locals, always careful to never kill anyone that was associated with the military.

Rolling Thunder

Over the years, bodies of the young, pretty women that Roach preferred were discovered in the Louisiana swamps miles from Barksdale Air Force Base, on two beaches on Okinawa, far from Kadena Air Base and in Germany's Black Forest, well away from Ramstein Air Base. While the local civilian investigators may have wondered about a connection to the US Military, there was never even a hint of a link to the three sprawling bases that were deemed too far away from the scene of the crimes.

He had only been at Arnold for a few months and, despite regular trips up to Nashville, which was flush with young, pretty women, he hadn't found the right one yet. He was considering stepping up his game after having been in a Honky Tonk on Broadway and seeing a couple of up and coming country music stars.

They were well known locally, but hadn't made the national scene yet. Unaware of the danger they were already in, the young women went out on the town with just a few friends and no security. Roach had no illusions about ever being able to get close to a big, nationally known star, but these girls were just starting out, making it on their looks and their voices. They didn't recognize that they were soft targets for someone like him.

Hand still on the phone, Roach let himself fantasize about Major Masuka. The pleasure he would feel as his hands wrapped around her small neck. Shaking the thought out of his head, he shouted for the Staff Sergeant that sat outside his office, issuing orders to get some men over to flight operations. With any of the other officers over him, the Sergeant would have asked for specifics about why they were needed. But he knew from experience that it would be pointless to ask Captain Roach. He just acknowledged the order and got on the radio to three Airmen who were on patrol near the flight line.

It was only a few minutes later when the first emergency calls for help started coming in from all over the base. The Sergeant was doing his best to answer them as quickly as he could, Roach standing in the doorway to his office listening to the growing chaos. There had been several Airmen in the office suite, working on arrest paperwork, but they had already been sent out by the Sergeant as the number of calls quickly exceeded the number of cops in the field. Roach and the Sergeant were alone.

The Sergeant was reaching for the radio when he suddenly stopped, grabbed his head in pain and fell out of the chair onto the shiny tile floor. Roach's only response was to place his

Rolling Thunder

hand on his holstered sidearm and watch. The man writhed in pain for a few moments before going still. The calm only lasted a brief time, the man snarling and sitting up, swiveling his head around. Roach calmly drew his pistol, stepped close and shot the Sergeant in the head.

He had read the reports that had been coming in over the past couple of weeks and knew what was happening. Knew the impact this would have on survivors. Like any predator, Roach saw a golden opportunity to satisfy his needs without worry of being discovered.

Hell, no one was going to look twice at a body any longer. He wouldn't even have to worry about disposing of them after he'd had his fun. Smiling, Roach walked out of the offices and climbed into a Security Forces Humvee. Starting the engine, he thought about where he should go. He was done with the Air Force.

But one debt needed to be paid first. Masuka. The bitch had rejected him, acted like he was beneath her. He'd show her the grave mistake she'd made, then be on his way. In the confusion of the outbreak, he'd be able to pull her aside into an office or stairwell. Once alone, he'd introduce her to the Japanese steel dagger strapped to his forearm beneath his uniform. It wouldn't be as satisfying as making her submit to him sexually, holding the gleaming blade to her throat while he thrust into her, but it was better than walking away without answering her disrespect.

Roach pulled out of the parking area and headed for flight operations on the far side of the base. As he drove, he started seeing infected males wearing Air Force uniforms shambling about and ran down a couple of females that charged the Hummer. His desire to kill Masuka momentarily wavered as the numbers of infected increased the farther he drove. But the need to mete out punishment outweighed the instinct for self-preservation.

The drive to flight operations took ten minutes. Roach parked in the front parking lot by the main entrance. Stepping out of the Humvee, he trotted up the steps to the double glass security doors. He paused, then changed direction at the last minute when he saw infected roaming the hallway inside the building.

At the rear, facing the flight line, was a single, steel door that the pilots used for quick access into flight operations. Roach ran around the building, keeping a close eye out for any more infected. As he pulled the door open, he heard

Rolling Thunder

the heavy thump of a helicopter coming in for a landing. Instead of turning to see who it was, he slipped through the door and pulled it shut behind him.

Moving quietly down the empty hall, Roach hadn't gone far when from deeper in the building a rifle started firing on full auto. Moments later it was joined by a second. When the rifles sounded, he had paused in front of an open office door. The infected that stumbled into the hallway to investigate the noise ran directly into him, wrapping him in its arms. Roach struggled to escape, nearly getting his throat torn out when he hesitated upon recognizing Brigadier General Samuels, the base commander.

The hesitation passed as quickly as it had come and Roach twisted, trying to break the grip of the infected General as he backpedaled towards the exit door to the flight line. He was a very physical man when it came to inflicting pain on those he had at a disadvantage, but he wasn't any good against an opponent that had no fear of him. Still scrambling, they reached the door and it burst open as Roach's back struck it. They tripped over the threshold and fell to the ground outside the door.

Dirk Patton

The General was on top of him. His lips were pressed to the side of Roach's neck, just above his carotid artery, when the infected's head was violently knocked to the side. The body immediately went limp on top of him. A moment later the weight came off his chest as the infected was lifted and tossed aside.

Roach looked up at the big fucker that had escaped from Atlanta and flown into Arnold the night before. The same guy that had humiliated him. He reached down, grabbed Roach's hand and yanked him onto his feet. Christ, the guy was strong. He was also now in uniform and wearing Major's oak leaves.

"You're on me," he said, turning and running to the steel door.

He pulled the door open, raised his rifle to the ready position and entered the building. Not sure why he was following, Roach fell in and softly closed the door behind them. The hallway was still empty and the sound of automatic rifle fire continued from the far end of the building.

Drawing his pistol, Roach moved to within a few feet of the man. Looking at the back of his shaved head, Roach raised the pistol as he paused and peered around a doorway into an office. One round in the back of the head and out the door.

Rolling Thunder

Never mind Masuka. Roach just wanted out of there.

Before he could pull the trigger, the man disappeared around the corner into the office. Curious, Roach poked his head out in time to see him pull a vicious looking combat machete and ram it into the back of the neck of a male infected. He did it so effortlessly that Roach experienced a visceral thrill just from watching.

Pulling his head back, he lowered the pistol into a two-handed, low ready position and scanned the hall to make sure there weren't any infected sneaking up on him. He was briefly startled when he looked back to his left and the man was standing in the hallway again, silently closing the office door. How the hell did someone so big move so quietly?

The rifles that had been firing had fallen silent as they moved down the hall. The big man cleared two more offices before closing their doors. Then they were at the stairs that led up to the flight operations center. With his rifle ready, the man led the way, aiming up the stairwell as he climbed.

At the landing, he fired a burst that killed a screaming female infected who tumbled down the steps and crashed into the wall. Roach would have been knocked down by the falling body if he hadn't jumped out of the way at the last second.

Climbing the rest of the way, the Major and Roach stepped over more infected bodies at the top of the stairs. They were nearly shot when some jackass fired through the wooden double doors that led into the operations center. The Major shouted out that they were friendlies and after a moment he carefully pushed through the doors into the room.

He was greeted by the fucking dog and the bitch that had flown in with him from Atlanta. She was Roach's type, but not young enough. He liked them in their teens or early twenties unless he was in the mood to dispense justice. In that case, age didn't matter, and she was another bitch that deserved it. She had mocked him the previous night when that fucking Army Colonel had intervened while Roach and his men were trying to disarm them as they got off the plane.

Roach snapped back to the current reality as the Major called the two Security Forces men over and started dressing them down over firing on full auto. When he was done, Roach took the men out to the hallway. He didn't really have any reason to do so other than wanting to get out of the room. There were three people in there he wanted to kill and the stress of the situation was getting to him.

He was actually considering shooting the two cops, taking one of their rifles and going back in the room to kill everyone. Could he do it? He knew he was emotionally capable, but the Major scared the shit out of him. The guy was big, strong and fast and Roach was willing to bet he was damn good with a rifle and pistol. He would have to be the first to go down. But what about the dog? And the bitch that was with the Major had a rifle too. Could he kill them all without getting shot himself?

Rifle fire from within the room ended his daydream. He charged back into the room with the two cops, the Major pointing at a dead infected female on the floor that he'd just shot. Roach stood by while he held a conversation with Masuka, seeing another opportunity when he heard there was a Globemaster about to land and pick all of them up.

The Major quickly organized the people into a group, getting them ready to move. He grabbed a rifle and spare magazines from the body of a dead Security Forces airman and handed them to Roach. Telling him to bring up the rear, he led the way into the hall.

Dirk Patton

There was firing as they moved, descending the stairs and turning into the hallway that led to the steel exit door. The group paused long enough to collect a young woman from the office where the Major had killed an infected on the way in, then they were at the door and moving out into the night. A massive fire was burning at the far end of the flight line, and Roach could see hundreds of infected shambling around between them and the runway.

Always one to watch for and take advantage of opportunities, Roach peeled off from the back of the group as soon as they exited the building. Wherever it was they were going on the Globemaster; he had no intention of joining them. Nashville was still alive and well and there were a couple of young women that had been on his mind. He wanted to pay them a visit before he headed west.

His only friend on the base worked for Air Force intelligence and had told him the location of the high-security site where the Pentagon had relocated. Roach intended to bluff his way inside and ride out the apocalypse in comfort. To do that he needed the right look, and it was lying on the ground at his feet.

Rolling Thunder

Grabbing General Samuels's body, he dragged it around the corner of the building into the dark. He quickly stripped it and changed into the new uniform. Five minutes later a Brigadier General climbed into the Security Forces Humvee and roared off towards the gate closest to the highway that led to Nashville.

30

A rumble of thunder caught my attention. I paused, listening, and realized it wasn't thunder. It was bombs and a lot of them. The Air Force was at it again.

"Is this the package that the Colonel was talking about?" I asked Jackson.

"It's the start. Carpet bombing the Nashville suburbs." He looked down at his watch. "There's a special package due in just under ten minutes."

I forgot all about Roach.

"What's a special package?" Rachel asked, looking between Jackson and me.

"Nuclear," I said.

Jackson nodded when Rachel turned to him with a shocked expression on her face.

"Are they crazy?"

Several heads around the car turned in our direction and I motioned for Rachel to keep her voice down.

Rolling Thunder

"They probably are, and a few days ago I would have thought this was a very bad idea. Now? I don't know. The only way to stop the infected is to kill them. If there's a hundred and you kill ninety-nine of them, the last one will be just as dangerous and keep coming until you kill him, too. If there're millions that will get taken out in the blast, well that's better odds for us."

I wasn't at all sure I was convinced by what I was saying, but I had little doubt this was the rationale being used to make the decision to drop the bomb.

"Blasts," Jackson said quietly.

"More than one? How many?" I asked incredulously.

"Three. City center, ten miles southeast and ten miles southwest."

"So we're going to do the goddamn Chinese's job for them? Is that it?" Rachel asked.

This conversation wasn't going anywhere. I could see the logic behind dropping nukes, but at the same time, I agreed with Rachel. However, Jackson was just the messenger. He was so far removed from the decision makers that he didn't deserve Rachel's indignation. Standing up, I held my hand out for her. She looked at me for a moment then grasped my forearm, giving my injured hand a break, and stood up with me.

"Where are we going?"

"Up on the roof. Other than old news reels, I've never seen a nuke go off," I answered softly enough to not be heard by any of the surrounding people.

Telling Dog to stay, I headed for the back of the car, Rachel hesitating before she followed. A narrow ladder led up from the platform and I climbed slowly, pausing to check for infected before climbing the rest of the way. Rachel followed and I helped her transition from the ladder to the roof before both of us sat down facing the rear of the train, legs dangling over the edge of the car.

The slipstream was strong, pushing hard on our backs, but it was refreshing to be out of the stench of the car beneath us. Between the roar of the rushing wind and the clatter made by the train, the only way we could talk was to lean towards each other and shout, so we sat there in silence.

I warned Rachel to keep her eyes averted until after the initial flashes of the detonations.

Rolling Thunder

We were fifty miles away by now, but I wasn't going to take any chances with having my eyesight burned out by the brilliant light emitted at the instant of a nuclear explosion. We sat there for a few more minutes. Rachel scooted as close to me as she could get and leaned her head over onto my shoulder. Talk about torn.

It felt good to have her close and at the same time I felt guilty as hell that it felt so good. It was like I was betraying Katie. I forgot all about my discomfort when there was a brilliant flash on the eastern horizon, like the world's largest camera just took a picture. It was quickly followed by two more.

Rachel raised her head off my shoulder, staring in awe. At first, it looked like the sun was coming up. Shades of orange fading into purple filled the entire horizon. Then three distinct mushroom clouds formed and boiled towards the heavens.

"Are we safe? I mean from the blast and radiation?"

Rachel shouted into my ear as she circled her arms around my right arm and held tightly. This didn't bother me. It wasn't affection. It was her reaction to the indescribable feeling of seeing an entire city wiped off the face of the earth in less than a heartbeat.

"We're at least fifty miles away. We'd be safe at ten. For a while, at least. Those three mushroom clouds are pumping debris into the upper atmosphere and that debris is highly radioactive. The problem will be when and where it starts coming back down."

One of the things my unit had trained for was the covert penetration of the old Soviet Union with an eighty-pound nuke in a backpack. The idea was that a two-man team could walk a bomb right into central Moscow, or any sensitive area, set a timer and get out before it detonated. The advantage was that the US could launch a pre-emptive nuclear strike without putting a single missile in the air which would trigger a Soviet response.

A big part of that training had been delivered by scientists from Los Alamos National Laboratory. They'd taught us more than we ever wanted to know about blast radii, overpressure waves, radiation hot zones, fallout and much more that I'd forgotten until now.

Sitting there, watching the fiery pillars still climbing into the night sky, I felt a wave of despair wash over me. I'm generally optimistic, or at least I don't quit until it's quite apparent there's nothing more that can be done, but when we start nuking our own cities, we're in a world of shit.

I probably would have kept sitting there, watching the fires burn if I hadn't been distracted by an Apache flying right over my head along the length of the train. He was so low, I involuntarily ducked. Turning my head, I watched him flare out near the front of the train and fire two hellfire missiles.

Hellfire missiles are probably the most aptly named weapon the military has ever devised. Originally conceived to be an air-launched weapon to destroy heavy armor, they have become the default choice to unleash hell on any ground-based target. They're also expensive and certainly don't exist in infinite numbers, so I knew if they were being used there was a pretty serious threat just up the tracks.

Definitely serious enough that I didn't want to be sitting out in the open on the roof of the train when we got there. Motioning Rachel down the ladder, I followed and bumped into her back when she stopped at the open door. Jackson was blocking the way as he came to find me.

"What's going on?" I asked as we sorted ourselves out, moving into the car and closing the door. The stench was worse than I remembered and I immediately started missing the fresh, outside air.

"There were a couple of trucks hauling ass for the tracks. After we took them out, we spotted the herd of infected following them. There's a lot."

"How the hell didn't we know the infected were there? Aren't we watching on satellite? What about scouting patrols with helicopters?" I was amazed we'd been caught unprepared for this.

"The terrain to the south of the tracks is heavily forested all the way down into Alabama and Mississippi. Even if the herd could have been spotted when they crossed highways, we've got about a tenth of the number of people looking at sat imagery as we did three weeks ago. We're short on resources. Shit gets missed."

Jackson shrugged, and I knew he was right.

"How many are we dealing with?"

Rolling Thunder

"We don't know yet, but we're speeding up to try and clear the area before they make it onto the tracks."

"What do you mean? A few bodies can't damage a train," Rachel said.

"A few bodies, no. But no one has a good idea what would happen if there were thousands of bodies on the tracks and tens of thousands more pushing in against the train. We don't want to find out."

While Jackson had been speaking, I'd noticed a change in the motion of the train. What had been a relatively gentle swaying back and forth as we rolled down the track was becoming sharper. Almost a jerking motion. Along with it, a vibration that hadn't been there before slowly built, everything that wasn't securely bolted down in the car starting to rattle.

I knew next to nothing about trains, but I did know that the US rail system wasn't built or maintained to support travel at high speeds. If we'd been going fifty miles an hour, we were now probably close to seventy and seemed to still be accelerating. If anything happened at this speed and a car jumped off the rails, we were all screwed. This was one hell of a lot of mass we were riding in. The worst part was there wasn't a damn thing I could do except be a passenger.

I don't do well when I have to take a passive role. Not that I need to be in charge, though that's usually what occurs. But just sitting back and letting things happen around me drives me nuts. I started pacing as the train continued to speed up, stopping and checking to make sure Roach was still secure and not causing any problems. He looked up at me like he wanted to say something but correctly read the look on my face and kept his mouth shut.

Pacing to the front of the car, I nodded to a few of the civilian evacuees who looked up at me and smiled. That was when I realized I had no idea what our destination was beyond Memphis. Turning around, I grabbed a seat back to steady myself as we went through a patch of rough track, or warped track, or whatever happened to train tracks, then went and found Jackson.

"What's our final destination?"

"Oklahoma City."

"Not Kansas City? I thought that was one of the refugee centers."

Rolling Thunder

"It is, or it was. Big herds coming out of St. Louis and Illinois heading that way. There's more carpet bombing going on in central Missouri to slow them down, and an evac is under way. They were harder hit with the second outbreak than Nashville, so there's not near as many people to get out."

"No second outbreak in Oklahoma?" I asked, curious.

"They weren't one of the original targets, so there weren't any infected there until the second outbreak. Has something to do with exposure to the original nerve gas versus contracting the virus. I don't understand it. Anyway, yes there's infection there, but they had time to get organized and have pretty ruthlessly enforced quarantines. That's the last I heard, but that was almost a day ago. No idea what's happening there right now."

"How long to OKC?" I asked, looking around at all the bodies in the car with us.

"It's around seven hundred and fifty miles, maybe a little less than seven hundred left to go. Say another ten hours at least, but probably more. I heard the engineers talking, and there's a lot of curves to get through Memphis and we're going to have to slow way down once we get close to the city."

And Memphis was one of the original targets of the nerve agent, I reminded myself. It was probably crawling with infected. The train engineers were worried about the herd blocking the track. What was it going to be like with an entire major city of infected converging on the rail yard?

"OK. So we've probably got another 12 hours minimum on this train, and that's if there're no delays," I said, turning and locating the man I wanted.

I waved the Sergeant from the National Guard squad over to where we were standing. For the first time, I bothered to read the name tape on his uniform.

"Sergeant King. We've got a long ride ahead and a lot of dead bodies riding along with us. They already smell, and it's going to get worse when the sun comes up in a few hours. I want you and your squad to conscript some of the civilians to help you get those bodies off the train. You meet any resistance from family members, I don't want you to force the issue. Come find me and I'll talk to them. Got it?"

Rolling Thunder

"What do we do with them, sir?"

Sergeants are usually pretty good at figuring things out. That's why they're Sergeants in the first place, but I was willing to give this guy some slack. This wasn't exactly the type of situation you trained for or even imagined you'd ever find yourself in.

"Out the doors and off the platform. It's not exactly a respectful burial, but it's the best we can do."

"Yes, sir."

He sounded less than enthusiastic, but turned away and called his squad together. I could tell by their body language that none of them were happy with the assignment. Regardless, bodies were soon being carried down the aisle and out the back door.

Some of the civilians looked disturbed by the way we were disposing of the dead, but no one spoke up or offered any resistance. There were many tearful goodbyes said, still without complaint at the disposal of loved ones. Again, I had to remind myself that there had been time for people to start adjusting to the new normal of our infected world.

31

The change in motion and vibration of the train woke me. I had managed to fall asleep in one of the seats. My head was lolled back and there was probably drool running down my chin. Rachel was in the seat next to me. Legs curled up beneath her the way only women can, her head pillowed on my shoulder. Dog was on his back, on my feet, legs splayed wide apart and snoring like an asthmatic steam engine.

Looking around, I saw most other people were also asleep. Jackson was the only person on his feet, standing at the windows looking south. Gently, I moved Rachel off my shoulder, had to poke Dog three times to get him to roll off my boots, then stood up and visited the small toilet at the front of the car. I opened the door and closed it almost instantly. Even though it was apparently out of order, people had been using it. A lot.

Walking to the back of the car, I stepped out onto the platform and relieved myself into the slipstream of wind created by the train. Immediate need taken care of, I went back in and stood next to Jackson. Glancing at my watch, I saw it was just after 0400. The sun would be up

Rolling Thunder

soon, just in time for us to negotiate Memphis and the Mississippi River crossing. It was still pitch black outside and I didn't know if Jackson was watching for something or just lost in thought.

"What's going on?" I asked, keeping my voice quiet so I didn't wake the sleeping people around us.

"We've passed the area the herd was transiting and the outskirts of Memphis are about thirty miles away. There's a sharp curve ahead as we turn into the city, and we have to slow to twenty and pretty much maintain that speed until we're over the bridge."

He kept staring out the windows as he spoke.

"How does Memphis look? Any reports?"

"The Colonel has a couple of Black Hawks flying recon, and it's the damndest thing. There's pea soup fog, and they can't see anything on the ground."

"They using FLIR?" I was talking about Forward Looking Infrared.

"Yep. And they've tried LWIR — Long Wave Infrared - too, but the fog is really messing with it. They keep thinking they see movement, but they reposition and whatever it was is gone. Don't know if it's real or the fog causing ghosts in the imagery equipment."

I knew now what he was watching for. Fog. Thick, blinding fog. Just fucking marvelous.

The train kept slowing, and the vibration finally ceased and we were back to the gentle swaying motion which continued to diminish as more speed bled off. Eventually, we seemed to settle into our new pace and soon I could feel the floor shift as we rolled into the curve Jackson had mentioned. Coming out of it, we suddenly entered the fog. One moment blank windows were staring back at us, the next we both blinked as thick, white fog enveloped the train and reflected the light back at us.

"Don't know about you, Master Sergeant, but I don't like this. Better get everybody up. And let's get some eyes up top, too."

"Yes, sir."

Jackson immediately turned and woke the National Guard soldiers, sending them through the car to wake the civilians. One of them got sent to the roof while the others headed into other cars to rouse the occupants. Wanting to get some fresh air, I joined the soldier on the roof of the car.

The fog was so thick it almost seemed like it had substance to it. Like I could scoop out a handful and a hole would remain. It was chilly and damp, quickly coating every inch of me with moisture which soaked right through to my skin. The clacking sound made by the train as it rolled down the tracks was muted, much like a heavy snowfall quietens the countryside. The only good thing was it fully woke me, and with the wind of our passage it helped flush the last of the stench from below out of my sinuses.

There were occasional gaps in the fog as we proceeded, but they were small and infrequent. When we passed through one, I could see flat terrain covered with thick bladed green grass. Once, I caught sight of two abandoned vehicles as we crossed a road but didn't see them long enough to identify their make or model.

Seeing those two cars made me think about the engineer driving the lead locomotive. He couldn't see any farther than I could. If there was a vehicle or something larger that was blocking the tracks, we'd plow right into it.

A check of my watch showed it was now after 0500. We had to be in Memphis, but the fog was still so thick I couldn't see a thing to prove it. I tried to remember how early the sun had come up in Atlanta, figuring Memphis couldn't be that much different. 0530, I thought. Well, I'd know soon if I had remembered correctly.

Pacing the roof of the car, I tried to peer through the fog but was still limited to the occasional break. I was getting momentary glimpses of buildings, streets, cars and empty lots. I wasn't seeing anything else and heard nothing other than the train.

The fog around me was lightening and I knew that somewhere above it the eastern horizon was glowing. Correcting myself, I remembered that the eastern horizon had been glowing all night. Jackson joined me, both of us looking up at the sound of a heavy rotor, unable to see the helicopter in the fog.

"That's the Colonel's Black Hawk," he said. "They're trying to see if the track in front of us is still clear, but if there's not something that's glowing red hot they aren't going to be able to see it in this shit."

He waved his hand through the fog in front of him.

Rolling Thunder

"How much farther to the river?"

"We're still east of the city. Probably another half hour at this speed."

That meant the bulk of Memphis was still ahead of us. We stood there in silence, the dampness seeping into our clothing, then deeper into my joints that weren't as young as they used to be.

Life as an SF operator is not easy on the body. Knees and shoulders seem to be what goes first. My left shoulder was reminding me it had been dislocated twice when I was younger. Reaching up and rubbing it, I froze when the feeling hit me. The same little sixth sense, whatever the hell it is, that had warned me there was an enemy behind a tree when I was south of Murfreesboro. It was screaming at me that something was wrong. Every hair on my body was standing on end and there was a creeping feeling all up and down the flesh on my back.

I looked around, but the fog was still too thick to see anything. The sun was up now, but the fog diffused the light so there were no shadows and nothing was well lit. I looked around for the soldier who had been on the roof when I came up and didn't see him. What the hell?

Dirk Patton

I was standing in roughly the middle of the car, which was close to a hundred feet long. Maybe he had moved to an end and I just couldn't see him. Raising my rifle, I took it off safe as I looked around. Jackson noticed and, like an experienced operator, didn't bother to ask what was wrong, just raised his as well.

We stood there, silent and unmoving, for a couple of moments before I hand signed to Jackson that the soldier was missing and I was going forward to look for him. He nodded and followed me, each of us stepping sideways so we were facing opposite sides of the car as we moved. It didn't take long to reach the front edge and we hadn't found the missing soldier. Reversing direction, Jackson led the way to the back. Again, it didn't take long to cover the short distance and we didn't find him.

The day was continuing to brighten as the sun climbed higher in the sky and a few moments later we came to another break in the fog. Jackson and I both cursed at the same time. Thousands of infected were right at the edge of the tracks, females leaping for any handhold on the train they could find. Then the fog swallowed us back up and we lost sight of our attackers.

32

I stepped to the edge of the rear of the car, looking down on the platform leading to the door. Two females were searching for a way inside. When they saw me, they both screamed. One of them leapt onto the ladder, covering half the distance to the roof in one bound. I already had my rifle pointed into the gap and shot her off the ladder.

Her body slammed into the other and both of them tumbled through the opening and under the wheels of the following car. I started to step onto the ladder to head below, pulling my foot back when another female grabbed the railing and swung onto the platform.

Behind me, I could hear Jackson on the radio reporting our situation to Colonel Crawford. I shot the new arrival, slapped him on the shoulder to let him know it was time to go, then stepped out and slid down the ladder to the platform. The instant my boots hit the metal, I stepped out of the way so Jackson could come down, raising my rifle in the same motion. Another female grabbed the railing to my right. She used the momentum of the train to whip herself up and around, but let go and fell away when I raised my foot and kicked her in the face.

That kick almost cost me my life as the one right behind her was able to reach around the rail and grab my ankle with a frighteningly strong grip. Shoving the rifle in her face, I pulled the trigger and she fell away, nearly dragging me off the narrow platform with her. Jackson thumped down next to me. I shouted for him to get the door open as I shot another female that was hanging on to the train with one hand and reaching for him with the other.

I snapped the rifle up at a scream from over my head, shooting a female that was about to leap at me from the roof of the car behind us. Damn it. They were everywhere. I fired at another as she scrambled for footing on the platform, then Jackson grabbed my vest and yanked me backwards through the open door. Pulling me out of the way, he slammed it shut as soon as I was clear.

Everyone in the car was on their feet, frightened conversations dying out as they turned to look at me. Ignoring them, I looked around to make sure Rachel and Dog were safe. They were still where I'd left them, Rachel now awake. Dog was sitting in my seat, looking at me like he was daring me to make him move.

Turning back to Jackson, I asked him if there was any way to speak directly to the engineer driving the train. He pulled out his radio and adjusted the frequency. He spoke briefly to the engineer then handed the unit to me.

"We need to speed up," I said over the radio. "At this speed, the infected are able to grab on and climb aboard."

"I can't go any faster." It was hard to hear the man's voice over the roar of machinery in the background. "There's a ninety coming up that lines us up for the bridge and I'm already at the max rated speed. I take that turn too fast, we go over."

"Can't you speed up then slow back down?"

"This ain't a fuckin' car. It takes miles to speed up and more miles to slow down. There's nothing I can do. We're committed and we can't go faster."

I didn't bother to answer, just ripped the earpiece out and handed the unit back to Jackson.

Dirk Patton

"We can't go faster. There's a sharp turn coming to get us onto the bridge, and if he goes faster, we roll."

Rachel had come to stand with us, listening to our conversation.

"Wait a minute," she said. "How far to the turn? And which way are we turning?"

I didn't know and looked at Jackson. He quickly called the engineer back.

"Twenty minutes and to the right," he reported when he got the answer.

All of us jumped at a loud thump on the door. Infected screams followed moments later, then we spun and raised our weapons when a pistol fired inside the car. A female had crawled in one of the windows that had been blown out earlier when the Apaches were firing next to the train. One of the men standing nearby had shot her before she made it all the way through.

Before we could resume our conversation, a window shattered as another infected battered her way inside. She was shot down by one of the National Guard soldiers, but not before reaching through the broken glass and slashing open the face of a child sitting on his mother's lap.

Rolling Thunder

"You've got an idea?" I asked Rachel.

"How many people on the train?" We both looked at Jackson.

"Not sure, but around eight thousand, I think."

"OK, eight thousand people, and if we say an average body weight of even just a hundred and fifty pounds per person that's…" Rachel paused and looked off into space while she did the math.

"One point two million pounds," she finally said with an excited smile that faded as Jackson and I just stood there looking at her.

"You Army guys aren't too imaginative, are you?" She looked back and forth at us. "Don't you get it? We've got well over a million pounds of ballast! Get everyone to move to the inside edge of the curve and we can counter the force that would tip us over. We can speed up!"

Rachel was excited, talking fast and using her hands to help make her point.

"Will that work?" Jackson looked at me.

"Hell if I know. I'm just a dumb, unimaginative grunt, but it makes sense. Call the engineer and ask him."

Jackson had a brief yet intense conversation with the engineer. While they were talking another infected broke through a window but was quickly shot before she could do any damage to the evacuees.

"He says it should work. He's pushing us up by fifteen miles an hour which will be fast enough to stop these damn things from climbing on..."

"Great!" I interrupted. "We need to spread the word..."

"One more thing." It was Jackson's turn to cut me off. "He says if it's not enough of a counterbalance, we will definitely derail at that speed."

"It's gotta work," I said. "Get on the radio and start spreading the word."

While Jackson started issuing orders to all the military personnel located throughout the train, I felt the sway and vibration increase as the engineer bumped our speed. That was good, stopping any more infected from boarding the train. But I was worried about how many had already climbed on and even now were breaking through windows and attacking defenseless people.

"The Colonel is briefed and wishes us luck," Jackson said, turning back to face me. "What now?"

I didn't know what now. The plan was in motion. The curve was fast approaching, and I couldn't think of another damn thing that needed doing. Ideally, I would have liked to go outside with Jackson and clear the infected off the skin of the train, but between our higher speed and the dense fog, I didn't think that was the wisest thing to do. They were a threat, but they were easier to deal with from inside as they tried to come through windows than they would be from the outside.

"We make sure everyone is on the right side of the train, and we sit tight."

I demonstrated by squeezing into half a seat next to Rachel and Dog. Two other people were crammed between them and the windows as all the passengers got shifted as far to the right as possible. Jackson settled onto the edge of the seat in front of me.

Dirk Patton

"Hey, Master Sergeant. Have you gotten any word about the bridge or the tracks on the far side of the river?"

Jackson turned in the seat to look at me, shook his head and got back on the radio.

"The fog is heaviest at the river. Thermal's not seeing anything on the bridge, but that doesn't mean a damn thing. The fog is thick for another ten miles on west of the river, then starts thinning. They're seeing movement a few miles out, but can't tell what the tracks are like for the first few miles west of the bridge."

Just great. All this amazing technology that let the US fight as effectively at night as in the daytime and it was rendered nearly useless by something as simple as fog. I understood that FLIR or thermal imaging worked by detecting heat sources. The dense fog, which was comprised of billions of fine droplets of water, did an excellent job of masking heat signatures. But, you'd think with the trillions of dollars we poured into the military that someone would have found a solution. Of course, we'd been wrapped up in wars in the desert for over a decade and fog wasn't a big issue where we'd been fighting.

33

The time to reach the curve passed slowly. If there's one thing the Army teaches you, it is patience. Not the kind of patience a kindly grandparent might have, more like the forced patience you learn from spending time waiting for something to happen even though you're primed and ready to go. Kind of like the interminable time spent in an Emergency Room waiting area, or dealing with a delayed flight at the airport.

It's not fun, but it's been an integral part of my life. I've frequently had the daydream fantasy of being filthy rich. Not so I could buy whatever bauble caught my eye, but so I could have enough money to never have to wait for anything or anyone, ever again. This and other ridiculous thoughts swirled through my head as I sat, waiting for us to reach the curve.

Rachel was nervous. The pressure of our lives depending on her idea was getting to her. She had a firm grip on my arm with both hands and a worried expression on her face. I patted her hand and gave her a reassuring smile. We either made it or we didn't, and the more you dwelled on the possible bad outcomes, the more energy you wasted that might be needed if things didn't go according to plan.

If you've been in combat, you learn to accept that fact very quickly or you wind up bouncing off the walls in a rubber room somewhere while the Army processes your Section 8 discharge paperwork. I've seen plenty of guys that were beasts in training turn into puddles of jelly while waiting for the bullets to start flying and bombs to go off. Not their fault. There's just some people that aren't built for the battlefield.

"The locomotive is just entering the curve," Jackson turned and informed me. "Our engineer is nervous as hell. He says there's thousands of infected on the tracks, but so far we're blasting through them without any issues."

I nodded and Rachel squeezed my arm tighter. I could feel a new vibration start up in the train as more cars entered the curve. I couldn't shake the mental image of the entire train slowly rising up onto the outside set of wheels as it rolled through the curve, then in exaggerated slow motion, we kept tipping until we were beyond the point of no return and crashed into a sea of waiting infected arms. I forced the image out of my head. Focusing on the inside of the car, I noticed Jackson's sweaty face. The man was nervous. After a moment, I realized I was too.

The vibration continued, worsening by the moment until I thought the train was going to shake itself to pieces. Then our car entered the curve. The change in motion was more sudden and sharper than I expected. A hard push to my left as the car was dragged through the turn. Several people let out gasps and cries of fear as they were jolted out of their seats to sprawl into the aisle.

Seemingly forever, we rocked back and forth, then I felt the car tip up slightly. The vibrations changed dramatically as the wheels along the right side came off the rails. For a moment, there was that semi-weightless feeling you get on a plane when it starts descending, then a hard impact as the wheels crashed back down. There was a brief scream of protesting metal then we were rolling again.

A collective sigh of relief and a few muted cheers sounded throughout the car, but the celebration was cut short as everyone was suddenly and violently thrown forward. There was a horrendous screeching of metal pushed beyond the point of failure, quickly followed by another sharp jerk to the left that snapped necks harder than any roller coaster I've ever ridden.

The car started to tip, slowly gaining momentum. I could feel it when the wheels left the track, a long moment later crashing to the ground. All around me people were screaming and crying out as we seemed to be moving forward, but the car was at a forty-five-degree angle to the direction of the tracks.

The sounds of metal being violently ripped apart and the bass rumble of the steel wheels dragging on the bare earth grew in intensity, then quickly faded as we came to a full stop. The car was tipped up at a dizzying angle with a lean to the left. I had the weight of the three people and the dog to my right trying to push me out of my seat and into the aisle.

Standing up, I had to hold on to the seats to maintain my footing on the sloping floor. I tried to see out the windows, but the fog was too thick to allow more than a dozen feet of visibility. The passengers in the car were eerily quiet. The only sounds were the crying of a few children and the underlying noises made as the overheated metal wheels cooled with a pinging sound not unlike popcorn in an old time kettle.

Rolling Thunder

"Master Sergeant, how far to the river?" I grabbed Jackson and pulled him to his feet.

"About five miles, if we follow the tracks."

"Let the Colonel know we're going to be on foot. I'm going to try and get an idea of just how many infected we've got to deal with. Also, get me a count of military personnel on this train and what their state of ammo is."

While Jackson got on the radio, I moved to the left side of the train and cautiously stuck my head out one of the broken windows. I was immediately greeted with the screams of hundreds of females. Some were clearly visible as they were very close to the train, others looked more like spirits as they moved through the fog. Stumbling through the throng of females were hundreds more males. We were crashed in the middle of a sea of death. Rachel had moved to the row of seats next to me and was also looking out a window, catching her breath when she saw the mess we were in.

"What the hell are we going to do?" She asked without taking her eyes off the milling infected.

"We're going to get everyone ready, then we're getting off this train and fighting our way to the river," I said.

"Are you nuts? There's too many of them. We won't make it!"

"Keep it down!" I said in a low voice before Rachel got the civilians in the car interested in our conversation. "We don't have a choice. There's no one to come get us. If we just sit here, they'll keep us trapped until we die of dehydration. When the sun burns the fog off, it's going to get damn hot in these cars and half these people will be dead by this time tomorrow. Our odds aren't much better, if any, out there amongst them, but at least we'll have a fighting chance. We stay here and we have none. And we need to get moving before more of them pile into the area."

Rachel didn't argue further, eventually nodding her head that she understood my reasoning. But I could tell she didn't want to go out there. Hell, neither did I, but I sure as shit didn't want to sit on my ass inside this train to just wait for a slow and certain death. Would a lot of us die outside? Absolutely. But some would escape, and that was better odds than if we did nothing.

Rolling Thunder

"Major, there's three hundred and twelve military on the train, including us," Jackson said, walking up. "Everyone is well provisioned, but we're too disorganized at the moment to get you accurate ammo counts. Each person is armed with a rifle and pistol and we've also got seven SAWs, – Squad Automatic Weapons or light machine guns – two up-armored Humvees and one Bradley. Also, the Colonel is overhead with a flight of five Black Hawks and twelve Apaches ready to provide air support when we need it, but it's going to be dicey as hell with the fog for them to be able to see where to shoot."

I nodded, wheels turning as I processed the information he'd just given me. Eight thousand people on the train and barely three hundred soldiers to protect them from what I guessed were going to be thousands, if not tens of thousands of infected. Infected that couldn't be scared off, beaten back or would even tire from the fight. They would just keep coming until every last one of them was dead. Or every last one of us was dead or beyond reach. And there was also the five miles to the bridge that we had to cross.

Covering five miles on foot was nothing for someone in the military. Just another day at work. The civilians, on the other hand, would be tired before we'd even gone a mile. Of course, there were the few that stayed in shape and could keep up or even set the pace, but America had gotten fat.

We drove everywhere we went. Found the parking spot closest to the door and consumed more calories for breakfast than millions of people around the world did in a day. Most of these people were going to be easy prey for the infected and I didn't have any bright ideas about how to protect them. I kept those thoughts to myself.

"Get that Bradley and those Humvees moving. Pair up the Hummers on the left side of the train to provide fire support and put the Bradley on the right. I want him to stop as many infected as he can that are coming from that direction. Get all the military personnel to spread the word. We move in five minutes."

I glanced at my watch to note the time, Jackson checking his as well.

"Everyone out and to the left side of the train. Get the Colonel to put half that flight of Apaches on the right side with the Bradley to keep the infected cleared out. Keep the other half in reserve to support them and the Black Hawks ready for air support on the left."

Rolling Thunder

Jackson had been making notes on a small spiral pad while I talked. Giving me a look that said he hoped I knew what I was doing, he nodded and turned away to get back on the radio and start issuing orders and a request to the Colonel.

I called the National Guard Sergeant over and gave him a thirty-second dump of what was going on and told him to get the civilians on this car ready to move.

"What about the prisoner?" He asked when I was finished.

Shit! I'd forgotten about Roach. Part of me wanted to leave him tied up right where he was and let the infected have him after we left, but it wasn't my call to make.

"Cut him loose," I said. "But he does not get a weapon. He can take his chances with the infected, just like the civilians."

The Sergeant nodded and started barking orders to the remaining members of his squad. With two minutes left, I walked over to where Jackson was wrapping up a conversation on the radio.

"Colonel Crawford wishes us luck," he said when I stopped in front of him. "He asked if we wanted him to pick us up in the Black Hawk. In fact, he strongly suggested that we'd be of more value to the country if he did pick us up rather than staying down here and becoming some poor infected bastard's breakfast."

"What did you say?"

"I told him we appreciated his offer, but we were right where we were needed most."

I clapped Jackson on the shoulder and gave him a big grin. I was really starting to like this guy.

34

It was only a couple of moments later when I heard the first rounds fired off outside the train. I recognized the sound of the Humvee-mounted machine gun and soon the second one joined in. Then the Bradley cut loose on the opposite side of the train with its twenty-five-millimeter chain gun and I could hear its machine gun start hammering as well. I glanced at my watch. One minute to go.

Involuntarily, I looked up as if I could see through the roof of the train car when a helicopter that had to be an Apache came into a hover right over us. It added its chin-mounted chain gun to the suppressive fire. We certainly had the fire support. But I also knew the air and ground units didn't have unlimited ammo, and not even the option of falling back to resupply.

Thirty seconds. I moved to the back door of the car and Jackson fell in on my left as if we'd been training together for years. Rachel moved in behind us and Dog took up station in the middle of the triangle we formed. The National Guard had all the civilians on their feet and ready to follow us out the door.

I hadn't seen Roach for a bit but had noted that the strips of fabric that had been used to secure him had been cut and he was out of his seat. I didn't like having him somewhere at my back. I only trusted him when he was close enough for me to kill.

Fifteen seconds. Jackson sent an alert call over the radio to prepare to move. I wanted every car evacuating at the same time, as many rifles as we could field ready to go simultaneously. If we weren't coordinated, it would give the infected an opportunity to fall on those that moved out early and wipe them out. I wanted their attention as spread out as possible. We were going to hit them hard the second we stepped out and do our best to keep the civilians in a tight group as we moved.

I glanced over my shoulder to check on Max. He was sitting in his wheelchair with a rifle in his hands, surrounded by his three sons who were also armed. Two large male civilians stood ready to lift Max down. They would stay with him when we hit the ground, a third man ready to go with Max's equipment cases.

Five seconds. The hammering of a machine gun sounded right outside the car and I was glad that one of the Humvees was in place

Rolling Thunder

and ready to take Max and his equipment on board. There was also a pregnant woman that would be joining him. I tried not to think about what the virus might be doing to the baby in her womb.

Unfortunately, there wasn't room for Max's sons in the Hummer. They were going to have to take their chances as we ran for the bridge. Jackson was on the radio, counting down to our go time. When he reached three, I grasped the emergency release in my hand. On one, I pulled it hard and the door slid open as Jackson began yelling, "Go! Go! Go!"

Three females waited for us on the other side of the door, screaming in anticipation as soon as the door started moving. Rachel, Jackson and I each fired at nearly the same instant. All three of them dropped dead into the seething mass of bodies that had forced its way into the gap between the cars.

I stepped through the door before any more could climb onto the platform, picking off targets that were so close I could actually see the powder burns from my shots on their mottled skin as they fell. Jackson was close on my shoulder and, between the two of us, we quickly cleared the gap and jumped down to engage targets that weren't close enough to touch.

The fog was a bitch. To my front the Humvee sat idling, waiting for its passengers. It was no more than fifteen feet away and it looked almost ethereal in the mist as the gunner fired the machine gun to keep the area clear. I was acquiring and firing on targets as fast as I could. At twenty feet, they were little more than an amorphous movement, suddenly sharpening into clarity as they charged closer.

"Reloading!"

I called out when my rifle's bolt locked open on an empty magazine and Rachel stepped to my side. She maintained the rate of fire and kept targets knocked down for the time it took me to drop the empty magazine, slap in a new one and release the bolt to chamber a fresh round. I turned to cover Jackson's area while he reloaded, then it was Rachel's turn. We kept this progression up, moving into the open space between the crashed train car and the Humvee. As we moved, we spread out to provide protection for the civilians that were streaming out of the train.

Max was rolled out the door onto the platform. The two men leapt to the ground and lifted him and his chair into the air and carried him to the waiting Humvee. The driver popped open the passenger door as they approached, reaching out and grabbing Max by the arms. He dragged him out of the chair and into the vehicle. There wasn't time for sensitivity.

The chair was collapsed and tossed into the back, then two of the National Guard soldiers hustled over with the pregnant woman between them. I was engaging three females charging directly at me when several screams sounded way too close. I couldn't look. Any loss of focus and the three infected would be on me in a heartbeat.

Firing three quick shots, I dropped them and spun. A female who had made it onto the hood of the Humvee launched herself directly at the pregnant woman who was being hurried along with a soldier gripping her under each arm. The infected slammed into her chest and ripped her arms out of their hands, knocking her flat on her back. Immediately she started tearing into her throat.

Before I could pivot and bring my rifle up, Dog leapt and ripped the infected off the woman's body. They rolled across the rough gravel and came to a stop against the front tire of the Hummer. He quickly dispatched the female, but I didn't have time to check on the pregnant woman as more shapes suddenly appeared in the fog to my front.

We kept up our rate of fire, along with the Hummer, and soon all the civilians were off the train and milling nervously in a tight group. Many of them were armed with varieties of weapons that ran the gamut from kitchen knives to a turn of the last century double barreled shotgun that was about five feet long. The group was pressed up against the car and the ones that were armed had positioned themselves at the edge to try and provide protection for the rest.

"Jackson, get everyone moving!" I shouted.

Despite the weapons being fired, the screams of the infected, and the roar of the hovering Apache, he heard me. The helicopter was firing short, controlled bursts on the far side of the train, the wash from its rotor whipping the fog around the area. Jackson shouted into his radio and as previously agreed, Rachel and I went to the front of our group. He would bring up the rear as we got them moving west along the shattered remains of the train. Firing from the group ahead of us was steady and it sounded like

Rolling Thunder

the Bradley was in a target rich environment, firing burst after burst.

Breaking into a slow jog, I kept firing as I ran, Rachel right beside me and doing the same. I was gratified to see how much her skills had improved as she was hitting most of her targets while on the move. Dog trotted between us, head on a swivel.

The group behind had to spread out to be able to run. Soon we were all moving at a slow but steady pace. Maybe four miles an hour. That meant over an hour just to get to the bridge.

Running through fog isn't pleasant when there aren't swarms of infected trying to kill you. Doing it when there are is absolutely terrifying. Your senses compress in as the fog blinds you and mutes sounds and smells. Like having a layer of gauze wrapped around your head. I was frequently being surprised by infected that suddenly appeared out of the mist, right in front of me as if by magic.

The fight was so close that I had slung my rifle in favor of my knife in my left hand and pistol in my right. We moved that way for a few minutes, Rachel still using her rifle and keeping up a steady rate of fire. I stabbed or shot any infected that were within visual range. A couple of times, I did both.

Screams from the females were continually sounding deeper in the fog than I could see, and the way sound was impacted, I couldn't tell the direction the majority of them were coming from. It took me a moment to realize there were screams from behind me that were both infected as well as terrorized people. Looking back, I could only see the first rank of evacuees closest to me, also turned and looking to their rear as they ran.

"Maintain the pace!" I shouted to Rachel as I dashed back toward the screams.

As I moved through the fog, I started encountering infected, both male and female, moving in from our flank. At least a dozen evacuees were already dead on the ground and the infected were still pouring in. I shot two females and three males as soon as they appeared.

Pushing on, I slashed the throat of a male who was fighting with a teenager and stabbed into the back of the head of another female who was trying to pull a heavyset man to the ground. Jackson ran up from the rear and killed two more females, nodded to me and headed back.

Rolling Thunder

"Faster!" I shouted to the group and turned and ran back to the front, sheathing the knife and doing a quick magazine change before holstering the pistol and grabbing my rifle.

The two Humvees were driving up and down the edge of the fleeing evacuees, mowing down infected with their machine guns as they moved. I matched pace with one as it went past, taking advantage of the fire support it provided as I ran to catch Rachel.

I was having to watch my footing so I didn't trip over a body, as well as be alert for infected popping up in the fog. Every few yards I was having to step over dead infected and more savaged evacuees than I wanted to see. I was moving too slow. But faster than the group of civilians. I shouted at them again to run faster.

I caught up with Rachel and Dog, Rachel nearly shooting me when I suddenly appeared out of the fog. Her hair was wet and plastered to her head. Long strands of it hung down across her face and she looked exhausted, but she still gave me a bright smile when she recognized me. Shooting an infected that was less than five feet to her left, I yelled for her to pick up the pace.

She ran faster and matched my speed. Dog was able to stay with us at no more than a trot, but then he had four legs and could cover a lot of ground very quickly without much effort. At our faster pace, it didn't take long for us to catch the group ahead. We had been dodging and stepping over bodies of both infected and evacuees for a few minutes before we caught them, frequently killing males that we encountered who were following in their wake.

When we first came upon them, Rachel and I both nearly shot the civilians at the back of the group when they coalesced out of the fog. We had grown accustomed to seeing and shooting infected males that were lumbering along. If it hadn't been for a little blonde girl holding her father's hand as they walked, we probably would have fired on them.

"Run! Move faster!" I started shouting as we approached the group from the rear.

Heads turned to look at me and one by one people broke into a slow jog. Rachel, Dog and I peeled off to the side and ran past. The group had apparently suffered a lot of losses as there weren't very many people left. The one we had been leading caught up and pushed into the back of them, urging them to a faster pace.

We were running close to the derailed train which offered a degree of protection. The

Rolling Thunder

Bradley and Apaches were doing a good job of clearing the far side of infected. But our exposed flank was under continuous attack and I couldn't kill infected fast enough to protect everyone. Our numbers were dwindling fast.

35

Captain Lee Roach was terrified. He had thought he was going to die when Major Chase put the knife to his throat. But for some reason, the big man hadn't killed him. Instead, they'd stripped him and tied him to a seat where he'd been interrogated by that jumped up Army Master Sergeant like a common criminal.

Roach didn't see that he'd done anything wrong by taking the General's uniform when he escaped from Arnold. That uniform had helped him survive. It had gotten him past roadblocks on his way to Nashville, then into a suite at the Hyatt where they had happily accommodated him. That damn star was like an all-access pass, getting him the best room in the hotel even though they weren't open for business.

The uniform had also gotten him into several of the nightclubs just down the street from the hotel. Despite the damage done to the country and the impending invasion by millions of infected, there were still people that wanted to party. Roach had enjoyed himself immensely, paying for drinks courtesy of the General's DOD issue American Express card. Amazingly, the systems that processed credit card payments were still up and running. He was playing the big shot that he'd always believed he was.

And the women. They were desperate. Frightened. Willing to latch onto anyone they thought could or would protect them. And three of them wound up back in Roach's suite, lured there with promises of military protection and priority evacuation when the time came.

Roach satisfied his carnal needs first. Then satisfied his demons. Two of the young women were left in the bathtub in the second bath of the large suite. The third still lay on the master bedroom's king-sized bed, blood from her slashed throat soaking deep into the mattress.

Roach had walked out of the hotel when the evacuation notice was issued, General's uniform freshly laundered and pressed. With head high and shoulders back, he looked the part he was playing. He had walked right through military and police checkpoints, then bypassed the long lines of civilians queued up to board the trains. He had even gotten an escort onto the train, one of the first to board. He didn't encounter any other officers, only enlisted and NCOs. None of them even thought about questioning why he was there and evacuating with the civilian population.

Dirk Patton

The train had loaded slowly, but Roach sat patiently in a comfortable business class seat in a passenger car. He watched the rain fall, soaking the evacuees and soldiers that were trying to control the frightened crowd. He had worked hard to suppress laughter when skirmishes between the panicked civilians and soldiers broke out, secretly delighting in seeing people shot as they charged the military lines.

The car he was in filled quickly with people, but the seat next to him stayed empty until the very last minute. He looked over at the young woman with an infant in her arms that sank into the seat and started fussing with her baby to make it comfortable. He had felt a tingle in his legs when he saw the young mother. She was exactly his type. He turned back to the window, trying to figure out how and where to get her alone. That was when he spotted the bitch that had arrived at Arnold with that asshole Major.

She was with a group of women and a man in a wheelchair. The entire contingent was being escorted by a squad of soldiers. Turning to watch, he saw them approach and board a car only a few behind his. He kept nervously scanning the crowd for the Major, knowing his charade would fall apart if the man saw him.

Rolling Thunder

Checking every male face that was approaching or boarding the train, he was relieved when they started moving, and the Major still hadn't shown. Had he not made it out of Arnold? Regardless of the reason, the bitch was alone. Roach forgot all about the woman seated next to him. Instead, he focused on the warm feeling of revenge he would take on the bitch, planning how he would make it happen.

The train picked up speed and Roach settled back. His head was turned to watch the dark countryside slide by, his mind busily plotting how to get his knife into the woman's body. He didn't know her name, thinking of her only as *the bitch*. He would learn it as he slid his blade into her belly and slowly twisted, making her feel every bit of the agony for the humiliation she had caused him.

It was sometime later, and Roach was nearly asleep from the monotonous rhythm of the train's wheels on the rails, when there was a roar of wind as the back door to the car opened. A short, black soldier with massive shoulders and an equally powerful chest entered the car with his rifle up and scanning. After a moment, he lowered the weapon and called out to the passengers that he was checking for infected. He came forward in the cramped aisle, two National Guard soldiers on his heels.

As soon as Roach saw the Special Forces soldier, he knew how he'd get to the bitch. He stood and stepped past the woman with the baby into the aisle and met the operator who straightened when he saw the uniform.

"Master Sergeant," Roach said. "I saw a woman board this train before we pulled out of Nashville. She is wanted for crimes committed at Arnold Air Force Base. Maybe you've seen her. Tall and very pretty, long brown hair. She's dressed in an Air Force tactical uniform and is four cars behind us."

"I have a good idea who you're describing, sir," Jackson answered.

He didn't let his face give anything away, but something just didn't seem right here. He was obviously describing Rachel, but... Regardless, he was face to face with a General, so he decided to see where things went.

"What do you want me to do?"

Roach smiled.

"Take me to her, Master Sergeant. We're going to arrest and restrain her until we reach somewhere where I can have her taken off the train."

Roach was making it up as he went along, but the first step was to get the bitch disarmed and tied up. After that, he'd find a way to get to her on the train or he'd maintain the pretense and slip away with her when they got out of Tennessee. Either way, he'd have his revenge. He felt his manhood rising with the thought and casually buttoned his jacket to hide the erection.

"Yes, sir, but we've had some infected breach the train and I have several more cars to clear first. She's not going anywhere in the meantime."

Roach wasn't a patient man, but knew if he insisted the soldier abandon his sweep of the train to go arrest the bitch it would raise questions he couldn't answer.

"Very well. Carry on with what you were doing. Come find me as soon as you're done with the sweep so we can arrest her. She's going to deny the accusation and I want to be there to confront her."

"Yes, sir."

Dirk Patton

Roach stepped out of Jackson's way and after a moment he and the other two soldiers squeezed past and moved into the next car forward. It wasn't long before Jackson returned and Roach fell in directly behind him as they worked their way down the length of the train. The transition from car to car was a little unnerving, stepping across open space with the ground rushing by only a few feet below. Roach steeled himself and followed close on the Master Sergeant's heels.

They passed through one car that was a charnel house, blood and gore splattered across the floor, walls, windows, and even the ceiling. Bodies lay sprawled across most of the seats. Roach stepped gingerly, making sure not to brush against anything that would get blood, or worse, on his uniform.

Leaving the death car behind, they moved across another gap and into the next car. The Master Sergeant glanced over his shoulder at Roach as they entered and started down the aisle. Roach was scanning for the bitch, checking each female face he saw. He was caught completely unprepared when the big Army Major pushed the Master Sergeant out of the way and lunged at him. He was knocked onto his back and the man landed on top of him. Roach could feel the tip of a knife digging into the flesh under his jaw. When he looked into the Major's eyes, he thought he was about to die.

Roach's charade quickly fell apart. The Master Sergeant believed the Major and the bitch when they accused him of deserting and revealed who he really was. In minutes, he found himself stripped to his underwear and tied to a seat like a common criminal. He stoically endured the humiliation, grinding his teeth as he spun a story when the Master Sergeant interrogated him.

After the interrogation, they left him alone, and Roach started to get scared. They didn't know about the women at the hotel in Nashville, did they? How could they? Were they only concerned with the bullshit desertion charge? It was bullshit because the base was going to fall. Everyone could see that. It isn't desertion if you're only trying to save your life, he told himself, deciding that would be his defense.

He knew the Globemaster with evacuees aboard had crashed on takeoff, and he would say that he knew it couldn't successfully get away. If he had stayed with them and boarded that aircraft, he would be dead too.

The Major and the bitch hadn't gotten on board. They must have known something. How could he be guilty of desertion if they weren't? Roach kept playing out the line of reasoning in his head, finally happy with the argument he would use when the time came.

The Major was the real criminal here. He'd doomed all those people by putting them on that plane. A plane that had no chance. That never should have landed to begin with. Roach had escaped safely in a Humvee, just like the Major had. Why hadn't the Major just put the evacuees in a vehicle and driven them to safety? The Major had a lot to answer for!

Roach sat planning his defense argument while most of the other passengers slept. He went over it in his head repeatedly until he was snapped out of his thoughts as the train violently derailed and came to a grinding stop. After a few minutes, one of the National Guard soldiers stepped in front of him and cut him loose, telling him to get ready to run.

He soon found himself pushing his way out of the car with the other evacuees, into a thick fog. Unarmed and dressed only in underwear and shoes, Roach started running in the middle of the group. Infected screams were all around, as was gunfire from vehicle mounted

Rolling Thunder

machine guns and the rifles of the soldiers running with them.

A female slipped past the defenses and charged the group, adjusting course to head directly at Roach. He saw her at the last moment and changed direction, pushing the man next to him into her path. She slammed into the man and they went down as she tore into his throat. Roach ran on with the larger group, continually looking around and working to stay as close to the center as possible.

He had lost sight of the Major and the bitch, but he knew they were somewhere around. They seemed to have an amazing knack for survival. Just ahead he saw a woman trip and fall over a shredded body that lay on the ground. Roach felt a thrill of exhilaration when he saw the uniform. And the rifle slung over the shoulders of the corpse.

Pausing, he grabbed the rifle, worked the tactical vest off the body and shrugged into it. The vest was well stocked with spare magazines, a couple of fragmentation grenades, a pistol and a Ka-Bar fighting knife. The Major and the bitch would be somewhere up ahead.

And they'd be facing away from the evacuees, fighting the infected. A quick bullet to the back of his head, then a knife blade across her throat to make her cooperate. When that happened, Roach would find a place where the two of them could have some fun.

36

We kept running. I never had the opportunity to look at my watch, but we ran for what had to be another thirty minutes. I was guessing we had covered two miles. Hundreds, if not thousands, of evacuees had already fallen to the infected. Mostly those that were out of shape and slow, but also the unfortunate ones. People who had been running and had an infected come screaming out of the fog and tear into them before they could defend themselves. Thousands more infected had been killed as well. As far as I could tell, we hadn't even made a dent in their numbers.

The train had been left behind and we now had two exposed flanks to protect. Our air support had peeled off. Visibility was too poor for them to risk firing on ground targets. That left us with the surviving military personnel that were on foot, two Humvees and one Bradley. The Bradley prowled up and down our right flank, but we were stretched out close to a quarter of a mile and it couldn't effectively cover the entire area.

Despite that limitation, we were losing less people to the right flank than we were to the left. Even with two Humvees racing up and down the side, thinning out the infected with their machine guns, we were under constant attack. The cries of dying evacuees were nearly a constant counterpoint to the screams of the infected females.

Since the groups had merged into one long mass of fleeing people, Jackson had joined Rachel, Dog and me on the left flank. We were still killing infected at a ferocious pace and were getting dangerously low on ammo. Jackson and I had switched to pistols and knives, preserving our rifle ammo for Rachel. My hands ached and I was pretty sure I'd torn stitches again, but there weren't a lot of options.

Every few minutes, one of the Humvees would pass our area. We'd get a momentary respite from the battle as it knocked down all the infected in the area, but before we knew it, we were back under attack.

The group was running. Really running, now that most of the slower people had fallen, and the pace had picked up. Less than three miles to go. Soon, we could send the Hummers ahead to clear any infected on the bridge while the Bradley protected our back as we made our way across and into Arkansas. At least that was what I planned to happen. That plan and five dollars would have gotten me a coffee at Starbucks once upon a time. Now the five bucks was useless for anything other than tinder to start a fire.

A group of females charged out of the fog, screaming as they ran at us. Rachel snapped off a shot, killing one of them before they got too close. Jackson and I waded in with pistols and blades. I shot two in the face before another one leapt directly at me. Twisting to the side, I avoided the full force of her attack. Bringing the knife up as she flashed past, I sliced her open from sternum to pelvis.

She tumbled to the ground and tried to stand, but slipped on the entrails spilling out of her abdomen. She started to scream at me, but fell over dead before a sound left her mouth. Jackson had preserved his pistol ammo and killed four of them with his knife. He was so strong, he could punch the blade directly through skulls or sternums, getting an instant kill with each thrust. One of the Humvees drove past at that moment and we took advantage of the lull in attacks to run and cover some more ground with the group.

"How many do you think are left?" I asked him as we ran. Rachel was close to my right shoulder and Dog trotted a few paces in front of me.

"Us or infected?"

"Us."

"If I had to guess, I'd say we've already lost at least half," Jackson said.

I had been thinking the same thing but was still dismayed to hear his assessment. Half was four thousand dead in less than an hour. And we still had a long way to go.

Ahead of us, a female appeared out of the fog, making a charge for a young man and woman that each had a small child riding on their shoulders as they ran. Dog dashed forward and slammed into her leg, tearing out her Achilles' tendon. Rachel was closest and shot the infected in the head without breaking stride.

"We can't keep losing people like this. Any ideas how we can get the flyboys into the battle?" I asked, snapping off two shots as a pair of males shambled out of the fog directly in my path.

Before Jackson could answer, he was tackled by a female that ran in behind him. They tumbled to the ground and into my legs, tripping me and sending me sprawling on the wet gravel. Another female was on me in a flash and I struggled with her briefly before she lunged forward and tried to bite down on my throat. At the last instant, I had seen what she was doing and raised my shoulder and tucked my chin to protect myself. Her mouth bounced off the side of my head and clamped onto my shoulder.

She bit down hard and started trying to tear a chunk out of me. Fuck that hurt! I had dropped my pistol when I hit the ground and was left with just my knife, rifle pinned under me and useless. Pushing with one hand to get some space, I started stabbing, hard and fast into her body. After what seemed like an eternity, I finally hit something vital and she released me and rolled away. A gout of blood poured out of her mouth as she died.

Looking around, I saw Jackson climbing to his feet, the female that had attacked him lying on the ground with a broken neck. He grabbed my arm and yanked me upright, the same arm the female had just tried to make a meal of. I scooped up my pistol and started running again.

We'd been slightly behind Rachel and Dog when the attack happened and there was so much noise in the environment that neither of them had noticed. As I ran, I tried to examine my shoulder for damage. After almost tripping over a dead infected while distracted, I chose to ignore it for now and concentrate on running.

We were passing through a particularly heavy patch of fog. It was even harder to see because it was lit by the sun and looked like a solid wall of white cotton candy. It was so thick that Rachel, who was only a single step in front of me, was almost completely shrouded in mist. Water ran down my forehead, into my eyes, as the mist condensed on the hot skin of my shaved head.

Firearms were basically useless as we couldn't see the infected until they were literally right in front of us. Jackson and I moved in front of Rachel, using our greater body weight and strength to bull aside any we encountered. Slashing and stabbing, we threw them out of our path.

We were covered in blood, some of it our own, but more of it from the infected. There were still screams of pain and fear coming from up and down the group as evacuees continued to fall. There wasn't anything more we could do to help. We could barely see five feet in front of us.

Rolling Thunder

One of the Hummers rolled by, invisible in the fog, but clearly audible as the machine gun spat out round after round. They were firing blind, but I had little doubt they were hitting targets. There were too many infected for them to not. I hoped that was all they were hitting. The vehicles gave me an idea.

"Jackson, those Humvees should have emergency roadside kits on board since they're stateside. Right?"

Military vehicles that are in the US are generally equipped with a small kit for roadside emergencies in case they break down while driving on civilian roads.

"They should. What are you thinking?"

"Those kits have roadside flares?"

"Sure as shit should! And those flares will burn hot enough for the pilots to see even in this pea soup!" He excitedly got on the radio and called the drivers of the vehicles. After a minute, "Yes, they both have them. What do you want to do?"

"Tell them to hand flares out to people on each flank of the group, every twenty to thirty yards, and have them light up. Once they're all lit, tell our air to target everything outside the perimeter of those flares."

Jackson relayed my orders as I killed another female and two males. I stumbled over the second male's legs as he went down and Rachel grabbed my vest to steady me.

"How much farther?" She asked, panting as she ran.

"Should be less than two miles by now, but it's about to get a little easier."

Ahead I could hear Dog take an infected down, but couldn't see him through the fog until I was almost right on top of him. A female lay on her back, screaming, leg torn open where Dog had disabled her. When she saw me, she stopped screaming and looked me right in the eye as I was raising my pistol. My blood ran cold. I was so unprepared for the sight of the woman that I came to a stop. Rachel, then Jackson ran into my back and nearly knocked me on top of the female.

"What?" Rachel asked.

I didn't answer, just stood there like an idiot staring at the female.

"Oh, for Christ's sake," Rachel said, pushed me aside and shot the infected in the head. "You pick the strangest damn times to let your soft spot come out."

Jackson snorted with a suppressed laugh at my expense as he trotted on behind Rachel and Dog. After a moment, I followed. I didn't care what they thought.

I hadn't hesitated because the female was helpless. She had looked like my wife, Katie. So much so that for an instant the thought had gone through my head that it was Katie. Even though I knew that wasn't possible.

37

It took a few minutes for the Humvee crews to distribute the flares. We lost a lot more people while that was happening. But then they were burning, hot enough to be clearly visible to the thermal imagers onboard the helicopters, even through the dense fog.

I felt a sense of relief when I heard multiple miniguns start firing. The door gunners in the hovering Black Hawks didn't have distinct targets, but they could see the crude perimeter we had created with the flares and just hosed down everything outside that area.

The occasional infected still leaked through and had to be dispatched. Some of them had horrific injuries that would have killed them in a short amount of time anyway, but their enraged brains hadn't let their bodies give up yet and they were still dangerous. As a group, we were picked up more speed. I wanted to get to the front so I could manage any surprises that were waiting for us.

I ran harder, Jackson and Dog easily staying with me and, after a moment, Rachel fell in right behind us. We dodged through gaps in

Rolling Thunder

the fleeing evacuees, finally reaching the ragged leading edge. A young Army Lieutenant was running point, a road flare held high over his head. An equally young Army Specialist stayed at his side with a rifle ready to defend both of them.

We settled in right behind, wisely not passing them as bursts of minigun fire were shredding the infected that were in our path only a few yards ahead. Next to me, Jackson was on the radio telling the other soldiers to pick up the pace and tighten up the group. Rachel was staying with us, breathing heavily but maintaining the pace. Dog was trotting along with his tongue hanging out, for all the world appearing to be enjoying the exercise.

The Hummers and Bradley had backed off when the Black Hawk's door gunners had opened up. They were trailing at a safe distance so they didn't wind up casualties of friendly fire. The bodies we ran over and around had been nearly pulped into hamburger by the heavy slugs from the miniguns.

I was glad we were running on the rough gravel that made up the road bed for the rail tracks. There was so much blood and other bodily fluids leaking out of the shattered remains that if this had been on a hard surface, like asphalt, we would have had a difficult time with our footing.

I was estimating we had less than half a mile to go to reach the bridge when I realized I was suddenly seeing farther through the fog. The sun had been up for over an hour and was starting to burn it off. With the fog thinning, we were able to get a better idea of how many infected stood between us and the bridge. I heard Jackson mutter a curse that matched my own thoughts.

A nearly solid wall of infected humanity seethed in front of us. Without the fire support from above, we'd be so hopelessly outnumbered that none of us would make it. The fog continued to thin, visibility improving by the minute. Soon we could see a ghostly outline of the bridge's steel girders in the distance.

"Jackson, get those Hummers to the bridge entrance so they can start clearing it."

Jackson made the call and soon the two heavy vehicles passed us on the left, smashing through and over infected as they moved. Their machine guns were silent, the gunners conserving their ammo for the work they would have to do once they reached the bridge. The bridge. It was built for trains, not vehicles.

Rolling Thunder

"Jackson, does the bridge have a solid deck with tracks on it, or just rails over girders? Are the vehicles going to be able to drive across? Are these people going to be able to cross it on foot?"

Jackson looked at me with a surprised expression on his face.

"Shit, Major. I don't know if anyone ever checked that out since the plan was to cross on the train."

"Call the Colonel. See if he knows."

Jackson nodded and started speaking into the radio. Rachel and I both continued firing on infected that made it through the withering minigun fire.

"He doesn't know either, Major."

Well, didn't that just fucking figure.

"OK, have one of the Humvees check it out when they get there and let us know."

I didn't know what good the information would do us at this point, but I sure as hell wanted to know what was ahead.

Dirk Patton

The visibility had improved dramatically in just the last couple of minutes and I could now see the three Black Hawks that were on station above us, providing fire support. The bridge was also clearly visible, sunlight shining brightly on the steel beams. I could see the Hummers push through the back of the ranks of infected and arrive at the bridge which was now less than a quarter of a mile away.

Their machine guns began firing, clearing pockets of infected that were too close to the bridge. One of the drivers hopped out and trotted out onto the bridge. We kept running, waiting for his report. While we ran, a pair of Apaches swooped into a hover behind us and opened up with their chain guns. They were firing on the solid mass of infected that was pursuing us, creating a buffer zone, so we had some breathing room as we came up to the river.

"We've got solid bridge deck a few hundred yards out over the river, then it changes to just girders supporting the rails."

Jackson had to shout for me to hear him over all the ordnance going off around us. A battlefield is a very noisy place.

"Are the girders close enough together for us to cross?" I shouted back, already wondering how the hell we were going to get Max in his wheelchair across.

"He's checking."

We kept up our pace and a minute later Jackson shouted back, "He says they're about four to five feet apart."

Shit. Max was a problem, as was Dog, not to mention the people with small children. Most of the people, for that matter. Leaping from girder to girder across four to five feet of open space with a river flowing sixty-five-feet below? The girders would be slick with moisture from the fog that had just lifted and there was also probably about seventy-five-years' worth of bird shit crusted on them.

Footing would be difficult for a young, agile athlete. Ninety-five percent of these people wouldn't make it. The group would slow down so much that if they didn't slip and fall into the river, then the infected would overwhelm our rear guard and tear them apart.

"Jackson, this isn't going to work," I shouted. "These people can't make it across. We'll lose damn near everyone, either to the river or to the infected."

"Agreed. Got any ideas?" He shouted back after dispatching a charging female.

"We've got to use the rails somehow. The locomotives looked like they were still on the tracks when we passed them, as well as maybe half a dozen cars before the derailment started. Do you know how to drive one of those things?"

"Hell, Major, today was the first time in my life I've ever even been on a train. I've got no clue how they work."

"I can!"

Neither Jackson nor I could have been more surprised that it was Rachel that spoke up. She was running behind us, tucked in close enough to hear our conversation. I nearly tripped as I kept my head turned to look at her a moment too long.

"I can drive one," she insisted. "My dad was an engineer for BNSF when I was a little girl. I used to spend summers on the train with him before he died. Trust me. I used to drive all the time when I was with him."

I didn't have time to think about it, just had to make the decision.

Rolling Thunder

"Jackson, tell the Colonel we need a chopper down here. Now! The three of us need a ride back to the train."

Jackson looked at me with big eyes for a moment before placing a call on the radio. While he was talking to the Colonel, I looked around and spotted Max's youngest boy. I called out to him and told him I needed him to watch out for Dog while I was busy. He nodded and reached out to pet Dog on the head as I firmly told him to stay with the kid.

I've had dogs all my life and I've never stopped being amazed at how much of what I say to them is really understood. Dog was no exception, giving me a look to rival any human. A look that said, "are you fucking nuts?"

"Ride's on the way," Jackson shouted over the roar of the Apache chain guns. "Evacuees are going to continue out onto the bridge so the Hummers and Bradley can set up a barrier to protect them while they wait for us. There's a Black Hawk and Apache on the far side of the bridge to make sure no infected come across."

I nodded, looking up as the hovering Black Hawks that were providing air support started shifting positions to make room for another one to come pick us up.

"How many people do you think are left?" I asked, even though we'd already has this discussion.

Jackson and Rachel looked around at the flood of evacuees that were streaming around us. I looked away from the descending helicopter and spotted Dog's furry tail as he ran with Max's son. I made a mental note to learn the kid's name.

"Maybe only a third," Jackson shouted back.

"We should be able to get everyone that's left in a few cars. Right?" Rachel spoke up.

"Sure as hell hope so," I said, stepping forward and grabbing the thick, weighted rope that had been pushed out of a hovering Black Hawk.

Jackson stepped up on the other side and put a boot into one of the loops woven into the rope as I did the same from my side. Waving Rachel forward, I helped her get a foot into a loop then put both her hands on the rope at chest height.

"Oh, shit. We're not really going up, are we?"

Rolling Thunder

She looked more afraid than I'd ever seen her. Her knuckles were white as she gripped the rope for all she was worth.

"Yep, we are. Don't let go," I said with a grin as Jackson and I circled our arms around her back and grabbed the rope to lock her in place. I twirled my free arm in the air. Rachel screamed like she was riding a roller coaster as we were lifted into the air faster than any elevator she'd ever been on.

38

The pilot was good and a second later we were fifty feet straight up before he slowly transitioned to forward flight back down the tracks toward the abandoned train. Jackson and I extended our free arms, which acted like small wings and stabilized us as we moved through the air at the end of the rope. This kept us from spinning as we flew and I was able to get a bird's eye view of the infected beneath my boots.

The crush of bodies reminded me of Murfreesboro. There were thousands, if not tens of thousands. The only reference point I could think of to use was remembering attending NFL games and seeing the sea of tightly packed fans that numbered in the range of seventy thousand. I tried to imagine all those people on the ground instead of stadium seats, jammed as tightly together as possible. Picturing that, I revised my estimate to hundreds of thousands.

There were infected as far as I could see in every direction. The train tracks cut through an industrial area, very much like the warehouse district we'd fought through back in Nashville. The wide streets and alleys were full beyond capacity with teeming bodies. As we transited over the herd, I said a little prayer to the gods of war that our rope was strong and in good condition. The fall wouldn't kill us, but the reception committee would make sure we didn't walk away.

"We're going to have to uncouple at the point where the first car is derailed," I shouted so both Rachel and Jackson could hear me. "How do we do that?"

"There's a lever on the coupler," Rachel shouted back, eyes looking straight ahead, so she didn't have to see the ground passing beneath her feet." Pull the lever when there's not a lot of pressure on the coupler, then disengage the pin in the center and the cars will separate when the train starts moving."

"Don't suppose there's any way to do this without going down there where all our friends are waiting, is there?" Jackson asked with a heavy dose of sarcasm.

Rachel looked at him and shook her head. By this time, we had reached the lead locomotive and the pilot brought us to a hover, maintaining altitude.

There was a total of four locomotives, the three behind the lead all facing the opposite direction. Looking back down the track, I could see seven cattle cars, still sitting on the rails, that were immediately behind the locomotives. Behind them, the first car that had derailed was a passenger car with a higher profile. Stretching beyond that, for as far as I could see, was a jumble of cars of all type that had jumped the rails. Some were upright, but most were on their side.

I looked up at the belly of the Black Hawk and saw a crewman's head sticking out the side door watching us. With his helmet and bulbous, tinted visor he looked like a giant insect. I twirled my arm again. A second later he flashed a thumbs up, then we were descending.

Jackson and I were ready, having been on this amusement park ride before, but Rachel let loose with a loud squeal of surprise when we dropped fast enough to momentarily leave our stomachs behind. A couple of seconds later, our boots hit the roof of the lead locomotive.

Rachel lost her balance and would have gone down if Jackson and I hadn't still had our arms linked behind her. We stepped out of the loops and helped Rachel clear the rope, making sure she had her balance and wasn't going to topple over as soon as we let go of her.

Rolling Thunder

"Let's get her in the cab, then we're going to go push that lever," I said to Jackson.

"How will we let her know when it's done?" He asked.

Shit. A not so minor detail I had overlooked.

"Call up and see if they've got a spare radio they can toss down," I said, gesturing at the Black Hawk that was still hovering.

All around, the mass of infected seethed. The screams were clearly audible even over the noise of the helicopter. We needed to move quickly before they started piling up along the sides of the locomotive and cutting off our access into the control cab.

"Heads up!" Jackson shouted over the commotion.

I looked up to see an object just leaving the hand of the crewman leaning out the aircraft's side door. Jackson tracked it with his eyes, adjusting his position on the locomotive's roof to catch the handheld radio. He moved too close to the edge and leaned too far as he snatched it out of the air. He overbalanced and would have fallen into the waiting hands below if

I hadn't grabbed his vest and yanked him back to the center of the roof after he made the catch.

"Thanks," he said, setting the frequency on the radio and handing it to Rachel. "Know how to use this?"

"Push to talk. Don't push to listen. Right?"

Jackson nodded and we moved to the front edge of the roof and looked down. There was a narrow catwalk that ran along the side and around the front of the cab. A large door was on the left and a much smaller door on the right. For the moment, the catwalk was clear, but the infected were swiftly piling up and would soon cut off access to the interior of the locomotive.

Rachel sat down with her legs dangling over the edge of the roof and held both hands up for help. Jackson grabbed her hands, and she slipped off the roof. Turning in the air, she faced the locomotive as Jackson squatted until her boots were only a couple of feet above the catwalk. He let go and she landed gracefully, then disappeared inside the cab. The heavy steel door slammed loudly behind her.

I hadn't noticed the muted rumble of the idling diesel engine while we were standing on the roof. Almost as soon as Rachel got into the cab, the engines in all four locomotives rumbled loudly and the roof under my feet moved backwards a few inches with a soft jerk.

"That should have taken the pressure off the coupler," Rachel called on the radio.

"Hell of a woman you've got there, Major," Jackson smiled at me before turning and running back down the train.

"Yes, she is," I mumbled to myself, following his broad back.

39

Jackson and I ran the length of the roof of the locomotive, leaping the gap to the next one and continuing on. The Black Hawk that had given us the ride had gained altitude so the rotor wash didn't blast us off into the waiting arms below. It followed as we ran for the beginning of the derailment.

I was glad they were hanging around like a guardian angel. The sea of infected that pushed up against both sides of the train was so thick I couldn't see the ground they were standing on.

Reaching the last car that was still on the rails, we trotted to the back and looked over the edge into the gap where the coupling was. I had to take it on faith that there was actually a coupler down there. I sure couldn't see it for all the writhing bodies that were jammed into the gap.

"Get our friend up there to start clearing a buffer zone so we can get to the coupler," I said to Jackson, gesturing at the hovering helicopter with a thumb.

He nodded and made the call on the radio. A moment later, the door mounted minigun jumped into the fight. The heavy, high-velocity slugs tore into the infected bodies surrounding the gap between the cars. In an instant, they were turned into steaming piles of meat, shattered bones poking up here and there.

While the door gunner did his job, Jackson and I dropped some grenades into the gap. We stepped away from the edge to avoid any shrapnel that might come our way when they detonated, then moved back forward and started picking off targets.

The area cleared, but we couldn't stop firing or the infected would flow back into the void. I tossed the last of our grenades, leaned away from the gap for the detonation, then resumed shooting. By now we had a pretty good pile of bodies on each side of the opening. It looked like there was no time like the present to go uncouple the cars.

I slung my rifle and squatted, reaching for the edge of the roof to help me swing down onto the platform below. Before I could move any further, Jackson placed a big hand on my shoulder, holding me in place.

"Sorry, sir. This is an NCO's job, not an officer's."

"Fuck off, Master Sergeant. I was doing this shit when you were still in diapers."

"Yes, sir. You were. And you were an NCO. You know how this works."

Before I could say anything else, he moved past me, grasped the edge of the roof and swung down with more agility than I would have guessed he possessed. Fuck me. Sitting back and letting someone else get the job done just wasn't the way I liked to operate. But, he was already down there and needed fire support.

Still on one knee, I brought my rifle around and started taking out infected as quickly as I could pull the trigger. I was acquiring targets at less than twenty-five-feet, hardly needing to aim at that range. Every time I pulled the trigger, an infected fell dead. The minigun was keeping a large buffer zone open on one side of the train and I was piling up bodies on the other.

Jackson hit the platform and drew his pistol, much better for defending himself in the tight confines. Shooting a female that was scrambling out from under one of the cars, he stepped out and put one foot on the derailed car's platform.

Rolling Thunder

Holstering the pistol, he bent and grabbed the decoupling lever. Try as he might, he couldn't make the lever budge. Apparently, it was jammed tight from the tremendous forces of the train going off the tracks.

Moving fully onto the rear car's platform, he squatted and rested his weight on his left leg. Using his right, he began hammering on the lever with the heel of his boot. The lever had just started to move when Jackson's boot was grabbed by a male infected that had crawled out from underneath the platform he was squatting on. He lost his balance and fell onto his ass, thankfully staying on the grating. I noted this out of the corner of my eye as I engaged four females that were charging in. I couldn't shift my aim, or they would be on him.

Fortunately, Jackson was far from needing help. Yanking his foot free, he whipped out his pistol, shot the male in the head before dispatching another one that was squirming its way out from under the front car. Squatting again, he drew his leg back and kicked out hard. The lever squealed in protest, popping free and swinging a full ninety degrees to bang against its stop.

Jackson didn't waste time, leaning forward quickly and grasping the coupling pin. With the trouble he'd had with the lever, I expected the pin to be jammed, but it came out easily enough. Apparently easier than he expected, too. The amount of force he used was far more than needed, the extra momentum sending him off balance. He stumbled sideways and was about to recover when a female came around the front corner of the rear car, leapt and wrapped him in an embrace.

They fell to the platform, the female tearing at Jackson's body and face. She was a big woman, heavy with rolls of fat, but she was tall too and I didn't doubt she outweighed him by a good fifty pounds. They rolled on the platform, Jackson futilely pounding her head with his fist.

I had stopped shooting for a second, hoping for a clean shot at his attacker, but they were moving around too violently for me to risk it. Shifting back to fire at more approaching infected, I noted out of the corner of my eye that Jackson and the female rolled off the platform, bounced off the coupling and fell to the ground between the two cars.

Damn it! Sitting down on the edge of the roof, legs dangling into the gap, I scooted forward and dropped onto the platform. Shooting three more infected, I looked down and saw Jackson still locked in battle with the female. Several more infected were crawling along the ground under the cars, about to join the fray. I shot the ones that I had angles on, then had to engage more females charging in.

A hand slapped onto the platform an inch from my boot as an infected reached for me and missed. I lifted my foot and stomped down, hard, feeling the bones break as I ground with all my weight on top of the fingers. I knew the pain wouldn't register in the infected brain, but no matter how immune to pain they are, they can't grab you with a broken hand. I stepped back as the other hand grasped the edge of the platform, then the face appeared and I put a bullet into the center of the forehead.

Glancing down, I saw that Jackson was in trouble. The large female still had him wrapped up and two males had a grip on his legs. They were pulling themselves up his lower body and trying to bite through his uniform pants.

Slinging my rifle, I jumped into the gap. Both feet came down hard on the back of one of the males. Pulling my pistol, I leaned, angled the weapon so the round wouldn't hit Jackson if it went through the infected's head, and pulled the trigger. I shot the second male in the side of the head and tried to get a bead on the female but still didn't have a shot. Stepping forward, I finally had a target but was tackled by another leaping female before I could pull the trigger.

She hit me square in the middle of my back, knocking me forward into the steel platform on the back of the front car, face first. Nose first, for the second time in twenty-four hours. Fuck that hurt!

And I was a little stunned, my forehead also having bounced off the metal. The female was on my back, her legs wrapped around my waist and arms around my throat as she shoved her mouth against the back of my neck.

Clothing and vest saved me from being torn open, but she had one of her forearms locked directly across my throat and was squeezing for all she was worth. I couldn't breathe and nearly panicked before I remembered my training. It doesn't make you superman, but it does prepare you to deal with unusual situations. Knowing what to do prevents panic, which is often more dangerous than your enemy.

Rolling Thunder

Remembering a lesson from hand to hand combat school a few million years ago, I turned away from the elbow of the arm that was pressing on my throat. I used the platform to prevent her from turning with my body. As I moved, I leaned forward and pushed her arm up and away, popping loose from the choke hold, but not from the legs locked around my waist.

She was pressed against me, flailing for a better grip as I got my left forearm under her chin and forced the snapping teeth away from my face. Scrambling with my right hand, I finally gripped the Kukri that was sheathed at the small of my back. Drawing it, I stopped the fight with a sharp thrust into her lower back. The blade severed her spine at the waist, her legs instantly going limp and releasing. She fell to the ground and I quickly dispatched her with another thrust to the throat and up into her skull.

I spun around and came face to face with Jackson. He had finally gotten the leverage he needed on the larger female and stabbed into her head with his Ka-Bar. More females were charging in and we shot them down as we scrambled up onto the front car's platform.

I bent at the waist and Jackson clambered up my back, stepped onto my shoulder and leapt to grab the edge of the roof. He quickly pulled himself the rest of the way up, turned around and, on his stomach, extended his arms down to help me. I was reaching for his hands when my feet were pulled out from under me. I crashed onto the platform before rolling into the space between the cars.

A male had crawled out from underneath the platform I was standing on and grabbed my ankles. I was now face to face with him, no weapons in hand as I'd already put them away for the climb onto the roof. Another male fell on me almost immediately and started trying to bite into my side.

Fortunately, he was only able to chomp down on my vest, but he was working his way towards my face. My legs were pinned under the weight of both infected. My rifle stuck under my body and none of my other weapons accessible. A female screamed as she charged in, heading directly for my unprotected head.

40

Captain Roach spotted the Major and the bitch. He was closing on them through the crush of evacuees when the Black Hawk appeared overhead, dropping a fast rope extraction line to them. He watched in frustration as they, along with the powerfully built black soldier, were lifted into the air and flown back towards the disabled train.

The idea to pick them off with his rifle was so tempting he started to raise it, then thought better of what he was doing. Sure, they were easy targets, hanging there only fifty feet in the air, but the crew in the Black Hawk would spot him and turn him into hamburger with their minigun. Lowering the rifle, he cursed, turned and started running with the evacuees again.

They weren't leaving. He knew that much about the Major. They were up to something, and they'd be back. He was certain of that when ahead he spied the bushy tail of the Major's dog waving as the animal trotted alongside a teenage boy. Roach would bide his time. He was good at that. Had all the patience of any successful predator.

As he ran, he shot several more infected, then intentionally aimed a little off target and brought down two women who were running by themselves. No one seemed to notice, at least no one said anything, and the thrill of killing amongst a group of people with apparent impunity brought out a small giggle that threatened to become full blown laughter.

Roach suppressed his joy, getting his emotions under control and reminded himself he had bigger plans. Plans for the bitch. If he played games now, he might be found out and lose his opportunity later.

Just ahead of him, people were streaming around two Hummers and a Bradley that were doing their best to fire over and around the evacuees at the infected that were in hot pursuit. A few dozen soldiers on foot tried to fill the gaps between the vehicles. Several more were on top of the Bradley, adding the fire from their rifles to the fight.

Roach pounded through the space between the two Humvees and slowed to a walk as the evacuees in front of him stopped running. They felt safe behind the big military vehicles.

Several soldiers were moving through the milling people. They were trying to herd the people, yelling for them to continue out onto the bridge to be ready for a train that was coming to pick them up. So that's where the Major went! He had some plan to get the train moving again to save the survivors that had made it this far. Roach smiled, excitedly anticipating the moment when he could put a bullet into the Major and get his hands on the bitch.

"Hey, what are you doing?" A young soldier was looking directly at Roach, approaching with his rifle held across his chest. "You aren't supposed to have a weapon!"

It was one of the National Guard soldiers that had stripped him and tied him to the seat on the train when the Major recognized him.

"I'm just trying to help," Roach said, moving directly towards the soldier.

The man stopped a couple of feet in front of him, not recognizing the danger as Roach kept coming. When he was right in the man's face, he grabbed the rifle to control it, whipped out the knife sheathed on his stolen vest and buried the blade into the man's stomach. With a swift twist and cut, he disemboweled him. Pulling the blade out, he stabbed through the mouth that was open in a silent scream of pain, piercing into the brain.

"Infected!" Roach shouted, pushing the body onto the ground and backing away.

People didn't even question or stop to look. They just gave the corpse a wide berth. A couple of them even slapped Roach on the back in thanks as they ran past.

41

Two shots rang out and the female's scream was cut off as her head deformed from the impact of high-velocity slugs. Her momentum was enough to carry the corpse forward to crash down across my upper body. I was now buried under infected, but at least the female's body was momentarily protecting me from the advance of the males.

I squirmed, struggling against the weight of three bodies lying on me and the grasps of the males as they tried to pull my arms to their hungry mouths. Adrenaline was surging, and I was on the verge of completely freaking out when there were more shots that sounded very close. Both males went still. A moment later, the female's corpse was lifted off me and I looked up into Jackson's grinning face.

"Forget how to fight when you pinned on those oak leaves?" He asked, hauling one of the males off my legs then twisting to shoot two females that were charging in.

"Blow me, asshole," I said, kicking the last body off and quickly climbing onto the platform.

We repeated the move of Jackson scrambling up my back and onto the roof, but this time I made sure I wasn't about to have my legs pulled out from under me before I took his outstretched hands. He grabbed me and we both pulled. Moments later, I climbed over him and the rest of the way onto the roof. I turned and brought my rifle up in case any females were making a leap for us. For the moment, we were clear and Jackson called Rachel on the radio to tell her we were ready to go.

The metal roof under my boots vibrated as the four locomotives throttled up and belched black diesel smoke. Then we were moving. Slowly at first, but we quickly gained speed until we seemed to be traveling at a steady twenty miles per hour. All around us, the infected pushed in against the train cars. Those that were too close were knocked to the ground and I was gratified to see the crushed bodies in our wake.

The Black Hawk that had maintained station over us fell in and was soon joined by another. Both used their miniguns to clear the infected around us. They were killing hundreds, the bodies packed in so tightly that they didn't even have to bother aiming. But for every one they killed, there were a dozen replacements.

Rolling Thunder

We quickly rolled past the line established by the Apaches, bodies and body parts piled up from the high explosive ordnance they were firing. The volume of infected was greatly reduced, but the Apaches couldn't stop all of them. Females were still in the area, running towards the bridge in pursuit of the remaining evacuees.

"Jackson, what happened to the second train?"

I had completely forgotten about the other train full of evacuees until that moment.

"Our engineer was able to get a warning out on the radio when we derailed. They stopped in time and the last I heard they had reversed away from Memphis. The Colonel is working on getting them airlifted across the river."

I looked at him sideways until he continued.

"Yeah, that's not going to happen. We don't have the air assets to move eight hundred people, let alone eight thousand. They aren't going to make it."

Thinking about all those people sitting there waiting for rescue until they eventually realized there wasn't any coming, only millions of raging infected, killed any further conversation as we approached the bridge. I spent the time staring off into the distance, trying to come up with any plan to save them. But there was nothing I could do.

The tracks were blocked with over a hundred derailed rail cars. Even in a perfect scenario, it would take hundreds of men, lots of heavy equipment and days to clear that much wreckage. Air assets were limited at best because of the loss of trained pilots and flight crews to the infection. I suspected that just like at Arnold, before the base had fallen, there were plenty of aircraft, just no one to fly them.

"Has the Colonel tried to find civilian pilots? Most of them will be former military anyway and can probably fly most of what's available."

Jackson smiled, but it was an acknowledgment that I had a good idea, not a display of humor.

"Yep. Been there already. Half the pilots flying these Apaches and Black Hawks are over sixty years old. Retired Army, Corps, Navy. You name it. The guy flying the bird we roped out of is a Vietnam vet. Flew medic evac in '68 and '69.

Rolling Thunder

Hell, it was a Korean war vet that flew the C-130 I was on when we evacuated Fort Campbell. He couldn't walk anymore, but I'll be damned if he didn't handle that plane like he was a kid again."

I nodded my head and kept my mouth shut. It was bad and people were going to continue to die. I couldn't save everyone. Out of frustration, I started to raise my rifle. I was thinking I would pick off the females that were running behind and beside us, then thought better of using up ammo that might be desperately needed later.

We rode, sitting on the roof, for a few minutes. It wasn't long before we could hear the machine guns at the entrance to the bridge, keeping the infected from swarming the waiting evacuees. As we approached, Rachel slowed the train and the Humvee that was straddling the tracks moved out of the way to let us pass. Four Black Hawks and a couple of Apaches were supporting the guarding action and for the moment, the infected were being held.

But, just like at the wall in Murfreesboro, they weren't being stopped. Mounds of bodies were piled high in a semi-circle around the bridge entrance, but the infected that were trying to get to the survivors just climbed over the piles of dead and kept on coming. Nothing deterred them. As soon as we ran out of ammo, or retreated, they would surge forward unabated and flood every inch of the bridge.

The rear of the train, where we were sitting, passed the last line of defense provided by the Hummers and the Bradley, then we were fully on the bridge. Slowing more, Rachel kept us rolling at about five miles an hour, evacuees standing on the bridge deck on either side of the tracks looking at the train with obvious relief on their faces. Jackson and I stood up as Rachel brought us to a gentle stop. She really did know what she was doing. Don't know why I was surprised.

Scanning the crowd, I spotted Dog standing on the left side of the train, next to Max's son. Max was in his chair and the rest of his boys stood in a protective circle around him. People started rushing forward when the train stopped and Jackson and I swung down to the ground to make sure we got everyone on board. Far down the train, I saw a figure climb up onto the lead locomotive and disappear into the cab where Rachel was, but didn't think any more of it as I was nearly knocked over by a very happy Dog.

Rolling Thunder

42

The evacuees had gone as far onto the bridge as they could. The solid steel decking that provided a bed for the tracks ended a few hundred yards out over the river, the rails continuing with only evenly spaced steel girders supporting them. Roach wandered up to the edge of the decking and looked down. He pulled back quickly when the swiftly rushing water far below started to make him dizzy. He didn't like heights, and a poor swimmer, he liked water even less.

Vibration in the steel beneath his feet caused him to look up as the first locomotive passed through the defensive perimeter that had been set up at the eastern entrance. The bridge gained elevation slightly as it approached the middle of the Mississippi River and he had a perfect vantage point to watch the train approach.

He couldn't see through the thick glass surrounding the cab where the train's engineer sat, but he could see the two figures sitting on the roof of the rearmost car. Even though he couldn't recognize features at this distance, he could tell from their relative size and shape that this was the Major and the Master Sergeant. That meant the bitch was driving the train? Surprised, Roach moved deeper into the tightly massed crowd of people, not wanting to be recognized as she approached.

The train slowed, seeming to take forever to reach where he was waiting. As it drew closer, Roach could see into the cab and smiled tightly when he saw the bitch at the controls. She brought the train to a stop and the people around him immediately moved towards the few cars that were in tow. He moved with them, cutting diagonally until he was at the access platform at the rear of the lead locomotive.

Stepping up, he quickly climbed the narrow, metal stairs onto an even narrower catwalk that clung to the side of the giant locomotive. He moved rapidly, not running, but as fast as he could walk on the narrow grating.

There was a large mirror outside the cab that would afford the engineer a view down the side of the train. If the bitch happened to look up, she would see him approaching. Despite the tactical vest he wore, Roach was still in just his boxers and she couldn't help but recognize him even if she didn't see his face.

Rolling Thunder

In the mirror, he could see her working a variety of controls with one hand while pushing long hair off her face with the other. She was distracted and felt secure for the moment, not watching her surroundings. But she could finish what she was doing at any second and look up. What would she do if she saw him? Lock the cab door? Was it already locked? Sound the horn and bring the Major running? He had to surprise her.

Roach was twenty feet from the door when Rachel flipped the final switch on the control panel and raised her head. She didn't look in the mirror, rather directly forward at the nearly four miles of bridge ahead of them. On the far side of the river, she could see several helicopters hovering, tracers from their weapons visible even in the bright sunlight as they kept the infected from flooding onto the bridge from the west. She looked to her right, north, up the river. It appeared to be running swift and strong, swollen by the same storm that had pounded Nashville.

She was turning to look to the south when the door to the cab was yanked open. Before she could react, Roach was in the cab, knife tip pressed to her neck. She caught her breath and thought about going for her pistol, but he pressed the blade against her flesh hard enough to hurt.

Rachel could feel warm blood trickling down her throat, continuing between her breasts. Without consciously thinking about it, she recognized that he'd only made a superficial cut. Nothing dangerous, but deep enough to command her complete attention and compliance.

"What the hell do you think this is going to accomplish?"

She stared into his eyes without moving a muscle. Madness stared back and her blood ran cold. There would be no reasoning with this man.

"You belong to me now, bitch! You think you're so fucking high and mighty because you're running around with that big fucker. You run your smart mouth, flash your tits, shake your ass and you've got him to make sure no one calls you on it. Well, he's not here, is he?"

Roach giggled. He couldn't help himself. He also had a raging erection and the solution for that was standing right in front of him.

"Look, I don't know what you think I did or said, but if I've offended you, I'm truly sorry."

Rolling Thunder

Rachel had no clue what he was going on about. Had she slighted the man during one of the few brief moments they'd ever seen each other? Not that she could remember, but he certainly thought she had.

Roach nodded and smiled, then punched her in the stomach with his left fist. Rachel was focused on his eyes and didn't see it coming. The blow knocked the wind out of her, doubling her over and momentarily paralyzing her diaphragm so she couldn't draw a breath.

Before she could recover, he grabbed and spun her around, savagely shoving her upper body across the control panel so she was bent at the waist. He moved behind, pressing hard against her ass with his manhood.

Something in Rachel snapped at that moment. She still couldn't breathe, but reacted faster than Roach thought possible. Slamming backwards with her lower body, Rachel knocked him away from her. She took another cut on her cheek as the knife moved past her face.

Spinning, she kicked out, heavy boot landing squarely in Roach's stomach and knocking him even farther away. Her diaphragm unfroze and she took a deep breath before screaming out all the pain and anguish she'd been carrying since having been attacked as they escaped from Atlanta. She moved in, intending to beat Roach to death with her fists.

He had been caught by surprise, but he'd had women fight him before. After the blow to his stomach, he'd been knocked back, taking another step and feigning that he was more helpless than he really was. When Rachel screamed and charged, leading with her fists, he stepped inside her reach and slammed the top of his head up into her face.

If she hadn't recently had two serious concussions, it might not have stopped her. But she wasn't in any condition for another blow to the head. The cab spun and Rachel dropped her arms, swaying on her feet. Her vision tunneled and all she could hear was the rush of her own heart beating a mile a minute.

She wanted to fight when Roach grabbed her from behind, but despite her brain's commands, her body remained loose and rubbery. She felt like throwing up and after a moment was unsure if she had or not.

Roach grabbed the bitch around the throat and slid around her body, keeping an arm locked around her neck. Glancing behind him, he looked over the controls for the train. Everything was clearly labeled and it didn't look like you needed to be a rocket scientist to drive the thing. Two levers were marked as brake, one for the train and one for the locomotives, and he moved both to the off position. Another lever was marked throttle and he shoved it forward as far as it would go.

43

Jackson and I had gotten maybe half the people loaded when I heard the massive diesels in the locomotive throttle up. A moment later, the train lurched and began slowly moving. I was caught completely unprepared and looked toward the front, thinking there must be something that had caused Rachel to start it rolling. But there was no one and nothing near the lead locomotive.

I started trotting towards the locomotive, slowly at first, then broke into a run. Jackson was right behind me and I could hear him calling Rachel on the radio. It didn't sound like he was getting an answer. Dog, who I had put in one of the cars with Max, must have seen me running because a moment later he fell in by my side. I was glad to have him along.

The train was picking up speed, but very slowly. The engines were making a lot of noise and belching thick clouds of smoke, but not moving faster than three or four miles an hour. I was running hard, slowly gaining on the rearmost locomotive, but I'm not a sprinter by any means. If the train picked up much more speed, I would be left behind.

Rolling Thunder

Ahead, I could see the end of the bridge deck and the open space down to the river. I tried to gauge if I was going to be able to catch the locomotive. I couldn't even guess and settled for putting on as much speed as I could.

"Go!" I shouted to Dog, who raced ahead of me and bounded onto the platform at the back of the locomotive.

He turned to look at me and for the first time since I had known him, started barking. Encouraging me to hurry.

Jackson, a decade younger, passed me and a few moments later grabbed the railing around the platform and swung up next to Dog. He turned and shouted, but I couldn't understand him over the roar of the diesels and my own breathing. I ran harder.

The edge of the deck was coming up fast and I dug deep, drawing on every reserve I had. A few more steps and I was past the point of no return. I couldn't stop in time to not go over the edge, so it was either jump for the train or go for a swim. I threw myself forward, fingertips brushing the rail and missing.

I felt myself starting to fall, then strong hands gripped my wrist and I was bodily yanked up onto the platform. I wound up on top of Jackson, breathing like I'd just run an Olympic sprint, which for me I guess I had. Dog was happily licking the side of my face. I rolled off Jackson and onto my feet.

"Guess I owe you one," I said.

"Two, but who's counting?" He grinned.

We quickly moved down the side of the fourth locomotive on a narrow catwalk. Transitioning to the next one in line was simple as they didn't have nearly as much of a gap between as the passenger cars did. We kept moving forward, got onto the second one and I trotted as fast as I could with the narrow footing. The train was still only moving at around four or five miles an hour, and I was really concerned something was very wrong with Rachel.

Reaching the front of the second locomotive, we moved onto the lead engine and headed for the cab. Ahead, I could see a large mirror that would allow the engineer to see down the side of the train behind him, without turning around. I should have been able to see into the cab, but it was pushed out at a crazy angle and I couldn't see anything except the open track and river below us.

Rolling Thunder

We slowed and moved to the cab, stopping at the back edge. Poking my head forward, I peered in through the side window. Nothing. No Rachel. Eyes glued on the interior, and pistol in hand, I moved slowly to the door. Dog stayed tight on my heels with Jackson right behind, keeping an eye on our rear.

I reached the door into the cab and still hadn't seen anything. I was starting to think Rachel hadn't been in there at all and maybe the train had just started on its own. Was that why it was going so slow?

Roach had seen the Major running to catch the train in the mirror. He had pushed on the throttle, trying to outdistance him, but the lever was all the way to its stop and the diesels were roaring. Why weren't they going faster? He scanned the controls, making sure the brakes were off, but couldn't find anything else to tell him what he was doing wrong. A myriad of lights blinked at him. Some were red, some yellow, and various gauges had needles pegged in the red zone. Something wasn't right, but he didn't have a clue what it was.

Turning back to the mirror, he saw the damn dog leap onto the train, then the Master

Sergeant. He wanted to watch, but didn't want them to see him. Dragging Rachel to the door, he popped it open, reached out and knocked the mirror out of adjustment so the Major couldn't see into the cab as he approached. That done, he slammed the door and looked for a way to secure it. There wasn't a lock on the door.

Knowing time was short, he dragged Rachel to the far side of the cab where a narrow door opened onto a small platform and pulled her through behind him. The door didn't have a window and he felt safe for the moment.

The platform was just wide enough for the two of them to stand, a lightweight chain all that prevented him from stepping off the edge and into space. The bridge had narrowed as they progressed and with just the slightest push, a person would be able to leap off the platform, clear the edge of the structure and plunge more than sixty-five-feet to the river below. Roach was frightened, but not as frightened as he was of the Major. He knew he wouldn't survive this encounter if he wasn't smart.

I opened the door to the cab and Dog immediately slipped through ahead of me. Following with my pistol up and ready, I scanned the entire area, finding no one. Lights were blinking on the massive control panel and alarms were buzzing, but I ignored them and thoroughly checked the space.

Dog was sniffing an area on the floor and I stepped over to look. Fresh blood was spotted on the metal decking. Too fresh to have been from the engineer in the event he had been injured when the train derailed earlier. Damn it. Where was Rachel? Jackson stepped into the cab and looked around, holstering his pistol when he was satisfied we were alone.

Dog kept sniffing the floor and made his way to a narrow door set into the right-hand side of the cab. He lifted his muzzle, sniffed the handle and growled. Jackson and I looked at each other and pulled our pistols back out.

Moving to the door, we put our backs against the bulkhead on either side. Jackson placed his thick hand on the steel lever that functioned as a handle. I took a step away, raised my pistol in both hands and aimed at what would be head height for most people. Jackson glanced at me, waiting, and I nodded. He pulled the lever and jerked the door open.

Immediately outside was a small platform, not more than three by three feet. When the door came open, the first thing I saw was Rachel. She stood there, swaying, looking barely conscious. An arm was locked around her neck, a knife point pressing against her throat right on top of the carotid artery. Part of a face was visible behind her head, peering through her long hair that was blowing in the breeze of the train's movement. Roach.

"Let her go and you live, Roach," I said as I tried to get a clear shot at his head.

Jackson stepped away from the door, pistol up and looking for a shot as well.

"Fuck you!" Roach screamed. "You'll kill me as soon as you have an opening."

He was staying tightly tucked behind Rachel and if not for her hair, I might have had a shot. But if I was off by even an inch, I could hit her instead of him.

"No shot," Jackson said to me in a low voice.

"Release her and you walk away. No one will touch you. You have my word," I said, not expecting him to believe me, but telling the truth.

Rolling Thunder

"Back out of the cab or I cut her! I'll walk away, but she's going with me. If you try to stop me, I'll bleed her right in front of you!"

His voice was pitched high, on the verge of hysteria. Despite his state of mind, he was making sure he was well protected behind her body and I wasn't coming up with any options.

"I got no shot," I said in a voice only Jackson could hear. "If you have one, take it."

"No," he replied a moment later.

"OK, Roach. We're backing out, but here's the deal. If you put even one more mark on her, I will kill you. Slowly and painfully. You want to live, make sure she's alive and healthy."

I didn't lower my pistol but took a couple of steps back, as did Jackson.

Rachel seemed to be more alert as I started to back away, eyes that had been rolling in her head finding and focusing on me.

"John..." she started to say, Roach cutting her off with a tightening of his arm.

Rachel gasped and reflexively raised her hands to the restriction on her throat. Roach had to use the hand holding the knife to control her arms. When the blade came away from her throat, I lunged. I reached for Rachel with one hand, pistol in the other seeking a target.

Dog had stayed within a few feet of Rachel and when I moved, he took the cue and leapt, slamming into her chest. As he impacted Rachel, Roach's knife hand flashed toward him. Dog was faster and locked his powerful jaws onto Roach's wrist. Roach screamed and the knife clattered to the floor as all three of them began to move.

Roach was standing with his heels at the edge of the platform. The small chain, pressed into the backs of his legs just below his hips was the only thing separating him from open space and the river below. When Dog's hundred plus pounds hit Rachel, he slammed her back into Roach. His upper body pushed back by the momentum, Roach tried to step back to maintain his balance, but the chain prevented him from moving his lower body as his upper kept tipping back. He finally overbalanced.

With his arm still wrapped around Rachel's throat, and Dog locked onto his wrist, Roach went over the chain, taking them with him as he fell. My lunge carried me to the platform just as the three of them flipped over the chain. My grab came up empty.

Rolling Thunder

I leaned over the edge, Jackson rushing to stand next to me. We watched as they fell past the narrow bridge. The three of them separated as they dropped, moments later making three splashes as they struck the surface of the river below and disappeared into the water. Moving and not thinking, I yanked my rifle sling over my head. Tossing the weapon to Jackson, I stepped over the chain and leapt into the Mississippi River.

Dirk Patton

Continue the adventure in Red Hammer: V Plague Book 4 now available from Amazon!

Printed in Great Britain
by Amazon